HEART OF CINDERS

Cinders in Midnight Glass

J. DARLENE EVERLY

To request use of the copyrighted material, please contact the author at jdarleneeverly.com

Hardcover: ISBN 978-1-954719-24-8
Paperback: ISBN 978-1-954719-23-1
Ebook: ISBN 978-1-954719-22-4
First paperback edition October 2021.
Edited by Jupiter Alley.
Cover art by Miblart.
Layout by Wishing Well Books.

J. DARLENE EVERLY

HEART OF CINDERS

CINDERS IN MIDNIGHT GLASS

For the stabby girls

INTRODUCTION

Heart of Cinders is just the beginning of the Cinders in Midnight Glass series, the second book, Heart of Shattered Glass is on preorder now! If you would like to be the first to hear about the next book in the series titled Heart of Midnight, get an exclusive prequel to this story and more free books, as well as see what else the author has written, please go to jdarleneeverly.com and sign up for her newsletter.

CHAPTER 1
THE LATE LORD FALL

The air was far too clean.

From my place in the rafters, I could see all the way to the Protectorate Mountains and across Thirteen Rivers Valley while night descended outside the windows. Throughout the valley, with their fair weather and clear skies, the people went on about their lives. So very different than back home. The islands dotted the landscape of waterways crisscrossed with bridges, houses and cities, fields and fisheries.

Being able to see so far, knowing that others could see all the way to the manor I waited in, made the small hairs along the nape of my neck stand on end. Of all the things I didn't want to be, seen was highest on the list.

A cramp seized on the muscle of my calf, forcing me to adjust my stance one tiny measure at a time, shifting my weight from one foot to the other while remaining crouched. I kept my upper body, braced along the beams of the ceiling, as still as the cobweb next to my left elbow.

Lord Fall was late.

I was told he always took to his bedroom before dinner. Yet

night was falling, and I was the only person here, perched above the opulent room with its soft, gauzy fabric.

Somewhere within the walls of this great manor, servants bustled about, his young wife convalesced, and the man himself was doing something out of his routine.

Eventually he was going to come to his bedroom.

He never slept in his wife's room. I knew that much for sure. And he couldn't now anyway, so all I had to do was be patient.

Not the easiest thing I had ever done.

The easiest was probably getting into the manor through the attic dormer and making my way here. Waiting in the attic wasn't a problem, especially since the floorboards of it had cracks between each of them that made it much easier to watch for a moment the servants weren't nearby.

How was it possible to live their lives? Was it the clear air and the ability to see so far that left the people of these lands so inattentive? Was it their focus on the waters around them, heads bent to the fishing so many people relied on?

Whatever the reason for it, it made my job almost boring.

Early that morning, the light low, after using the night to hide my passage through the towns, I had made my way over the walls of the manor grounds, across the wide lawns, and up the side of the manor itself without raising a single alarm.

Amateurs.

Maybe they found out I was here. Maybe that was why he wasn't keeping to his schedule.

But I dismissed that idea. If they knew, they would have been looking for me. They would have been ringing the bells and sending armed guards to search every nook and cranny.

No, it was something else.

My brother would want to know what it was when I got home. He would want all the specifics of what I had witnessed in the region. He would want to know every last detail. That wasn't my job. Not that it mattered to my brother.

I swallowed rising bile and squeezed my hand into a fist thinking about what my brother would do if I didn't at least try to find out what was causing the deviation from routine. He wouldn't have been sated by news of the fine furnishings, or the ways in which the people of the valley used reeds for most of their buildings.

Reconnaissance for the kind of information my brother wanted was on my to do list, although the chances of me getting exactly the right detail to slake his thirst for secrets was small.

A long, slow breath was all I could afford myself to quell the anxiety that rippled through me at my thoughts of returning home.

First, I needed this done.

The door to the bedroom swung open and Lord Fall stormed into the room, his gray hair thinned on the top and his riding cloaked caked in mud down one side.

He threw his crop at his desk, sending the stack of papers on top flying, the sound of them fluttering as if a thousand ravens took flight at once.

"Sodded horse," he yelled, his voice enraged. "I asked for a gelding. Is that what I get? No. Of course not. Make me ride a fucking green broke stallion. I need a new trainer."

Ah, so nothing more than an accidental delay.

My body and mind set aside all other thoughts and worries, my muscles bunched and ready.

If no servant followed on his heels to help him disrobe, this was my chance.

Boots thudded against the imported carved wood door, one after the other. The door was black, so it had to be made of raven wood. The nearest raven wood forest was more than a week's journey from the outer edges of the valley.

Those boots could have fed a family for a week, but he tossed them against the door like so much trash, not even bothering to knock off some of the caked-on mud.

No doubt he was going to have his servants take care of the dirt. If they didn't get to it in time, a guy like him would just buy a new pair and toss the old.

I narrowed my eyes as he took off his soiled cloak and started to remove his other clothes.

He mumbled to himself about his groom and stable hands while I grinned in the shadows above him.

Any second...all he had to do was...

Lord Fall moved to the armoire in the corner. It was my cue.

I dropped from the rafters and landed with barely a sound, light as I could on my toes, and rolled down to the balls of my feet at the same time my fingertips touched the floor. With my other hand I pulled the spike from the holster on my leg.

The passage of the air directly behind him must have set off the alarm bells in his head, because he started to turn toward me.

Before he got his eyes all the way around, before he could actually see me, I surged up from the floor and in one swift movement drove the spike between his ribs and right into his heart.

My other hand caught his head and I carefully lowered him to the floor, his last exhalation coming out as soft as a snowflake landing as I did.

His eyes were open and staring. Looking at them, no one would ever guess exactly the kind of man he was.

"Good riddance. May the Gods and Goddesses reject your soul so you find no peace until you return and pay your debts in pain," I whispered to his corpse.

The only regret in doing what I did as well as I did, was that it was too easy a death for people like Lord Fall.

Stretching, I stood and made a study of the room.

He was such a fool, so sure of his superiority, there seemed no secret places for papers. But I had to check.

Under the bed yielded nothing. The armoire was also empty. Among the papers scattered on the floor were statements of the valley's production and the trade it engaged in.

Pocketing those, I turned my eyes to the desk.

The drawers didn't hold anything of value, but one seemed oddly shallow. I took a moment to listen to the manor around me. No footsteps sounded in the hall. There was no hint that anyone was likely going to find me. So I set the contents of the drawer on the desktop in neat stacks.

Sure enough, there was a false bottom, but the only thing under it was an envelope with the dragon head seal of the King of Onyx, and two different wax seal stamps.

One of them was the seal of the Thirteen Rivers Valley, but the other…I didn't know what it was.

Onyx had been at war so many times, and I knew little of the kingdoms outside our borders. Could it have related to something involving those wars?

I didn't know, and it didn't matter.

Everything went into the pocket inside my short cloak, and I put the drawer back to rights before turning to face the corpse of the former Lord Fall.

I yanked the spike out of his side. A small bloom of blood formed, but not large enough to explain his death. Hopefully it would be counted as part of his tumble from his horse. A quick swipe of the spike along my black pants, and back in the holster it went.

My smile widened.

No doctor had yet to cut open one of my kills, none of them had yet figured out how I did it.

Lord Fall's death would probably be counted along with the others as a small trauma leading to a sudden attack of the heart.

They were right, of course. Just not in the way they believed.

Climbing back up the wall using the thick wooden beams as easy handholds and footholds was the easiest bit of the next part.

What I needed was for the light to finally die outside, but first I was supposed to go to see another member of the household.

I looked out the window again, just for a moment, longing to go home and be done with this manor and this land of too clear skies.

CHAPTER 2
LIBERTY SLEEPS

Making my way through the house via the attic was far too easy.

I had no idea what builder thought it was a good idea to put access to it from the hall directly outside the Lord's bedroom, but they should seek a new line of work.

Once I reached the area above the room I needed to get into next, I peeked through the spaces between the floorboards.

While the Lord's bedroom was all light opulence with some of the best furnishings available, this room was cramped and spare. The fabric looked like wool, but it was threadbare in places. All the furnishings were rough-hewn wood.

The spaces between the attic and this room had more cobwebs and more dust than the ones in the Lord's bedroom. They made it only a fraction more difficult to take in what was going on below.

But that wasn't why my heart twisted and I wished more than ever he had suffered more.

In the room below me, a servant deposited a small bundle

and exited the room carrying a tray, leaving behind the occupant of the bed.

I found two planks that seemed loose enough, and used a dagger to dig out the nails holding them in place, taking my time so I didn't make too much noise.

Checking once more for any surprise visitors, I pulled up the boards. After I tucked my short cloak in around me, it left a space just wide enough for me to feed my body through, clad in the lean-fitting black suit I always wore for this work. I didn't bother to pull them back into place behind me. There was no reason to hide from this occupant of the manor.

Part of me wondered if she was so heavily sedated that she wouldn't be able to wake up and hear that she was free. I licked my lips and sent a plea to the souls of my parents that she would wake up if only for a moment.

She deserved to know.

"Solaria," I whispered, leaning on the edge of the bed and taking the hand of the person ensconced in bedding. She used to be my cousin. Now she was Lady Fall, but it wasn't her title that made her barely recognizable.

Her eyelids fluttered although opening them must have hurt.

Every part of her face was bruised, swollen, scabbed, or all three. Her delicate features and soft skin hidden by the abuse she suffered.

The injuries, bright and lurid, made the blood in my body turn to ice. In a perfect world, I would have been able to parade her husband through the streets while everyone screamed at him. In a perfect world, she would have been able to beat him to death in front of everyone, his crimes against her the shield and weapon for his punishment at her hands.

But this was only our world, and I was her only weapon.

"My arm, your hand. It is done," I said, placing the seal of the Valley in her palm.

Solaria curled her fingers around the cold metal of it, her grip strong.

Finally, her eyes opened. The pale blue of them normally looked like a cloudless sky, now it looked more like melted ice, something that was once solid and had been undone.

"He's gone, Solaria," I said, my voice as gentle as I could make it.

She took a deep shuddering breath. Although it must have been agony, a smile played on her split and swollen lips.

"Thank you, Cinder," she said, turning her head just enough to look at the cradle along the wall. "I named her Liberty."

Of course, she named her Liberty. He was too angry that she had been born a girl to even suggest a name for his own daughter before he beat her mother as a birthing gift.

I closed my eyes and fought back the tears until I knew I could school my face.

Looking back at her, I said, "Welcome Liberty, the future Lady of Thirteen Rivers Valley."

"Yes." Solaria's eyes fluttered shut again and I gave her hand one last squeeze. Her other hand was wrapped in bandages and trapped in the sling for her broken arm.

The baby—swaddled and sound asleep—had the same diminutive features as her mother.

Closing my eyes again, I put a hand over Liberty's tiny heart. The blanket was as soft as a cloud and my touch almost as light as I prayed to my parents to protect the baby, allow her to grow healthy and happy, and never experience the kind of trauma her mother had.

Part of me hesitated, it wanted to add the blessing of the Gods and Goddesses on the child, but I wasn't the one to give it.

I opened my eyes and pulled my hand back from the child.

"Hopefully, one day I will watch you do great things as a happy adult."

One more look at Solaria resting under the blanket was all I allowed myself to take before climbing to perch on the footboard of the bed. Standing on it gave me just enough height to leap and catch the edge of the opening in the attic.

Pulling myself up, I turned around and couldn't stop myself from taking a moment to look back on Solaria, and close my eyes. In my mind the image of her and Liberty living happily, healed and whole in themselves, bloomed. They swam in one of the rivers on the edge of the manor's grounds, the people around them not guards, but the people of the valley.

She would have no need of guards when she managed the valley with love, light, and a deeper understanding of hardship than her people would ever know.

The floorboards slipped back into place, but I didn't pound the nails back in, they would come home with me in my pocket.

Most of my work was for payment. Not that I saw the funds —my brother handled all of that so he could help our people. I didn't know what Solaria had promised Ash, but I would have done this job for free.

Below me, the alarm went up, screams traveled from one frantic voice to another, and boots pounded through the halls.

I didn't bother to suppress my smile.

Good. They found the body.

That bastard deserved it, and any minute one of them would remember there was a Lady of the house and an heir.

Maybe Solaria would start receiving better treatment even before I had to leave.

Not that it mattered if it happened tonight or tomorrow, either way she had the seal in her hand, the heir in her room, and the wedding vows to make her claim.

Lord Fall's family, no matter how grasping they might be, would never rule over the valley again. Now, it would be the descendants of the Lady Fall.

Whatever name she chose to continue with, Lady of the Valley, Lady Fall, Lady Solaria, or even retake the name of our family and be Lady Ahmya, it would be hers and she would be remembered long after he was forgotten.

All that was left for me to do, was wait for night to fall completely.

No one would think to look for me up here.

If they did, I would be ready.

But they wouldn't.

One of the things I had learned during this trip to the valley was that Lord Fall kept his people's eyes downcast for so long that none of them even thought to look up.

Death, however, was like fire. It could spark and burn where it wanted and flame up from the ground. Or it could fall from the sky like cinders.

CHAPTER 3
WELCOME HOME

I couldn't see any real demarcation in the land, yet I still knew the moment my feet were on the grounds of my family's estate again.

The monotonous gray covering all around and falling from the sky, made everything meld together and reduced the world around me to hulking shapes of shadow and vague movements as if I were surrounded by wraiths.

My breath caught in my chest, scratching and gnawing until I coughed again.

Every time I left the duchy, every time I was away long enough for my lungs to forget how to breathe this air, my return left me gasping and hacking.

I was able to smell the overpowering tang of the hellfire water burning. Hellfire water burned spicy with a hint of sweet, like the fancy breakfast treats everyone else in the kingdom ate. None of my people made the damn things. But every morning when I was in a different region or a different Lord's land, I got waves of the smell that reminded me of home wafting from other people's ovens.

Passing the blackened trunk of a tree, its bark long turned harder than the metal of most blades, I ducked one of the rare leaves it grew. The leaf was wilted, brown, and furred in some kind of soft layer that no one knew the purpose of.

All the trees in our lands were like this one, whatever species they had once been. Since the war seven years ago, nothing green survived on these rolling hills that used to grow so much.

Now, all that was left for plants were the iron hard trees and their occasional leaf that never lasted more than a season.

Just beyond the line of trees, the ruins of my home rose as a deep, black shadow in the sky.

I leaned my head back and looked up at the last intact spire as I always did. The ash falling from the sky landed as light as a sigh on my cheeks before I made my way to the front doors.

Our proof of life spire—the one that signaled to the survivors of the battle that our duchy still stood—still lived in some way. Char marks licked at its lower edges on one side, but somehow there it remained.

Walking across the yard to the doors, the dogs didn't run to greet me, which meant they were inside with my brother.

"Damn it," I muttered, taking a deep breath which made my chest ache and forced me to cough. I shoved at the rough wood door that he replaced the old one with five years ago.

Of all the days to get home, of all the times, it had to be when Ash was holding court.

As soon as I was inside with the door shut behind me, the silence sent the hairs along the nape of my neck rising.

I swallowed and stood up straighter, grabbing the extra seal and the papers from Lord Fall in hands that immediately balled into fists around them.

The muscles in my arms wanted to shake, my hands began to sweat. But Ash couldn't know.

If he knew, it would be worse.

Around a corner, the front hall ended in the jagged and broken stone opening where doors to the receiving chamber used to be.

My brother sat on the metal frame of what once was our mother's beautiful and lush receiving chair. His deep brown hair fell long over his forehead, brushing the thick top lashes of his hooded eyes.

He sat forward, his arms resting on his knees as if he was ready to leap from the chair and attack any of the half dozen people arrayed in front of him.

"Cinder, it's so good of you to come during reception," he said, his voice edged at the mention of reception, clipping the word short at the end.

"Apologies, Duke Ash," I said, knowing better than to try to explain why I interrupted, and knowing that coming anywhere near the suggestion he should have had someone posted outside to warn me about barging in was the stupidest thing I could do.

Narrowing his eyes, a smug grin spread on his face before he leaned back in the chair, slouching to the side.

"Everyone, I would like to greet my sister privately for a moment. You can go into the antechamber, and someone will get you refreshments while you wait."

I swallowed, sweat broke out along my hairline, and my teeth ground together. I wanted to call out to them, please don't go.

But only one person risked a glance at me as they all filed out of the room and had the door shut behind them by Brix, Ash's best friend and the captain of the guard.

As soon as the door clicked shut after them, Ash jumped up from his seat and stomped off the dais to meet me in the middle of the room.

I walked toward him because that was what I had been

trained to do—follow my liege, anticipate his needs. But I wanted to run in the other direction.

"Tell me," he commanded, as soon as we were face to face, his eyes only a couple inches higher than mine.

Rounding my shoulders and keeping my back looking straight, I shrank and handed over the papers and the seal.

"He's dead, and Solaria and her baby are safe."

Ash waved a hand as if he was brushing aside the most important parts of the story, but Brix smiled behind him.

But what started as a smile slowly morphed into a leer.

I couldn't help curling my upper lip.

Somehow, I would find a way to never be married to any of Ash's friends. Even if it meant one day, I was going to have to use something even more subtle than my spike.

"What is this seal?" he asked, turning it and raising it to the light so he could inspect it from all angles.

"After I was done, I looked through his desk. That was in a false bottom of a drawer. I have no idea what the seal means, I've never seen it before." All of that was true, but by the way his eyes flicked from it to me, all I could do was hope he didn't hear the omission hiding in my words.

"Nothing else?"

"Nothing. I found that, and the envelope from the King. The other papers were on the desktop." I looked him in the eye as I said it, willing nothing but veracity to show on my face.

"Did you look in the envelope?" His voice was low and the weight of it settled in my stomach sending it careening to my feet.

"No," I said, the truth was easy. I knew better than to look through the papers too much.

His hand shot out, and although I saw it coming, although I had time to block him or to clench my muscles to take the blow, I didn't.

Fingers hard and straight as if they were his version of my spike, he slammed them into my stomach, doubling me over, the air rushing out of me in one big gush.

"Lies are unbecoming," he said, his voice the same as it had been when he asked me for my report.

Don't respond, Cinder.

There was no right answer, there was only the right way to take *his* response.

I nodded, my eyes still on the floor, my hands on my stomach where I could already tell a bruise would form.

"Mother and Father would never approve of a lie," he said, his voice soft and sad.

"They…" I said, my voice shallow and more like a breath in the shape of a far-off echo than an actual word. "They would be proud."

He stepped back then, and I allowed myself a peek up at him. Would it work?

But he was onto the papers in his hands, pouring over the information in them.

It was my cue to go, so I straightened as much as I dared and turned to leave the room, to find my bed.

"Cinder," he called after me and I wrapped my hands tighter on my stomach.

With a deep breath, I turned around.

"I have another job for you." He smiled, his face soft like it used to be when he looked at me. He looked like he did when I was still just his adorable baby sister and he loved me.

Like every time before, I looked at him with bare hope all over my face. I couldn't help it. Every time his face was like that, like he truly saw me again, I wanted to cling to him and beg him to stay that way.

"This job is a little different, and it will be your most important yet."

CHAPTER 4
SWORD ARM

'D on't interrupt, Cinder,' I told myself. Although I wanted him to stop playing games and just spit it out.

Instead of speaking and bringing more of his wrath down on me, instead of risking the loving look falling from his face, I stayed silent but cocked my head and raised my brows. I let my face be the question while I kept silent.

"Instructions will be sent to you as soon as I take care of some things," Ash said, looking me up and down, his eyes studying me in a way that made my skin itch. What in the world would this new job be?

"For now," he broke off his perusal of my body and leaned back in his chair, looking down at the papers in his hands, "go have a bath."

Part of me didn't trust that I was dismissed.

Last time I turned my back on my brother when I thought he was done speaking I couldn't lift anything with my sword arm for a week.

But a glance Brix's way didn't tell me anything, and my brother's face gave no clue that he was waiting to strike.

Finally, I turned to leave.

"And Cinder," he called, stopping me mid-step so my muscles bunched, and I turned to look at him over my shoulder, "Get well cleaned."

Well cleaned?

My stomach flipped over, the feeling so focused on my abdomen that the bruise forming there screamed in pain.

But I nodded and left the receiving room, heading down the hall past the broken doorway toward the stairs while I tried to disconnect from my body.

I tried not to think about what he was going to make me do. I tried not to imagine it was even worse than the things I was capable of coming up with, because the myriad possibilities running through my head as I plodded down the stairs into the sweltering heat of the lower levels were bad enough.

One story under the ground, just below the stones everyone usually walked on, was the secret heart of my home.

Down here, the reason snow fell from the sky in the deep of winter but never collected on the ground was made plain. Down here, where the stones of the foundations were held up only by the viscosity of the source of hellfire water, the heat was oppressive.

Why and how our ancestors built directly over the almost solid sludge of the hellfire water that filtered itself through underground rivers, mixing with other things to form the usable, easier-flowing fuel we mined throughout our lands, was a mystery to everyone.

Maybe when the day came that my brother got the justice he hungered for, I would be able to ask him if that was why he didn't repair our home. Maybe it just wasn't possible.

But I still laid awake most nights looking through the

broken wall of my bedroom where a window used to be, and imagined it whole again.

For right now, all I could do was help him see the future he craved, and be his blade in the slow battle to avenge our parents.

"I am his sword arm," I said to the walls of the pool chamber as I entered the room at the bottom of the last set of steps.

Around me the vaults of stone gleamed even as shrouded in steam as they were. While the rest of my home bore the scars and wounds of our traumatic past, this space hidden deep within it, remained untouched. Instead of gray and muted, or scorched black and broken, the stone down here was white as the sun and the blue gems embedded periodically among the white looked like stars in a pale sky.

Even though the air was so hot and humid it lay on my skin like the thickest of my quilts, there was comfort in its embrace. A return.

"Lady Cinder, can I get you a bath ready?" Meg asked, appearing out of the steam in her white gown and matching white hair, her dainty face flushed and her hazel eyes daring to meet mine.

"Yes, thank you, Meg." I started to take off my cloak and many weapons as she walked away toward the back corner pool I preferred.

Pausing with my knife belt only partially undone, I watched her go.

She was only a few years younger than me at nineteen, but the way she carried herself seemed to me to deem her even younger than that.

I couldn't help but wonder if I would look and move the same if the war had not come to my home in exactly the way it had.

My mother and father trained me before they were killed, but I was still expected to wear dresses and be presentable at court. Now, there was no way the corded muscles of my arms or the scars criss-crossing my stomach would ever allow me to wear some of the most popular fashions. And I had no idea if I could even walk in the shoes anymore. I certainly wouldn't know the dances.

Meg would probably be forgiven any clumsiness because she was lovely. While I would be a strange clod who people would probably compare to a horse.

Shaking my head at the odd thoughts running through my tired mind, I finished taking off the many layers of clothing and weapons I always traveled with, placing them carefully along one of the long benches carved into the stone walls.

By the time I finished, I turned around naked to see candles lit all along my bathing pool and Meg lining up the oils and salts for the kind of thorough scrubbing I didn't usually bother with.

"Well cleaned," I mumbled to myself, a shiver running down my spine despite the heat.

Meg didn't look at me as I made my way to the pool and down the steps into the water so close to the same temperature as the air that my body didn't register a difference. It just sluiced over me as if the air itself had simply grown thicker.

"Ahhh." I leaned back into the water and let my body float on top, my long hair floating all around me.

"Lady Cinder, your brother gave me very specific instructions. When you're ready, let me know." Meg's voice came to me through the water, distorted and more like the waves were speaking to me.

I sighed, but stood in the pool, the water up to my collarbones, before I made my way over to the bench just below where she perched so I could remain mostly submerged.

"What exactly were his instructions? He didn't give me much information." I tried to sound jovial and conversational, but I think it came off as more confrontational because her small mouth formed into a frown.

"Pardon me, my Lady." Her voice was small and there was a quake in it that had not been there before.

"Meg, I'm sorry. It's not your fault. My brother was just busy with the reception and didn't have time to explain." There, my second attempt was closer to the tone I was reaching for.

She nodded and picked up the hair wash, so I didn't push it.

For the next few hours, I simply moved where she directed me to, few words spoken between us in the process.

By the time she was done, there was no staining left around the edges of my fingernails or my toenails and my skin looked smoother than it had in ages. All the ash was gone from the tiny crevices and cracks.

Well cleaned, my brother said.

I still wasn't entirely sure what that meant, or why he would have thought it necessary when I was just going to go back to my room.

All the ash and soot of this place, my home, was going to coat my entire body again. It was already making its way back into my lungs. Soon I wouldn't even cough anymore.

Unless the next assignment would take me out of the duchy for a long period again.

Maybe that was his intention.

It didn't matter.

Whatever his assignment for me, I was his tool, the best way for both of us to get revenge and right the wrongs committed when our parents were killed.

I was his sword arm.

He would use me as he saw fit.

CHAPTER 5
OUR WORK

B y the time I was shaved and washed and scrubbed, my
entire body started to feel like the pads of my fingers
after being submerged for too long.

I sighed and stepped out of the pool, but footsteps sounded
on the stone nearby. I dropped back with barely a splash.

My ears and eyes waited for another sound. My hands
curled to fists.

If Brix or one of my brother's idiot friends thought spying
on me down here was going to work out in his favor because I
was nude, they would find how very not unarmed I was when a
blade wasn't in my hand.

"You should know that I wouldn't waste an opportunity on
one of them," Ash said, reading my mind.

"What opportunity?" I asked, climbing from the pool to grab
a drying sheet and wrap it tight around myself.

Brix and his lot weren't great to be around ever. Let alone
while naked and unarmed. Ash was worse.

A drying sheet was at least a small layer of protection
from him.

"It's about your new assignment." He materialized from behind a pillar, as if it wasn't weird for him to be hiding there.

"Which pampered want-to-be-princeling will I be visiting next?" I asked, pretending I didn't want Ash to just go and let me relax for a minute.

"Funny you should say, 'princeling.'" He paced back and forth, a frenetic kind of energy emanating from his whole body.

He was excited about something. Ash was always so contained, so carefully controlled. This unnecessary level of movement sent all the alarms bells ringing in my head.

My muscles responded, tightening and bracing, while I rose onto my toes and unlocked my knees, bending just so. Preparing to move swiftly if needed.

"All this time, our work," he said, mostly to himself.

Our work.

What he meant was, his direction, his choices, my risk, and my labor.

But I shoved down the bitter tang of my place and took a deep breath.

I was his sword arm.

I accepted that position a long time ago. I was used as he saw fit. There was no reason to wish it different.

Especially not when the cause was just and the best way for us to get it was through this arrangement. So he could keep his hands clean and our lands could stay in this family. Under his rule.

"Listen, Cinder, what has been the goal? All along?" he asked, turning to look at me. He stopped pacing.

"To make it to the King. To get revenge for our parents." My words were rote and automatic by now.

It was all he could talk about for a year after their deaths. The need, the way to get it all back. But he finally came up with a plan. I was the plan, and I went to work. What started as my diversion became my mission: training. At least after he decided on the plan he was more stable for the duchy and the people in it.

After that the only person he usually took his rage out on was the one person who would love him no matter what. The one person who understood his anger.

Me.

"Yes. Exactly. And has that worked out? Our way of trying to find the network, of trying to find a way in to get to the King?" he asked. This time his eyes danced, and a smile tugged on his mouth which sent goosebumps rippling down my arms and legs despite the oppressive heat all around me.

"Not yet." Why was he asking me this? Like it was some kind of strange quiz. These answers were easy. They weren't like the usual things he questioned me about. The impossible things. No, these were things he knew I was fully aware of.

He nodded his head, the fevered light still in his eyes.

"Finally," he said, stepping closer to me.

I fought the urge to flinch as he took my hands. His were soft and almost loving.

Although I tried not to think about it, being down here with him, his hold on my hands. It reminded me of that day. The day I sent everyone down here. The day he had to tell me our parents were dead.

Swallowing hard and fighting back the tears collecting in the backs of my eyes, I looked up at my brother as I had that day. Our eyes were so close to the same height now, but he was still my big brother. And all the faith and care I had for him then welled within me anew.

"There is a way for you to get to the King. There is a way for us to finally get the justice we seek."

CHAPTER 6
NEED A QUEEN

"How?" I asked, my throat only allowing the word to come out thin and tight.

"Apparently King Tristan is in need of a Queen," he said.

I outright laughed in his face.

But I reigned in my reaction. I never pushed Ash, risked his ire like that. It was an impulse I couldn't control.

"You can't be serious. King Tristan would never pick me. We can't offer him anything. He'll marry for an alliance, for some kind of benefit. It's the way it's done." I scrambled for a way to soften the harsh guffaw, to avoid Ash's anger.

Nothing I said seemed to bother him though. Not even my laughter seemed to pull a response from him.

His face remained...not impassive, but almost...content.

More than anything he said or did since I got home, that look on his face—the one that belonged to someone else entirely—sent my heart plummeting to my toes.

"What's really going on?" I asked, all the humor gone from me, my voice cold and low.

"King Tristan needs a Queen and an heir. The neighbors are starting to think Onyx is ripe for takeover since he is all that remains of the royal family."

My mouth dropped open and the horrors of the last war ran through my head.

"Another war? Already?" My question was barely audible. We usually had at least a decade of peace for the people, but it was true that most royals never thought of their people when they made those decisions. Only their own increase in power.

"Not if we can help it." He let go of my hands and resumed pacing.

"But how would we ever stop it? You can't be serious that you want me to marry him. You said he's the reason our parents are dead." I wrapped my arms around myself, despite the heat down here, the whole world seemed colder.

"I don't want you to marry him. Even if the other kingdoms don't know what the line of succession is, it doesn't mean we don't have one."

He ran a hand through his hair. It had been such a long time since he did that, and it reminded me of before. When he was just my brother, and I was just his sister instead of a Duke and his sword arm.

"So you want me to somehow get the King to marry me, even though he would really need an alliance with a family and land, with far more influence than ours? And then you want me to kill him and allow the succession to take place?" I asked, trying to follow how in the hell that would ever work.

"Actually…" he paused and looked at me, his head cocked to the side. He plainly studied my face, as if delving into the depths of my brain.

I swallowed. The idea of him giving me that mission made me want to run, run as far and as fast from my brother as I could reach.

There was no way to succeed in that mission. There was no way to avoid his wrath if I failed. Not in this. Not in the closest mission to accomplish what we had been working for these last seven years.

But Ash shook his head, and I took in a shuddering breath.

"No, that isn't the plan. You're right that they'll look for some kind of advantage that we just can't offer."

Part of me wanted to relax, but the rest of me knew this wasn't the end of the conversation. And I had no idea where it was going.

"King Tristan has invited all the eligible women to the Obsidian Palace so he can get to know them," Ash said.

My brain went blank.

"So," I started, trying to work out how that was giving my brother so much joy, "You want me to accept this invitation and kill him in front of all those people?"

No, my brother wouldn't give me this impossible task, not in this way.

But he smiled.

I swallowed and wanted to vomit.

"His plan, from what I've been able to gather, is to have all the women go to the palace, attend an opening ball, and then have those he likes stay on for a time. It seems to be like a competition, but I can't gather how that will work just yet."

"A competition? Really? Some kind of sick trick to get more from the families before he commits to one of the alliances that can give him the best advantages?" How did his advisors think this was a good idea?

"Yes. As far as I know, it seems many think he'll get promises from more than one family this way."

But at the end, when only one alliance was made, the others would go home with their high hopes dashed and start plotting.

"What is my part in all this?" Was it as simple as ingratiating myself with all the losers so that when they hatched their plots for revenge they came to my brother?

He put a hand on my upper arm, all the muscles in my back tightening in response.

"Cinder, my beautiful sister, you are going to use this chance to get close to the King. You are going to find a way to be alone with him while the rest are posturing. You are going to kill him before they can be disappointed. And you are going to get away from the palace before anyone realizes what happened."

Somewhere in my body ice formed in my veins and my muscles buzzed as if they were falling asleep. Somewhere in me the protests that this plan would never work, that I would get caught, that this was a suicide mission, all screamed to be acknowledged and rectified.

But Ash stood before me, his hope, our work, the last seven years painted on his face in such detail, I couldn't say no.

"I am your sword arm. I will kill the King."

Even if it means going to my own death in the process.

CHAPTER 7
THROUGH THE ASHES

Ash let me sleep one night in my own bed and my own room.

But the morning came too soon.

I watched as the gray outside began to lighten, and the individual flakes falling through the broken part of my ceiling and wall dropped to the floor.

My lungs no longer ached for me to cough, and the coating of my home had settled again into the tiny lines in my skin. It was soft and became a snug-fitting blanket protecting me from the outside world.

And I had no idea how long it would be until I would feel it again, how long it would be before I could sleep under blankets chosen by my mother, in a bed she would have recognized.

Now, I faced a trip unlike the others I made.

It wouldn't be a mere few days, not long enough to make my lungs feel the full brunt if my eventual return.

My longest trip took months. But this one…

There was no way of telling when I would see my home

again, when I would feel the heat from the ground and the coating from the sky.

King Tristan's ball was just over a month away. In that time, I needed to travel close to the Obsidian Palace, turn myself into the kind of woman the King would want to keep around long enough to be alone with, and become my brother's sword.

Again.

"Mother, Father, please help me see this through. Please help me make the kingdom better. Please let the next royals care for the people," I whispered aloud into the lightening sky.

But, as always, I left out one of the things I wanted most after fulfilling my role as the sword arm.

No one needed to know that.

Even though my parents were gone, they would not have wanted me to hope for it, and I never wanted Ash to know that I did.

Someday, when I wasn't needed as a sword arm, maybe I would admit it. Until then, I tried to shove the hope all the way down into the mattress.

Maybe I would be able to leave it behind on this trip.

And when the King was dead, I could pick it up again.

Until then, I needed to try and remember what it was like to be a Lady at court.

On the other side of the door, footsteps rang down the stone hallway, stopping at my room and knocking.

"Lady Cinder, the carriage is waiting," Jocelyn said from the other side of the door, the clink of the sword at her side against her greaves made me smile.

"Coming, Jocelyn. I'll be down in a minute."

She walked away, her steps less hurried than before, but the clinking remained.

It meant she was in a good mood. A habit she picked up when she first arrived in her flashing fighter's cloak.

Whatever made her happy, I was glad of it.

Happy was too rare an emotion around this place lately

I climbed out of bed and donned my clothes, staring at the much less formal items I normally wore on a mission.

"Damn it," I muttered, sighing and dropping my head back to stare at the ceiling.

This was going to be a more difficult assignment than any simple assassination.

Making my way out of my room, running my fingers through my hair as I walked, I wondered when I would be able to wear something I could move in again. A dress wouldn't let me move the way I wanted to. And I had no idea how long I would be trapped in skirts.

"Good morning, Cinder," Ash said from behind me, making me freeze and pray that my thoughts didn't show on my face.

"Brother," I said, with a tilt of my head.

He smiled and shook his head.

"Darling sister, you are going to need to do better than that in court. A curtsy, a demure face. But you know all of this. It hasn't been that long." He clucked his tongue and slipped my hand into the crook of his elbow, tugging me the rest of the way out into the courtyard.

It had been that long, though. Seven years—from fifteen to twenty-two—was a lifetime.

"When you get to Bridgeton, I'll have someone instruct you and refresh your memory." He looked me up and down, but his smile didn't waver. There was no sign of the irritation I feared, the kind that usually preceded a blow.

"Yes, that would be helpful, thank you," I said, as fast as my lips would move.

Ash was being nice. It was so out of character it made my skin crawl a little bit, but I wasn't going to remind him that he should probably be hurting me.

"How long do you think I will be part of this? I mean, what if he doesn't want to meet with me alone, and I never get the opportunity to fulfill my assignment?" It was a risk to ask the question, but in the mood he was in, it was my best option to put a seed in his mind to forgive me this impossible task.

"Cinder," he said, patting the back of my hand as he held the other in his and tsked at me. "If you don't manage to complete this assignment, so be it."

I relaxed and let out a heavy breath before I squeezed my eyes shut for a moment.

"Just having you there will afford you some kind of opportunity to either take his head, or take someone else's and blame it on him. Either way, you bring our vengeance home." His voice had a thrill in it, the kind he used to have before a tournament, or some other game.

But this wasn't a game.

And now I knew.

I wasn't allowed to fail.

There was only one thing that would bring me home, only one thing that would mean my brother wouldn't resort to the worst of his punishments.

Maybe my status as his sister would no longer matter, even though it had protected me in some ways.

He smiled and kissed my forehead. All the relaxation in my body a moment ago focused into a sharp stab where he kissed me and radiated out to fill my whole body.

"Yes, Duke Ash," I mumbled, my voice as gray and desolate as the landscape around us.

"So, now you'll go and get trained in the things you need to do for the first step. And, I know, this isn't as fun as the training you have been doing." He grinned and winked at me while the back of my mouth filled with the taste of bile.

I nodded.

There were no words left inside me as he let go of me. Around us, the process of packing the carriage, and preparing for the journey finished up.

"Go, Little Sword, may your aim be true so your home be blessed." Ash's words followed me up the steps and in through the open door as I settled on the bench inside the carriage. It creaked beneath me from disuse and age.

Little Sword.

Ash never called me that, he called me his sword arm.

Little Sword was Mother's nickname for me. Tempered in fire, she said.

I never understood entirely what she meant by it, because she said it before the war, before the mine was set ablaze, and my corner of the world burned. Before she succumbed to the flames.

But now, sitting in the carriage, on my way to what might be an impossible mission, armed more with my lacking refinements than a blade, it felt more like a lie than it ever had.

Swords were tempered by fire, but if they were brought to temperature and left too long in the heat, they would shatter.

As the carriage rattled through the drifts of gray ash over the broken and irreparable cobblestones of the courtyard, every part of me felt as brittle as glass.

CHAPTER 8

FRESH FLOWERS

Bridgeton was just across the river from the Obsidian Palace, home of the Dragon Kings of Onyx.

Legend said that once, long ago, the Kings of Onyx formed the Obsidian Palace using their own power over flame.

But no one I had ever known believed that story.

And most believed that the reason we were so often the target of attack from other kingdoms was because we lacked any royal magic.

Other kingdoms thought that because our king couldn't attack with a tornado or throw a horse at someone, then we must be easy to defeat.

They always seemed to forget that few royals ever went to the battlefield themselves.

But the biggest effect of their erroneous assumption was that Onyx's population shrunk with every war, and it was now difficult for those left in some trades to supply all the work we needed to make a country run.

Everyone was tired of war.

Well, everyone that wasn't my brother.

Ash wanted to go to war as long as it was his sword arm against someone else's. As long as I was the one who was at risk and not him.

How he thought that would work out, I never heard him say. But watching out of the carriage window as we slowed to a stop in front of a thin, brick house just outside the city's jewelry row, I wondered again about his singular commitment to this plan.

Getting out of the carriage, I wrapped my cloak tight against a cold bite on the wind.

For the first time I could remember, this sword arm was going to be sleeping in a fancy private home while on assignment.

The tall front door opened on the brick house and a woman stepped out in a much more austere gown of gray with no frills or adornments I could see.

It was like the dress equivalent of my short cloak. Utilitarian.

"Lady Cinder, please come inside," the woman said, looking up and down the street as if my grime and travel-coated presence would offend the neighbors.

"Yes, Lady…" I let the implied question mark at the end of my sentence hang in the air between us, not taking a step in her direction.

Servants appeared to bring inside the trunks sent along by Ash.

What was in them, I couldn't imagine.

I had no clothes in current fashion at court.

And unless King Tristan was in the mood for speaking with a woman wearing more weapons than he did, I doubted Ash sent along much in the way of weapons.

"Lady Cinder, you can call me Madam Valentin. Now I must insist you come in and get settled. There is much to do."

The way she said 'much to do' sounded like judgement, but I took a breath and followed her inside.

She kept walking once I was right behind her, giving me little time to take in the shocking number of flowers in the foyer, or to be totally overwhelmed by the heady scent of them all.

A curved and ornate staircase wrapped around the foyer and up to the second story. In the rounded section of the floor at the base of the turn of the stairs, a round table sat with what had to be a dozen flower arrangements on it. Although they made no sense.

I didn't have time to puzzle them out, or to make any sense of the tiny images on the wallpaper we passed in the short hall to a grand dining room.

Madam Valentin, the name of someone with wealth but without a title or lands or people of her own to look after.

No, she wouldn't have received an invitation for some daughter or niece to participate in the search for a queen. So what was she doing helping me?

And how much did it cost Ash? Or would it cost me?

"Please, sit. I have taken the liberty of choosing the options for dinner today." She gestured to the chair at the end of the table.

I took the seat she offered, although I rounded my shoulders while keeping my spine straight like I always did when I was expecting a blow from Ash.

He wasn't here, but if I sat at the head of the table at home— even when he wasn't around—he would have made me pay for the mistake.

While now I was in no danger of this woman hitting me, it would take more than distance for me to forget the lessons Ash taught me.

Servants set down a full array in front of me, complete with a tiny finger bowl. They also brought out four dishes and placed them in front of me.

I looked at Madam Valentin, waiting for her to give me a clue of what was appropriate here in her home.

Would she sit and eat with me?

But all she did was tilt her head a fraction.

Okay. If she wanted me to help myself, I would oblige. Even if she was just going to stand there and watch me while I did it.

I scooped up more food than I normally ate in two meals, piling my plate high.

The road to Bridgeton had taken days.

Days of dry, boring traveling food and water left me ready to gorge myself on the flavors in front of me.

I swallowed down the ale leaving little in the bottom of the cup, and turned to the food in front of me.

Madam Valentin faded into the background as I made my way too fast through the food on my plate. At some point, I would be eating in the palace where I couldn't do this.

Before I became the ornamental rapier version of Ash's sword arm, I wanted to be a broadsword for just this meal. Just long enough to be full and ready for what came next.

Finally, the plate was almost empty, and I wanted to curl into a ball and sleep there on the chair.

"May I get some rest now. After the travel I find I'm exhausted." Well, the travel and the amount of food stretching my stomach.

"You may after you have bathed and changed into clean clothes. No one wants to sleep in a travel-marred outfit," she said, her face impassive, and I wondered for a moment if she would stand to the side while I bathed too.

I dipped my head to her and stood from the table, following her through the foyer of too many blooms and up to the second story.

She led me down a long hall with paintings of more flowers hanging all the way down.

Finally, she opened the door to a bedroom with pale, almost gray wood, and purple fabric on the bed.

My trunks with their mystery contents were already along one wall. I wanted to fall across the bed and go to sleep right then.

But she kept moving, through the bedroom to a bath that was as white as my home in Lehar was gray. Every surface seemed white and shiny.

It made me feel dirty in comparison and I wondered if anyone ever used this bathroom.

A bath was already drawn. Steam billowed from the water where flowers floated, their scent lacing the air.

What was going on with all the flowers?

None of my curious questions actually mattered, not when I needed to get this bath done so I could sleep.

Getting in the water stung the small nicks along my hands and arms from my last assignment in a way that the pool at home never did.

I sucked in a breath, the hiss of it echoing off the walls in a way that made the room sinister—no matter how clean and pretty—and set my hands to aching for a blade.

At least Madam Valentin let me bathe by myself. The only problem with that was it gave me little time to even attempt to relax. Between the charge in the air that made me look over my shoulder more than once, the faint sting still happening on all my scrapes and bruises, and the fact that I didn't trust myself not to fall asleep in the water if I leaned back, the whole thing turned into a job of its own.

By the time I got out, the water was still plenty warm, but I needed to sleep more than I needed to remain in it.

Hopefully the large bed would be comfortable enough for me to not wake up every half hour to check on my surroundings. It was my pattern when I was away from home to not allow myself to be off my guard for too long. Usually, the only time I was able to put away my own vigilance, was in my room at home.

Even there, with Ash around…

Seven years was a long time to never fully relax.

With the bath sheet wrapped around me and my clothes in my hands, I opened the door to the bedroom.

Madam Valentin was standing next to the enormous bed with a tray of brushes and pots of lotion. Next to her, draped across the bed, was a light piece of silk I feared was a nightgown.

So, it began already, the process of turning me into a woman who was supposed to fit in at the court of the King.

The King who was responsible for killing my parents.

CHAPTER 9
GIFTS

I straightened, my feet stepping apart into a stronger defensive position and my hands tightening their grip on my clothes, feeling the reassuring weight of my spike tucked within.

Madam Valentin pursed her lips.

"Please put your things on that chair there and get this nightgown on. I need to brush out your hair and prepare your skin," she said, glancing at a plain wooden chair by the door I just walked through.

I did as she asked, but tried not to feel like I was a small child following the directions of the tutor while I did it. And I was only mildly successful.

She sat me down in front of a vanity on a velvet stool that reminded me of one my mother once had.

Madam's treatment of my skin and hair wasn't rough, but it wasn't gentle either. In firm, brisk movements, she teased out all the knots, rubbed in different lotions for each of my limbs, and still another for my face.

When she was done with me, I looked down at my own arms

and realized that somewhere between the bath and her minis-trations, all my scrapes and bruises had faded.

One on my arm—which was a lurid red line only an hour before—was now a faint pink and showed no signs of forming a scar.

I grabbed my leg and checked the old scar from the last war. Even it, after all this time, was less obvious. Thinner and so faint in color it blended with my skin, a pang shot through my heart at losing it.

"How?" I asked, not expecting her to answer.

"Your brother made it very clear that I am to turn you into the proper Lady you are." She nodded to herself, like she was agreeing with her own statement.

It took a lot of willpower not to tell her that wasn't ladylike at all. In fact, it was damn irritating.

At least I had the mirror between us and only had to watch her through the reflection. If she did it directly in front of me it would have been more difficult to hold my tongue.

But Ash would be furious if I crossed her. If she was employed by him, I had to keep my thoughts to myself.

"What will that entail exactly?" I asked, because no matter how not smart it was, I needed some kind of answer, some kind of way to know what to expect.

"Hmm," she mumbled, her mouth pressed into a thin line as she ran a hand through my long brown hair and looked me up and down. Finally, she made eye contact with me in the mirror.

"You are pretty enough," she said, and I held perfectly still, realizing a little late that I invited a ton of judgement to fall on my head, "And you have an attractive shape to your figure, but you are far too muscular."

She stepped to the side, looking down at me, and all I could do was follow her in the mirror with my eyes. Part of me wanted to show her how deadly those faults she was busy accounting actually were.

But Madam wasn't my target, and I needed to stay on mission.

"When you move through a room, you are like a cat stalking a mouse. But when you eat you are like a wild and ravenous twelve-year-old boy."

Eat? She judged how hungry I was? Who would judge someone based on how hungry they were after days of shit food and shittier travel with few stops?

"To say nothing of your sullen and stubborn lack of conversation."

Right. Because that was fair. If I had known she was going to judge me negatively based on my choice to remain quiet instead of the opposite I would have…

No. I wouldn't have.

How was I supposed to magically learn how to engage with people in conversation, especially about inane small talk that was okay in polite society when I was better prepared to talk about when to use which blade?

"But more than all of that—each of which might take me six months that we do not have to properly train you in—is the fact that you stand like you are about to be in a fist fight." She shook her head and straightened her shoulders while I cringed inside.

The worst thing about me was the thing I did to save myself.

Of course it was.

I wilted and it was my turn to nod.

"Madam Valentin, I want to thank you for your assessment. I intend to improve in all areas. But I think I must get some sleep now. It was a difficult journey, and I am afraid I am exhausted," I said, standing and turning to face her.

She dipped her head and left the room without saying a

word, without acknowledging anything about how maybe, just maybe, she might have been incorrect.

Although…maybe she was right. Maybe my mission was over before it started.

Yanking the blankets down, I climbed into the bed.

But too many pillows were in my way. I chucked them, one after another, as far as they would fly through the room.

Ungainly pillows covered in frilly and ridiculous cases, flopped, end over end, landing on the floor, knocked over pots on the vanity, and resting up against the chair that held my clothes from home.

Next to the chair was one of the trunks Ash sent with me.

I was tired. That wasn't a lie.

But I didn't lay down right away. I sat there and stared at the trunks.

They had to be empty.

We didn't have anything that would make sense for Ash to pack for me.

He would never allow my best assignment clothes to be sent along to court, no matter what I was actually there to do. And none of my decent clothes for company at home would be appropriate here.

Or…

"Shit," I mumbled, climbing from the bed, rubbing the heels of my hands into my eyes, leaving them blurry and blinking.

When I opened the first trunk, it was empty like I thought they were.

Ash would have someone come and outfit me. Those clothes would fill this trunk and accompany me into the Obsidian Palace.

I flung open the next trunk, shaking my head that I was even checking. I knew it would be empty too.

But it wasn't.

On one end was a bundle of aged and withered velvet, and at the other was a pair of satin slippers with our family's flame sigil on them in bright green beading.

"Mother's shoes," I said to the empty room.

Picking them up, they were as light and soft as I remembered them.

When I was very small, I would get them out of her drawer in her room and slip my feet inside even though they were far too big. She wore them for her wedding to Father and only once after that.

But I didn't think about that time.

Not anymore.

I thought about her wearing them as she stood next to Father and took his sigil as her own, something she wore with pride until the day she died.

Her family were merchants, traveling even beyond the borders of Onyx, and among the things they traded was hellfire water.

Mother met Father via hellfire water, and died the same way. Alongside him.

But I held the slippers to my chest where an ache—one that never completely went away—flared up bright.

"Thank you, Ash."

I would at least have something from home with me when I entered the palace.

Placing the slippers to the side, I took out the velvet bundle.

It was heavier than I anticipated, but when I unwrapped it, I still wasn't prepared for what I found.

My spike, folded within my soiled clothes, was an almost constant companion. But there was no way I would be able to conceal it in a gown. My dagger, which was also with me, was likewise a problem.

This was perfect.

A small, double leather belt with a thinner, sharper version of my spike strapped to it was laying in the soft fabric.

I tried it on, knowing this wasn't supposed to go around my waist. It was much too small for that, so I tried it on my calf.

Not small enough.

When I strapped it on my thigh, though, it fit perfectly. And when I twisted it around so that the spike-like blade laid flat against my inner thigh, held in place by the leather on top and on bottom, even in my nightgown it was imperceptible.

Perfect.

All I had to do now was follow Madam Valentin's instruction so I could get close enough to the King.

CHAPTER 10

LADY

Morning came too early.

Light splintered my dreams, forcing its way in as the sun rose, shining in my window.

"Of course they put me on this side of the house." I rubbed my eyes and rolled over, trying to eke out even a few more moments of rest, even if there was no way to get more sleep.

Today I had work to do.

Ash may have given me my mission days ago, and I may have thought I was starting then. But I was wrong.

Right now, this morning, was the beginning of my real assignment. And I needed to prepare for it.

I sat up and bent forward, stretching my arms down to hold my toes under the blanket. In that position, I went through my body, one area at a time, tightening and releasing the muscles.

When I was done, I sat up and stretched my arms over my head, taking a deep breath and holding it for a moment, letting the birth of the morning light pour through me.

Finally, I released my breath and dropped my arms.

Madam Valentin might believe I was as close to a lost cause

as any woman entering the palace had ever been. But I was stronger than she thought.

If I could train and master a new weapon faster than my brother—something I did all the time when we were children—then I could master her lessons too.

No matter what they were.

The bathroom was my next stop. The chill on the floor reached up through my toes to give me goosebumps.

By the time I was done, and walking back into my room, Madam Valentin waited next to the vanity with three servants and two strangers in outfits that looked like a cross between my work clothes and a court suit.

I tried to stand like my mother did, hoping I would get close to being more like what Madam wanted.

"Pardon me, I did not know you were waiting," I said with a tip of my head.

One of Madam's eyebrows rose to a point, but she tilted her head back at me.

"Good morning. We need to start by getting you fitted for a new wardrobe and having at least one piece for you to wear while we prepare you," she said.

I glanced at the two strangers, understanding they were the dressmakers. She was careful in her word choice so they didn't understand the full extent of what was going on.

What exactly had she told them?

"Come over here and we can get started. I'm sure you're thrilled to be going to the palace, and I'm thrilled you'll be wearing our clothes," one of the strangers said, still not introducing themselves or giving me any hint as to who they were or what I was supposed to call them. Their voice was a velvety coo, low and soft. It felt strangely intimate and made the hairs on my arms stand on end.

But I followed their directions and stood behind the vanity

stool, looking into the mirror as they walked around my back, lifted my hair, and muttered amongst themselves in low enough tones I couldn't make out their words.

It was everything I could do not to brace myself the way I wanted to, not to curl my shoulders just enough.

Keeping my shoulders back, my head high, and my back straight, I thought about my mother, and all the things she made sure I learned from her and my tutors when I wasn't in training or thinking about training.

Which...wasn't often enough.

I'm sorry I didn't pay more attention, Mom. Please help me with this.

Throwing my hasty prayer to my mother for forgiveness, I hoped that my lack of respect for those long-ago lessons would not be something that would destroy me now.

One of the strangers went to the door and spoke to yet another servant waiting in the hall.

Finally, they deigned to address me.

"You need to eat more, but lucky for you we have some tricks to fix most of your challenges."

Tricks to fix most...it was so hard not to pick up the strangers and throw them through the window that I clasped my hands together in front of me and squeezed until two of my knuckles popped.

"Now, please take these," one of them said, taking three dresses from a servant and holding them out to me, "to wear until we return with our best options."

I stretched out my arms to take the proffered garments. Madam waved a hand, and a servant took them instead.

"Lady Cinder, let me walk them out and I will right back," she said, holding her arm out to them and giving me a pointed look that said I already failed.

When the door shut behind them, I wilted onto the stool.

"My Lady, I'm sorry, but are you alright?" a servant said.

She fidgeted in front of me, tugging on the hem of a jacket that didn't quite fit her properly.

I wanted to ask the dressmakers back and have them fix her uniform for her. If Madam was going to force all the servants to wear the same ugly outfits, made of what looked like an itchy, rough wool, she could have at least made sure they fit.

"Not unless you think Madam will let me eat something..." I let my sentence hang, waiting for her to fill in her name, but she didn't.

Instead, she looked over her shoulder toward the door, biting her lip.

"What's your name?" I asked, throwing out the formalities for a second. I didn't like not referring to people by name and the stilted, roundabout way of speaking I knew I would be forced to engage with for the foreseeable future. Maybe I could find at least someone here to talk to like a normal person.

"Oh," she said, turning it into a chirping sound that made me smile as she straightened. A blush took over her face. "My name is Augustina."

"Augustina?" That was a lot of name, and it didn't fit her at all.

She was soft and round, her blush was intense, and her hair bright red. If Madam Valentin, with her skin so dark it shined a black-blue along her cheek bones and looked like obsidian, stood next to Augustina, they would have looked almost as opposite as two people could.

Madam Valentin was thin, all angles and edges, with her hair pulled tight against her head, and of some indeterminate age that still conveyed wisdom of many years.

This girl was pale and pink, soft and plump and even if she wasn't as young as I thought, she exuded a naïveté I found disarming.

"Do you mind if I call you…" What would a good nickname be for her? Something playful and maybe a touch cute…"Gus?"

"I like that," she said, her voice a small squeak as she clapped her hands together.

"Good. Well, Gus, I appreciate you asking me. I'll be fine. I promise." I winked at her and crinkled her nose in a grin. "I'm pretty tough."

She cocked her head to the side, but whatever she was thinking would have to wait. The door to the bedroom opened and I sat up straight on the stool.

Madam walked in and looked around the room.

"Please help Lady Cinder get dressed," Madam said, with a wave of her hand.

Gus ran off to the bathroom and I held back a sigh.

"When you are ready for the day, please come down to the dining room for breakfast."

She turned and swept out of the room, and I tried to figure out if I was supposed to remember how to get to the dining room or not.

I did, of course, but what would a usual Lady of the court remember? Was I supposed to be brainless? Bad at directions?

Rubbing my hands over my face, I got up and headed to the bathroom.

No matter what I was supposed to be, I was hungry.

And that was the most important part. After I ate, I could try and find out from Madam…well, I could ask Gus.

CHAPTER 11

SOFTENING

The dress wasn't bad as far as dresses went. But I still wanted to burn it.

Why was it not proper for me to wear the same clothes my brother would wear to court?

Sure, he had to wear the ridiculous shoes the men did with their heels and their stupid buckles. And yeah, he had to wear all the frilly crap that made my neck itch just thinking about it constantly being right under his chin.

But at least he got to wear pants.

How was I supposed to defend myself in a dress with heavy brocade skirts? My legs felt like they were weighed down as I made my way down the stairs to the dining room.

Gus trailed behind me and I wondered if she was going to stay with me as my maid.

As weird as it was to have a maid just to answer my every command, at least it was Gus and not someone insufferable following me around.

Somehow, I was going to need to get Gus something else to wear.

Part of me wanted to start training her too, but the way she bounded as she walked and the perpetual wide-eyed look on her face would probably disappear as she gained fighting skills. And I couldn't destroy something so beautiful.

By the time we arrived in the dining room, Madam stood behind a chair, waiting for me. I made up my mind to keep it to the clothes.

Gus swept around me and pulled a chair out for me at the other setting already laid out.

I tipped my head to her, the rules about ignoring servants be damned, and took my seat, using every bit of my memories of my mother as my guide.

When the food was delivered, I kept my hands folded in my lap until Madam waved a hand and said, "Please. Enjoy your breakfast."

"Thank you," I said, taking up the proper utensils and proceeding to cut my food into the tiniest bites possible before finally, finally bringing the food to my mouth.

Between the build up to the meal and the emptiness of my stomach, it was everything I could do to hold back a noise that I was positive Madam would not deem appropriate.

But I didn't want my time here to be spent in these tense meals, or to focus on my table manners when there were far more important things I still needed to work on.

"Today, I must commend you on your change in attitude. Perhaps we can agree that we will get to work on other aspects of court life you will need to know and perform properly." Madam took another bite of her food and then set down her utensils and leaned back in her seat.

Fucking hell.

Was that it? Was I supposed to stop eating too? Because I was fucking hungry, and if she insisted on starving me, I was going to have to resort to sneaking out in the middle of the night and finding my own damn food.

"Yes, Madam Valentin." I set my own utensils down and followed suit while I imagined one hundred ways I could kill her with just the items in the room.

"No, Lady Cinder. You must eat more. I am not in your position and so I will have more coffee," she said, waving a hand. Another servant stepped out of the room, returning a second later with a carafe.

It had to be a trick.

"Please, Lady Cinder, eat up. You could use some softening." She took a drink of her coffee and closed her eyes while I snatched up my utensils and did as I was told.

Never in my life had I been happier to follow orders.

"Tell me, just out of my own curiosity, is it true that you have been training with your experts in all the arts of fighting and not preparing to go to court one day?" she asked, her hands wrapped around her cup, holding it up in front of her mouth so only her eyes showed over the rim.

It was definitely a trick. But I didn't know how to answer with anything other than the truth. It wasn't like she knew that meant I went all over the kingdom killing people. The last war ended the night my parents died. Even with skirmishes along the borders on a semi constant basis and the threat of other kingdoms looming, she wouldn't know that I had an opportunity to use my training. Let alone that I did all the time.

"Yes. The last war ended on my doorstep." That tended to change a person's priorities.

She raised that eyebrow at me, but didn't otherwise respond.

"I would think the safest place would be at court. I am surprised Duke Ash did not send you four years ago on your eighteenth birthday to present you to the King like so many do."

Her tone was indifferent, but only in the way a snake looks like it doesn't care about your presence right before it strikes.

"My brother and I are all we have left. I do not think he was ready for that kind of separation." And I didn't want to go now. Why did she think I would have wanted to go at only eighteen years old?

"Well," she said, taking a sip and putting down her cup. A smile played on her lips that reminded me of Ash right before he made his move. It was an act of will not to brace myself for the impact. "It might prove to be to your advantage."

The fork scratched along the plate sending a screech into the air, and I couldn't tell if the goosebumps on my arms were because of my slip up or because of her words.

"Pardon me, I am not sure what you mean," I said, pretending it wasn't a big deal and taking a bite.

She didn't seem upset by the ugly sound, or my reaction. In fact, her smile grew. And so did my goosebumps.

"All the neighboring kingdoms are sending some of their young women to the ball, of course, but I happen to know that some of the council want King Tristan to pick a bride from among our own."

Our own.

They wanted him to pick someone from Onyx, but why would that give me any kind of leg up?

"I still do not see how that means I might benefit." I shook my head and took another bite, trying to find a way through her thinking and to understand what exactly her motivation was.

"Every other eligible young woman has already been presented at court. He did not take to them before. He might not be any more likely to now. You, on the other hand…"

Didn't go to court. The rest of her sentence hung in the air, and I focused on my meal, on eating it exactly how she wanted me to, so I didn't have to watch as the marriage of the King and

I played out in her head. She had no idea why I was really going to be there.

As I took the last bite from my plate, I met her eyes again.

She had the same expression as before and it sent all my senses up so high it was hard to finish chewing the now too-flavorful bite.

"When you go to court, if I can prepare you properly then the chances of you being the next queen are high. You are going to take two Ladies in Waiting with you, as custom dictates."

Custom may have dictated that, but I didn't have any Ladies in Waiting. I didn't even have any ladies to ask.

"One of them will be my daughter."

CHAPTER 12
IN WAITING

I swallowed the last bite, careful not to choke.

Why would she send her daughter with me? And how was I going to complete my mission without endangering her?

"Your daughter?" I asked, my throat tight.

A young woman, thin and statuesque like her mother with the same dark skin and deep eyes, walked out from the same doorway the coffee came through. But she wasn't nearly as sharp at the edges as her mother.

She wore a yellow gown that was more striking on her than anything I had ever seen on a person before. Maybe the King would want to marry her. If I was him, I would choose her over me.

"This is Jacquetta," Madam said, her whole face changing as she looked on her daughter. All the careful coil of tension and veiled threat in her was gone and the only thing left was pride and joy.

"It is nice to meet you, Jacquetta," I said, tipping my head and trying not to grimace. This girl needed to be far away from me. She needed to stay home with her mother.

But this was probably the price Ash paid for me to get this training. Somehow, I needed to make sure it wouldn't cost her life.

"Lady Cinder, I am so excited I get to go with you. This will be a great adventure." She smiled and the light in her face eclipsed bright shine of her dress.

"Pardon me," I said, placing my hands on the arms of my chair and glancing at Gus who ran up and pulled my chair back. Once standing, I smiled at both of them, hoping it didn't look too brittle. "I must excuse myself."

"Come back down to the parlor when you are ready." Madam said, not a hint of anything wrong in her voice.

But as I turned and started back to my room, it was everything I could do not to run out the front door.

My hands shook more with each step up the stairs until I wrapped them together in front of me. My feet picked up speed as I got closer to the safety of the only door I could close.

Finally, I reached my bathroom and slammed the door behind me, leaning against it and sliding down to sit on the floor.

I ran through the possibilities in my head. The ways I planned to kill him, and discarded each.

Before they were dangerous. But only for me.

The risk to myself was worth the chance to finally have our revenge. But if I killed him and I was found out, the women who went with me as Ladies in Waiting would be labeled accomplices and there would be no escape for them.

Especially not Jacquetta who was clearly not a servant. No one would believe she wasn't a coconspirator.

I banged my head against the door.

Somehow, someway, I had to manufacture a moment, or take advantage of a moment when it would be blamed on someone else, so I and the women with me wouldn't come under suspicion.

Right. Because that was going to be easy.

First, though, I had to make it through Madam Valentin's training and be asked to stay after the ball.

Ash might have thought this was the perfect chance for us to get revenge, but I was starting to think it would have been easier just to try my usual way.

Even if it didn't work, it wouldn't have risked all this.

I shoved myself up from the floor, my lungs squeezed in the process, leaving me coughing.

Soon the coughing would stop, but for now it was a reminder I didn't belong here. I belonged at home, in the remnants of my past.

But instead of breathing in and walking through my home and the pieces of my life that perpetually fell from the sky, I was here.

Here near the capitol, to bring that same desolation to the Obsidian Palace.

And I needed to keep the end goal in mind. No matter how much I wanted to protect Jacquetta.

First, I had a job to do.

Leaving the bathroom, I hid myself inside who I was supposed to be for the palace, who Madam Valentin wanted me to be, while the real me tried not to cough and cry.

Gus smiled at me and turned to walk away as if nothing had happened.

But, of course, that meant I was successful.

At least as far as masking myself went.

I sighed, walking behind her to the parlor. Hopefully whatever we were doing next would be something I could do.

How much was there left to court life? All they did all day was preen, right?

The parlor was a grand space, not as large as our receiving room at home, but close. It could have held quite a party. And the way Jacquetta swayed side to side at the window, I thought it probably had.

Brightly colored velvets and silks were the main show in the room. Polished wood surfaces gleamed behind them, and the stone shimmered as if a vein of gold ran through it.

Madam sat on a chaise, not leaning back into it like it was designed for, but upright and stiff as always.

"Your arrival, as far as the King is concerned, will be at the ball itself, and all the young women will be staying that evening. So, the first thing we need to tackle is—can you dance?" Madam asked, that eyebrow raised high.

I laughed. It was short, and I managed to get it under control before I really offended her, but it was close. Under normal circumstances, if someone had asked me that, I don't think I would have been able to stop laughing.

"Forgive me, but I have not spent any time dancing in the last seven years," I said, leaving her to fill in the blanks about what I was doing instead. She had to suspect. Her own assessment that I carried myself like I was about to be in a fight rang in my ears, but I wasn't going to elaborate.

"The last seven years?" Jacquetta asked, her hands over her mouth, her face wearing an expression that was equal parts horrified and sad—as if I just told them I was a slave in the Corvid Kingdom the whole time.

No amount of willpower could allow me to school my face entirely. I was positive it registered the shock that ran through me realizing she was so upset because I didn't dance.

Was it that big of a problem? Was I that much of a freak?

I wasn't Corvidian. I was still Onyxian. That had to mean something.

"Did you ever learn to dance from your mother or your tutors?" Madam asked, none of the same reaction as her daughter even flitted across her features.

"Yes, of course." Not that I was a particularly good student of the dances. Books? Yes. Loved all the opportunities to learn new things and pore over a book. Unless they were the stuffy old tomes about royals and lineages. But painting or dancing? No. The weapons training was far more compelling to me.

"Well," Madam said, planting her hands on either side of her chair and shoving herself up to standing. She looked down her nose from me to Jacquetta and back.

"For today, we are going to run through the most common dances being performed now and hope that you know some of them. Jacquetta will act as your partner." She waved a hand and Jacquetta darted across the room, a smile now taking over her whole face.

When she got to me, Madam clapped her hands together and Jacquetta curtsied. So I did too.

"First, the quartanza," Madam said, and Jacquetta turned so her side was toward me with a hand in the air.

I tried to run through every memory I had of dancing and there wasn't a single thing in them to give me a clue as to what a quartanza was or how I was supposed to perform it.

Jacquetta's smile faltered, and she slowly dropped her hand.

"You do not know this dance?" she asked, her voice low and despondent.

"No. I…" I shook my head. There was nothing there, nothing in my mind to help me.

"Okay, I will do the dance for you to watch, and then you can try it with me?" Jacquetta offered, her bright smile back.

How did she have such a font of indefatigable hope and belief?

I stumbled back until the backs of my thighs hit a table and I pulled up short. For seven years, I didn't learn new things besides weapons. I mastered the things my parents taught me. But this…I didn't know if I could do this.

Jacquetta put herself in the same stance as before, with her side facing me and her hand up.

At first, the steps were simple. She moved in and out from a center point, all the while making her way as if around a circle.

Every step I tried to memorize, every way she tilted her head, every turn of her hand. But there was too much.

Then she sped up.

She turned and spun her hands above her head, jumped from one foot to the other and from one side of her circle of movement to the other. She landed with a dip, a swoop, and back up to her toes.

And she still wasn't done. She bent to the outside with both hands outstretched, and returned to the inside, back in the position she started.

Madam Valentin smiled at her daughter with a tilt of her head and then looked to me.

Jacquetta grinned and raised her brows at me, as if her little display was supposed to unlock some buried memory of the choreography in my brain.

"I…" Looking back and forth between them, my stomach flopped over, and I had to scream inside my head to keep standing straight because I wanted to brace myself for a blow so badly it hurt. "I am sorry. I have never seen that dance before."

Madam's smile disappeared and her mouth returned to a thin line while Jacquetta wilted. Her gaze softened like she was looking at a crying child.

"But I know the valz," I said, without any reaction at all in return, "and I will learn the rest."

Whether that was a lie about my ability to learn it or not, I didn't know. It didn't matter. Somehow, even if it broke me in half to do it, I had to find a way. If they were right to put so much emphasis on dancing, my whole mission might depend on it.

CHAPTER 13
ONE STEP

I tried. I followed every move she made. One at a time, she taught me how she swooped and spun, the exact way she moved her toes and feet.

The moves themselves, executing them, wasn't a problem.

"You are very graceful, Lady Cinder," Madam said, circling us as we practiced one of the more complicated swoops. "More than I was expecting considering your musculature."

My musculature. Right. Because someone who spent their life training was supposed to somehow not know how to move their body. That didn't make any sense, but I shoved it aside and focused on the moves.

After a day of work that left my toes aching, sweat collecting in my bodice, and me wishing for my assignment clothes more than I ever thought possible, we finally got to eat again.

But, of course, it was another affair where I had to spend energy on every minute move of my body, eating exactly as I was supposed to.

It didn't matter that I was exhausted, or that we had more than earned a relaxed meal. That wasn't Madam's way.

Finally, the meal was done, and at least my stomach was full. Although the sweat coating me inside my dress was clammy, and a chill was growing through my body by the time we were done.

"Now, let us see if you can put it all together," Madam said, getting up from the table, not bothering to wait for us to agree.

Jacquetta smiled at me. Gus tried to look positive as I walked by her, but I suspected they were as dubious of my chances of success as I was.

In the parlor, Jacquetta set herself up across from me, her hand in mine, palm to palm.

"Just remember that you know how to do every one of these moves," she said with a single nod.

With a deep breath, I nodded back to her.

And we began.

The first section, I did okay. Not perfect. I made mistakes, but I didn't do too bad either.

But then we sped up.

Jacquetta flowed so seamlessly from one move to another, and it didn't seem to matter that I knew all the moves too. I couldn't put them together. I kept trying the wrong steps, losing my place in the sequence.

When we returned to our starting positions, I was sucking down air, and a cramp seized my side.

"Hmm." Madam's face looked like she smelled something bad, and she shook her head before she turned away and took a seat. "We will try again tomorrow. I will send someone up with dinner when it is time. For now, go get cleaned up."

A wave of her hand in dismissal and Jacquetta slumped from the room.

I stood for a moment longer, waiting for her to say more.

But she didn't look my way.

Finally, I had to admit to myself that I let us all down and this was the way Madam handled my sad performance.

I stomped up the stairs, Gus on my heels, not bothering to keep myself in perfect form anymore.

One day. I had known the damn dance existed for one day and she expected me to learn it and perform it perfectly in that time.

Shaking my head, I made my way into my room and kicked off my shoes before flopping onto the bed face first.

"Lady Cinder, is there anything I can get you?" Gus asked, sounding genuinely worried.

I groaned into the blankets and rolled to the side to look at her.

"Can you draw me a bath? That's all I need right now. Thank you, Gus."

She hustled away. Her smile had returned, like she was sure she was helping.

Little did she know, the only thing that could really help me was if she could convince Madam I didn't need to spend the month preparing for the ball like I was preparing for a well-dressed war.

Training was one thing. I knew how to train, and it made sense to me. If someone like me didn't work hard in training, I could get caught. I could die.

But for a stupid ball and to win the favor of a man?

It all made me want to swear and run away. The only men I knew were Ash and his friends. The only ones outside them I had any experience with in the last seven years were the fighters who trained me and the men I killed.

Not exactly paragons of virtue, my marks.

My father, a truly decent person, was a rare man in my experience. And this King was a murderer. He was the reason my parents were dead.

The idea that I needed to put effort into impressing him specifically just made me want to start punching.

Why did it always have to be about the damn royalty? Even with my brother, there were things no one could question, no one could say, because he was the Duke. And I was a Lady, next in line.

It sounded like a lot. To be next in line to have all the responsibility of the lands of Lehar and the people in them while having no one to rely on to tell you the truth if you were making a mistake. But it wasn't. I was just another subject. Just another person who couldn't afford to do anything but try to impress.

Shoving myself up to sitting on the bed, I pushed aside the bitterness coursing through me.

No, I didn't want to learn how to be who Madam thought I needed to be. No, I didn't care about ever learning to dance or that she thought I had too much muscle.

I cared about my family, getting justice for my parents, and the people who lived in Lehar. And I couldn't do anything for any of those concerns while laying on the bed.

"Damn it." I got up and began undressing, peeling fabric away from my damp skin. When my training clothes became gross with sweat, it never struck me as quite so weird as when the pretty purple day dress that probably cost more than the rest of my wardrobe combined was saturated.

"Lady Cinder, your bath is ready," Gus said from the doorway to the bathroom, averting her gaze from my naked body.

I looked down at myself and back at her, cocking my head to the side, trying to make her look back at me.

Were my scars still too obvious? Was the shape of me that shockingly different?

No matter how she reacted, I needed to wash, and I couldn't worry about the things I didn't have control over.

Maybe the years of training and killing had left their mark on me more than I realized. Maybe my mission was doomed before it began.

I smiled getting into the heat of the bath, even with the stinging of the flowers, thinking about that possibility. If I didn't get invited to stay on after the ball, I could go back to trying to get close enough to mete out justice my way. With pants. And my spike.

STOP CALLING ME THAT

We practiced different dances every day for two weeks. It always ended the same way. I could do the separate steps and moves just fine, but put them all together into a set pattern, a routine, and I was a disaster.

And I hated every second of it.

"Damn it all to the fucking hellfires," I yelled, throwing a shoe across my room after another day of zero positive gain toward my dancing goals. It bounced off a wall and landed on the vanity, knocking over some of the makeup pots.

One rolled across the floor and came to rest next to my mostly empty trunk.

Flopping down on the bed in my temporary dress, I itched to be done with all of this.

"Lady Cinder," Jacquetta asked, peeking her head around the edge of the doorframe with Gus looking over her shoulder, bobbing and weaving to get a better view.

"If you come in here, you have to stop calling me that," I said, not moving from my position, sprawled out on the bed with my head hanging off the edge.

They came in and shut the door behind them. Both of them rushed to my side and crouched on the floor near my face.

"You do so well at all the steps, it's only a matter of time," Jacquetta said, her smile too big.

"I'm sure when you get to the ball it will all be valz's anyway, which you do perfectly. And he will want to keep you for more than your dancing ability," Gus added, her eyebrows so high they were hidden by her bangs. She was truly, a terrible liar.

"So, the two of you decided to team up to get me to be happy about this whole mess?" I asked, not giving in to their ridiculous levels of positivity. Not today.

They looked at each other and turned back to me, shaking their heads like they were attached to each other.

"Very convincing," I said, deciding again not to tell them that I wasn't upset for the reasons they thought I was.

Yes, I wanted to prove Madam Velentin wrong in her assessment of me, but it wasn't because I wanted King Tristan to like me. I just wanted him to keep me on long enough to find my opportunity.

In some other world my statement was sincere, and they actually were convincing. Gus lived in that world. Her smile grew larger still. But Jacquetta's mouth turned into a straight line. She had never looked more like her mother.

"How about I draw you a bath?" Gus stood up and left the room.

Jacquetta grabbed my hands and hauled me to a sitting position.

"Whatever you do, you need to stop letting Mother see you like this. She senses weakness and will exploit it if she thinks it can get her something," Jacquetta whispered before she heaved me to my feet.

Madam Valentin was clearly the kind of person her daughter described. I knew that a long time ago, but hearing her say it made my mouth fall open and I looked at my friend differently.

"Do…but…" I couldn't form the words to ask her what I wanted to. My brain was stuck on trying to place this version of her with who I thought she was for the last two weeks.

She laughed and slipped her arm through mine, locking us together at the elbows before she started toward the bathroom.

"Come on, Cinder. We need to make a battle plan. Because Mother is an accomplished general of personal and court warfare."

Battle plan.

Warfare.

If there was anything I understood, it was fighting.

By the time I was undressed and in the water, bubbles tickled the bottom of my chin, and I was blissfully without the stinging of the flowers. Through the open bathroom door, I could hear the chatter of Jacquetta and Gus. My mind was filled with all my years of preparation to fight.

Maybe I was going about this all wrong.

Dancing, at least learning the sequence of the steps, and putting it all together had been beyond me. But what if I thought of it as just another kind of battle?

When I learned how to use a short sword, I learned the moves first, built up my strength and my aptitude with those by themselves, and then I put them together into larger movements and patterns.

If I could do that, and do it well, with something as important and complicated as sword fighting, I could do that with dance.

A peal of laughter floated in from the other room and I sunk lower in the water, allowing it to slip over my head.

Under the water, with the bubbles blocking the light from above, I was in a cocoon of quiet warmth.

For the first time since I got here, I felt at home. The heat surrounding me from the tips of my hair down to my toes felt like being in the air at home on top of the hellfire source.

When I emerged from my bath, steam rolling off me, and a robe wrapped around me, my two Ladies in Waiting were sitting on my bed and chatting.

Their smiles were as genuine as they always were, but I knew them a little better now.

Gus was curious and Jacquetta was smart.

Between these two women and my remembering who I was and what I was capable of, success on my assignment—at least getting past the first hurdle—suddenly seemed a little more possible.

"Ladies, I have something important to ask you," I said, taking a seat on the bed between them.

"If we can help you brush out your hair. Because right now that's a tangled mess." Jacquetta gestured to my head, and I smiled while Gus tried, unsuccessfully, to stifle a laugh.

"No. But I'll take that under advisement." I got up and grabbed a brush from the vanity before I turned back to try again.

Brushing my hair while I asked was a good idea. It made this seem less formal, which as far as I was concerned was always the better option.

"Will you both come with me to the Obsidian Palace?"

Jacquetta grinned and Gus slammed her hands over her mouth while she bounced on the bed.

"I have to warn you," I said, and stopped. Because I did want to tell them how dangerous this really was. And that I was taking them with me knowing it meant I had to be more careful, more perfect in the execution of my mission. And I was doing it because I couldn't trust anyone else to keep their eyes open for me. But I couldn't tell them any of that. "Going to the palace sounds like fun, but this is going to be a huge challenge."

They nodded, both of them setting their faces to lines of grim determination and thoughtfulness.

Moving to the bed, I sat between them again, pausing in my brushing to focus on them, taking in Jacquetta's dark eyes and Gus's green ones before I went on.

"And more than a challenge, the people there are dangerous. Some of the women who will be there, for sure beyond the ball, are from places like the Corvid Kingdom."

Just mentioning the Corvids was enough to make Jacquetta swallow and shrink while Gus blanched and sucked in a breath.

"Exactly. This thing, this possibility to marry into the throne of Onyx is going to make some people ruthless." As ruthless as I was, even if their goals were different.

"Corvids are already willing to be the worst people in the world for no reason," Gus said, her voice dark.

I couldn't add anything to that. She wasn't wrong.

"So, what you need us to do isn't just help you with your hair or remember the schedule." Jacquetta sat up straight again, her chin in the air like she was already going to war.

"Right."

They exchanged glances and both looked back at me.

I swallowed and held as still as I could. This was their chance to back out, to tell me no. Part of me hoped they would. That they would protect themselves from the dangers of the moment. And from me.

"None of those women stand a chance," Jacquetta said.

"We'll be extra eyes for you. No one ever suspects someone like me to be anything other than what I say I am," Gus said.

She had a point. Maybe everyone at the palace would underestimate them. I hoped so.

CHAPTER 15

WRONG

Walking to the parlor from the dining room after breakfast didn't take as long as it had the day before. It didn't seem to anyway.

Not when I had a plan, and this string of failures was not going to defeat me again today.

In the parlor, Madam Valentin was stationed on the chaise, like usual. Her face was fixed into the constipated look she had taken on since the first time I tried to put all the steps together.

While Jacquetta looked so smug it knocked me back a step and made me question if I would let her down.

But this had to work.

"How about the quartanza again. We have not tried that in a while," Jacquetta said, looking to her mother.

Madam Valentin pinched her mouth even tighter together, but she nodded.

Jacquetta raised her hand to the starting position, and I followed suit. We faced away from each other, our hands together.

"Go slow. We will try it half time first." Jacquetta's voice betrayed her nerves, and I lifted my chin in response.

This had to work.

Following Jacquetta's movements, I made my way through the dance imagining I had a short sword in my hand.

All through the leaps and twirls, that imaginary short sword parried and thrusted, an extension of my arm. And the air itself became an attacker, someone trying to get though my graceful defenses.

By the time we were done, it was an effort to flatten my palm against Jacquetta's instead of wrapping my fingers into a fist that held my phantom sword tight.

Madam Valentin stood to the side, her face a mask I couldn't read. Her eyebrow was high, and her hand touched the brooch at her throat.

Her stance was different than it had been when we finished our dance of the day before, or the one before that.

I was frozen, waiting for her response.

But she didn't comment, just waved her hand to her daughter.

"Okay, Lady Cinder," Jacquetta said, and I let out the breath I was holding, "We shall go at full speed now."

Dropping my hand and stepping to the side, I nodded.

This was what I wanted, but it took a moment for me to reset myself. I took the time to run through all the steps in my mind, using that sword as my guide. I formulated all the moves an attacker would make in response, how it could be a choreographed fighting sequence like some of the sequences I learned in training.

A deep breath, as I flexed my hands and balled them into fists, and I was ready.

I stepped back into place. Jacquetta smiled, and placed her palm on mine.

We started and I lost myself to the imagined battle, allowing it to play over me and my body, to use it to do what I needed to.

My hand landed against Jacquetta's at the end, our timing perfect, and I sucked down air like I really was training. Nothing was the same as it was last time.

Sweat didn't soak my clothes, my feet didn't ache, and I wasn't afraid to look at Madam.

Madam smiled, her whole face changing. She almost looked...proud.

I grinned at Jacquetta, and she bounced, barely containing what I suspected was the urge to full on jump up and down.

"Now that was dancing," Madam said, "Well done. If you perform like that at the ball, I will not worry. Show me another one."

Jacquetta and I danced the rest of the day, starting with half time movements and speeding them up.

Each of the dances we covered became the exercise of a different weapon in my mind. Throwing knives, a mace, even a spear. It helped me keep them all separate in my head. A couple moves might actually be useful in a fight.

But no matter how hard I tried, I still couldn't stop wishing for my normal clothes.

At the end of the day, I asked, "Is that all the dances I will need to know?"

Madam laughed.

"Since you have found your feet, you are eager to learn more, I see," Madam said as she stood up from the chaise. "I am sorry, Lady Cinder, but those are all the dances currently being done at court. And now I think it is time for us to have dinner. Will you join us for the evening?"

"Yes, thank you." There was no more reason to hide in my room and the bath could wait.

Eating with Madam Valentin remained a stiff affair which

made me question my decision to not retreat to my room. At least there I didn't have to use the correct knife.

But even though Madam continued to scrutinize every move I made through dinner, that small smile didn't leave her face.

After dinner, when I set down my untensils, Madam said, "Tomorrow your wardrobe arrives, and I am having someone come to work on your hair. So, it is good we finished with the dances today. But I do want you to practice again before you leave for the palace."

I nodded and excused myself. Whatever came of the wardrobe and hair, I didn't care. I wasn't going to be comfortable for the foreseeable future. And I had an accomplishment to bask in. That was what mattered.

Heading into my room, Gus jumped in front of me.

On instinct, my hands shot forward to slam into her chest and shove her away. I managed to stop them a fraction before making contact.

"You did it. I don't know how you did it, but you did," Gus squealed, unaware how close she came.

I stepped back and pressed my shaking hands to my stomach, sucking down air like I was drowning.

"The bath is all ready, and your nightgown is laid out. I'm so happy for you, but I have to go." She grabbed my arm and I tensed, trying not to cringe away.

But a second later she was gone, the door shut behind her, and I could collapse onto the floor and rub my hands over my face.

"We need rules, damn it," I muttered to the empty room.

Somehow, I had to make sure that never happened again. I didn't want to hurt Gus.

My conversation from the night before—asking them to come with me—floated through my mind and I wanted to throw something. What was I thinking?

I was right the first time. It was too dangerous for them to be safe with me.

The bath was ready, but instead of getting in it, I pulled the plug and got dressed in my clothes from home. They weren't my assignment clothes. They were much stiffer and more formal, and they still had the grime of travel on them. But at least it wasn't a dress.

Strapping my spike on and donning my cloak, I looked out the window as the last of the light died.

Maybe I didn't need to go to the ball at all. Maybe Ash's information about the palace was wrong.

There was only one way to find out.

CHAPTER 16
NOT AN OPTION

My window didn't make a sound as I swung it open. The faint light of the half-moon shone down on the yard and the garden at the back of the house.

But I could see the outline of the Obsidian palace.

It was a deeper black than the night around it, dotted in places with the glow of lights inside.

What kind of security stood between me and the palace grounds?

After a moment of study, I looked down into the yard below and watched a guard sweep a light stone along the fence before heading to the front of the property. The light stone was a perfect way for me to keep tabs on their whereabouts, the idiots.

Most people didn't know proper defensive patrol practices, but for a guard to be that stupid...I could handle that situation another day.

For now, I lifted my leg up to stand on the sill and gripped the stone along the edge of the window before I swung myself to the side, grabbing the stone surrounding the next window over.

Using the edges and dips within the stones of the house and the grout around them, I made my way down to the ground and crouched in the shadows of the bushes surrounding most of the house.

The stupid guard passed again after a few moments, still on his rounds, still with the light stone leading the way, making him easy to avoid.

As soon as he was around the front of the house, I darted to the edge of the yard and jumped to grab the top of the fence. I swung side to side, using my momentum to launch myself over.

On the other side of the fence was a line of short shrubs. I landed in the branches of them and rolled my eyes.

Climbing down and making my way to the street, I made a mental note to try and get Madam to cut them all down.

The road, like most in Bridgeton, led to the main thorough-fare which led to the bridge and the palace beyond.

But I didn't want to walk right up to the bridge and the guards who had to be posted there.

I was a lot of things, but stupid enough to be that blatant wasn't one of them.

Along the edge of the river, some shipping depots and ware-houses sat in the cheaper parts of town. But in this neighbor-hood, the buildings along the water were the government offices and banks—the places some of the richest members of citizenry who weren't royal went to during the day to work.

Whoever allowed that to happen, thinking that lining the entire beach with buildings that were empty at night just to ensure the beaches stayed open for everyone's use during the day, should have gone into a different line of work.

City planners and administrators should have at least posted guards along the beach at night.

But I didn't see any sign of them through the gaps between the buildings.

Finally, I picked a space between two of the fancy offices and made my way to the riverside, pausing, crouched in the darkness, to scan up and down the river's edge.

The only movement anywhere was further down on one side by the docks and up on the bridge.

Idiots.

How had no one killed King Tristan yet?

Was he loved by everyone in Bridgeton? In the rest of the kingdom except at home in Lehar?

At home he was reviled by more than just me and Ash. But how was it possible for the security to be so lax?

I made my way slowly along the water's edge, placing my feet one by one on the black sand so I didn't make a noise louder than the sound of the water passing by.

Once I got to the bridge, I waited until the guard left the side I was on. Where he was headed, I didn't know and didn't care, just as long as he was focused away from me.

Grabbing the supports of the bridge I pulled my way up, careful to not drag my feet along the sand and make any noise.

Swinging my leg over the beam, the rough edges dug into my inner thigh, but it allowed me to stretch my arms to the next beam. As I moved from beam to beam, they grew smooth and slick with moisture splashed up from the river hitting the bridge's stone supports.

There had to be a way for the bridge builders to make them less easy to use for people like me, even though it was great for me that they didn't think like I did.

I thanked them silently in my mind as I swung down off the last beam, suspended above the sand on the other bank until I could plant my feet on it and not make noise.

This side of the river was better lit, but there were still big swaths of shadow between the lights.

Darting through the street, using one of the shadows as my cover, I made my way to the first building I came to. It didn't matter what it was, the building was dark and had thick window ledges perfect for climbing.

And guards were more plentiful on the ground here. My best chance to get to the palace itself, just the other side of the ring of buildings, was to go to the roofs.

Climbing up the side of the building, my fingers ached on the rough ledges, but I had to pause as a guard passed by below me.

If Bridgeton was quiet, the island of the Obsidian palace was silent as a tomb.

Nothing should be that easy, let alone getting to the King.

Grabbing onto the edge of the roof, I paused.

Was that a sound?

Something in the night sent the hairs on the back of my neck standing on end, and made every muscle in my body—even the ones I wasn't using—bunch up like my body was preparing for a blow.

I pulled myself up, a tiny fraction at a time, until I could see over the edge to the rest of the flat roof.

Guards. Lots of them.

No, not guards. Not normal city guards like the ones stationed on the bridge and the ones I already passed on their patrols through the street.

These were soldiers. And every last one of them held their crossbows as they scanned the street on the other side of the building and the side of the palace.

I lowered myself back down so that if one did look to this side, they wouldn't see me. And I took extra care not to make even the tiniest sound on my way back down the side of the building.

At one of the windows, I took a moment to rest, glancing inside as I passed the glass.

Next time I climbed up a building, I would remember how much it did matter what the building was.

This was a garrison. Row upon row of soldiers sleeping in their beds were illuminated in a faint glow from a stone light in a small space off the room that must have been a bathroom.

It took everything in me not to go faster as I made my way down to the street.

Crouching in the deepest shadow at the corner of the wall and the street, I checked that none of the guards headed my way. The closest one walked away from my position, his footsteps loud on the road.

Making my way back to Bridgeton was harder than getting across the first time.

After too long practicing dancing and doing zero training, my muscles weren't as used to the exertion. They ached and my arms shook before I even got to the end of the beams.

At the end, my legs wrapped around the last beam. I shook one arm out at a time, trying to prepare for the arduous task of lowering myself to the sand. I couldn't see on the bridge to even know if one of the guards was looking this way, and I didn't think I had the strength left to pull myself silently up the edge to peek.

So, after taking a moment to rest, I dropped my legs down, slow and controlled, until I hung above the sand. Lowering myself down, my arms screamed, and I went deep into my mind to the place where I didn't feel the pain.

After my toes hit the sand, I let my arms relax and relied on my legs to hold me on tip toes as I dropped the rest of the way.

It all left me dragging in breaths and trying to do it without alerting anyone nearby to my presence.

Balls, dancing, and stupid dresses were my best bet to get into the palace after all. Taking on a garrison by myself didn't sound like a great idea.

With a sigh, I realized that all I had to do once I got inside would be hampered by my attempt to do what I needed to get there. If tonight was any judge, I had to find a way to keep training at both.

First, I needed to get back inside my room without anyone noticing.

CHAPTER 17
LONG LAST

Morning came too early.

Gus shook my shoulder, calling my name.

"No," I said. Or I meant to say anyway. It came out more like, "Ungh."

"Why are you so sleepy? Get up. Madam wants you ready for the dressmakers later. We need to get you cleaned up," she said, her voice trailing away on the last two words. I imagined what my hair looked like after my late-night outing.

"Just let me sleep," I muttered into the pillow. "The dressmakers can wait until tomorrow."

"They're booked solid. So, no, they can't. Get up." She grabbed the edge of the blanket and used it to roll me off the bed.

"Damn it, Gus." I wanted to curse more, but the words were shocked away from me at the sight of her.

She was wearing a day dress far fancier than her usual clothes, even if it was a touch too small. The size was more obvious as she stood there with her hands planted one her hips, staring down at me, the usual good-natured look on her face replaced with something closer to one of Madam's.

"I was told to get you ready. Now. So, you're getting up," she said.

"Okay," I said, untangling myself from the blankets and getting to my feet, "I'm up."

Gus turned to walk into the bathroom without another word and I followed, trying to understand what happened to her while I was sleeping.

The bath was already full and smelled the same as the first one I had when I got to Madam's house.

"What are you wearing?" I asked, the words popping out of my mouth before I could stop them while I climbed into the water. The heat immediately unknotted some of my muscles.

"You chose me as one of your Ladies in Waiting. I need to look the part," she said, glancing down at herself and hunching like she was trying to make the dress fit better. "The tailor is supposed to come today to work on dresses for me."

"Not the dressmakers? Why don't they do it?" I tilted my head back to wet my hair. Straightening up again, water sluicing down my head, I saw her smile and stand up tall again.

"I think you meant that, but you have to know, the dress-makers are way too expensive for people like me." She came around to my back and helped me wash my hair.

A piece of leaf that didn't start out in the bath, floated by me, and I wondered how I was going to train without tipping off Gus or Jacquetta. Especially once we got to the palace.

For that moment, I scrubbed beneath my fingernails, let the tingling and stinging sensation of the ingredients of the bath soak deep into my skin, healing any little scrapes and improving old scars. I tried to enjoy myself.

Maybe today I wouldn't have to dance. Maybe after the dressmakers left, I could go to sleep early.

Gus helped me finish getting ready, but I couldn't suppress the yawn as she followed me toward the dining room for breakfast.

Jacquetta and Madam Valentin were already seated by the time I took my seat. Gus surprised me further by taking a seat next to Jacquetta.

"Do not look shocked," Madam said, her eyes narrowed at me, "She will make a fine Lady in Waiting and all of you need to be prepared for life in the palace."

I nodded and smiled. Just because I wasn't expecting Madam to treat one of her servants the same as her daughter didn't mean I didn't appreciate it.

Life in the palace…

While we ate and Madam gave tips—shockingly gentle in their delivery to Gus on the nitpicky points of table manner rules—Madam's words ran through my head.

Even with Jacquetta and Gus along with me, how was I going to 'live' in the palace?

The likelihood I would be able to find any time away from the girls to train in my room was nil. The chances I would be able to train in the open were less than nil. And after last night, I worried that when the time came for me to make my move, I wouldn't be in the condition to do it.

Besides, how was I supposed to do anything at all in the elaborate dresses the dressmakers were probably going to make me wear?

I stifled a sigh as I took the last bite of my breakfast.

No matter how dubious I was beginning to find this plan, I had to see it through. Like every other impossible mission Ash sent me on. Somehow.

"You three can wait in Lady Cinder's room. The dressmakers will be here any moment and the tailor will be here soon. I think we can stage both in there," Madam said, getting to her feet.

We all nodded and left the dining room, but Jacquetta and Gus seemed excited about the day ahead, whereas I...I wasn't sure what to think. And I didn't know what I was doing anymore.

Plans for assignments were always clear in my mind. I ran through them over and over again before I had to actually act. But now...

Once we were in my room with the door shut, Jacquetta flopped onto the bed with a giant grin.

"Ladies, we're going to have so much fun," Jacquetta said. "I can't wait to see all the dresses."

"I can't wait for one that fits," Gus said, sitting next to Jacquetta while they both laughed.

No matter how hard I tried to be as jovial as they were, the smile on my face felt broken and tremulous. Nothing about this made me think it was going to be fun. Especially not when we got to the palace.

"Do you get new clothes too, Jacquetta?" Gus asked, tugging on the sleeve of her temporary dress.

"Yes. But Mother says they won't come until tomorrow." She clapped her hands together. "Besides, I'm more excited to see yours."

She looked back and forth between us, her grin taking over her whole face.

Gus smiled back, and I kept trying to.

"And just think how much fun it will be, and what the dress will look like when Cinder marries the King," Gus said, and Jacquetta cooed.

Marry King Tristan?

Both of them thought this was real. Every time I was reminded, it hit me anew.

The door behind me swung open at the same time a knock sounded.

Madam walked in, followed by the dressmakers, assistants, and more dresses on racks than I had ever seen in one place at the same time.

Ranging from frills and gems to simple and sedate day dresses, there was every kind of dress I had ever seen and some I hadn't imagined on the racks. I even spotted what I thought were the hems of some nightgowns.

She thought it was real too. She thought this was going on for as long as possible. Forever.

CHAPTER 18
CHANGING POLITICAL WINDS

Every day of the next week and a half we spent under Madam's tutelage. From practice in conversation while not using contractions and using the proper titles, to the kind of greeting each person required according to our station and theirs, including the best curtsy.

And every night, more enraged, despondent, and closer to the edge of panic, I trained in my room with my new, thin spike. It was the only weapon that I had with me that I would be able to use at the palace. It was so light I had to modify most of my forms, but it kept me strong better than nothing.

If the midnight lesson in my own weakness made anything perfectly clear, it was that I needed to keep training.

The morning we were to go, the sweat from my workout the night before created a clammy film that covered my whole body and made me shiver when I crawled from the covers of the bed.

Gus didn't come for me that morning. Instead, moments after I woke, another servant walked in the room and prepared my bath.

"Where is G—I mean, Augustina?" I asked, tripping over her real name.

"Both of your Ladies are being prepared, just as you are. Today is a big day," she said.

A big day.

Yes. And no one knew exactly what I planned for the days after today.

The ball was tomorrow night.

Part of me wanted it to be here already, to get it over with, to know if I failed or not. And the rest of me never wanted it to arrive.

No matter how strange it was being trussed, primped, and monitored all day, it staved off a tiny fraction of the worry that I wouldn't be able to make this happen.

And it chased some of the gnawing sensation that if I was successful at fulfilling the whole mission, Jacquetta and Gus would be punished for it.

By the time I was dressed and ready, in a gown far more formal and elaborate than I thought appropriate to wear during the day, my stomach hurt. I shook from my knees down.

My gown hugged tight to my waist, and made me look like I had larger breasts than I actually did. They weren't small no matter how much training I did, but they didn't normally create a shelf either.

The dress had a slit up the side of the full and flowing skirts, and off the shoulder lace sleeves that made me want to rip them off. Reaching my arms up enough to even touch my own elaborate hairdo was impossible.

And my hair…hurt. There were gem-encrusted combs in it and my loose curls were tightened so they piled on my head and cascaded down my back.

Nothing about the clothes I wore, the makeup on my face, or my hairstyle made me feel like me.

Before we went down to breakfast, I dismissed the servants under the guise of using the bathroom, and struggled with my dress until I could strap my spike to the leg without the slit.

Looking down at myself, I could only hope that the slit of the skirts running almost the entire length of my thigh on one side wouldn't give away my weapon.

I took a deep breath, closed my trunk now filled with all manner of new wardrobe items, and pretended I was someone else as I walked out of my room.

Madam Valentin, Jacquetta, and Gus, all resplendent in their fine clothes, waited at the bottom of the stairs with drinks in their hands.

Drinks?

Were we going to have a party before we left for the palace?

Ash sometimes had parties, and I was well practiced at pretending to drink. But maybe today I would have something. Maybe it would help with the weakness in my legs as I made my way down the stairs. My knees felt like they wanted to buckle with every step.

"Oh, Cinder," Jacquetta said, looking up at me as I climbed down the last two steps. But one look at her mother's stern face and she amended her informality, "Sorry, Lady Cinder. You look amazing."

"Thank you. All of you look incredible," I said, smiling at each of them although I still might have toppled over.

"It is a special day," Madam said, with a tilt of her head and a smile on her face, "And I thought we might have an informal brunch and go over some court gossip before all of you need to go to the palace."

"Court gossip?" Gus asked, her eyes bright, like this was the best news since I asked her to come with me.

Biting my bottom lip, I stopped the laugh that wanted to

bubble out of me. I suspected if I did laugh, it would sound hysterical.

We gathered around a low table in the parlor instead of the dining room and I tried to relax, tried not to be the one to dampen everyone else's spirits.

"Okay, Mother," Jacquetta said, picking up a small tart and popping it into her mouth, grinning around her treat.

Madam shook her head, but her smile stayed in place.

"From what I understand, Corvid is sending a young woman potential."

Her words landed like a blow in the middle of my stomach even though I thought this might happen.

"Corvid? There will be a slaver at the palace?" Gus asked, her mouth dropping open and her shoulders rounding.

I balled my hand into a fist and placed my other hand on Gus's shoulder. If that damn slaver thought she was going to come to this kingdom and take one of ours, I would hunt her through her own cursed lands until my dying breath.

"Unfortunately, yes. The Corvids seem to think that their constant menacing along the northern border makes her a good choice for King Tristan to take as a bride."

Wasn't this exactly what I thought? That no matter what anyone believed he should do, his advisors would try and pair him with someone they thought would be most politically advantageous.

"King Tristan will never marry a slaver. She might start sending Onyxians back to Corvid, or bringing her slaves here," Jacquetta said, shaking her head, her mouth twisting around the remnants of her tart.

"Oh, no," Gus moaned while I cringed.

"What?" Jacquetta asked.

"She might already bring slaves with her to be her Ladies in

Waiting," I said as Gus dropped her head, wringing her hands together.

Of all of us, Gus was most likely to know someone or be related to someone that would be enslaved if Onyx turned into a slave trading kingdom like Amethyst, or a slaver kingdom like Corvid.

My hands ached for a blade and my dress chafed for want of my assignment clothes and a target list.

"There is not a chance that the King would allow that," Madam said, but she swallowed and looked away, her fingers tapping on her glass.

"Are there any others we need to know about?" I asked, leaning forward and planting my feet. Maybe it wasn't just the King I needed to take care of.

Madam nodded and sat back. It was the most relaxed I had ever seen her. She studied me, making no secret of her eyes roaming up and down my body.

"Yes," she said, motioning for the servants to bring in the rest of the meal as she took a small sandwich and pointed it at me, "You."

CHAPTER 19
THE MOST DANGEROUS

"Me?" I asked, sitting up straight.

Gus popped her head up, her hands dropping into her lap and Jacquetta furrowed her brow at her mother.

"Of all the women I know to be there—the ruthless Corvid one, the weak and spoiled Amethyst one, the other vapid rich and powerful, even the sorcerer's daughter from the Protectorate—you, Lady Cinder, are the most dangerous."

I didn't know what to react to first: The fact I was going to be in the same palace with, and probably have to pretend that I didn't want to kill a Corvid woman. Or the fact that one of the closed-off sorcerers of the Protectorate Mountains—who lived outside of any kingdom's laws and no one understood—sent his daughter, who may very well have been a witch. Or that she thought that I was the issue in that kind of crowd.

"How is Cinder the most dangerous?" Jacquetta asked, looking more interested than shocked.

"You see, if one of those stupid girls becomes Queen—one of the ones so spoiled she only sees the palace and the King as a fairytale—we may well lose the next war," Madam said, taking a bite of her sandwich like she had not just invoked a terrifying possibility and put it at the feet of some imagined woman when it wouldn't be her who got us into the mess she talked about.

"But still," Gus said, her hands continuing wringing together in her lap, "Corvid would have to be the most dangerous."

"I know you do not want an Amethyst queen, or a Protectorate witch queen. And I know the last thing you want is a Corvid queen," Madam said. We all nodded, including me.

Even though I knew the King was never going to live long enough to take a queen—that I wasn't going to let him—the idea of any of those kinds of women taking over the kingdom set my stomach to twisting.

"So, what is the best way for us to avoid that?" Madam asked, taking another bite.

"For the one he chooses to be from Onyx," I said, my voice flat, because none of this said anything about me.

"Yes." Madam smiled at me and said no more.

I looked back and forth between Gus and Jacquetta.

Gus looked as confused as I did, but Jacquetta...

She was beaming at me, her smile so wide it looked like it hurt her face.

"And the best person from Onyx is Lady Cinder," Jacquetta said. Gus smiled, breaking out of the horror caused at the mere thought of Corvid.

"Come on," I said, shaking my head. I didn't want to upset Gus again, but they had to get realistic. "We could hate each other. You do not know that I would even be a good choice, let alone the best."

The truth was, I was the worst choice if they wanted the King to live.

"Lady Cinder," Madam said, her mouth flattening into a thin line which made me go still awaiting her negative judgement.

"You have managed to perform at a level I admit I did not think you capable of when you first arrived. And more than that, I know you are strong. I believe you are capable of providing good council and fair rule. That is all that matters between a king and a queen."

All that mattered between royals was what one could offer another. I knew that. But...

"I have nothing to offer. My duchy is not well to do, and if someone was looking for a return of the mythical dragon magic, I have zero magic in my blood." How did they not understand that I couldn't take this...hope?

Madam's face squished together—her whole face furrowed, not just her brow—and the others went blank.

"What?" I asked, looking from one to another.

"The hellfire water trade is very profitable," Jacquetta said.

"Not enough. Not since the war, there is too much damage," I said, my voice thin. I didn't want to discuss this. Not now. Maybe not ever. If my brother paid for all the dresses and Madam Valentin's effort on my behalf, it was already a devastating blow to the finances of Lehar.

"Madam Valentin, it is time," a footman said, standing in the doorway to the parlor.

His simple remark sent my stomach dropping down into my toes.

"Ah, well," Madam said, getting to her feet and smiling at us as we scrambled to ours, "I trust each of you will be successful in all the responsibilities placed upon you in the coming days."

Responsibilities.

The mission was my only real responsibility. And I needed to remember that.

"Jacquetta, I am very proud of you. Lady in Waiting to the future Queen. I know you will continue to make me proud,"

Madam said, taking Jacquetta's hand. She kissed her mother on the cheek in return.

"Augustina, I will continue to send your increased pay home to your family. You have done so well, and I am sure you will continue to be of great service to your Lady." Madam tucked a stray curl of Gus's hair behind her ear, smiled at her, and patted her shoulder.

Of all the ways I had considered I might hurt the women standing with me, the fact that they both might have their lives changed completely if this was real, and that they were counting on that, wasn't one of them.

Hope was a killer.

And I was the deliverer of death. Again.

It was everything I could do to remain upright and keep my face from crumpling, only managing to keep it clear by imagining that we weren't going to the palace at all, that it was just another day.

"Lady Cinder," Madam Valentin said, her face soft and her smile so warm I took in a shaky breath, "You will make a remarkable queen. Thank you for taking these women with you, giving them their titles, and working so hard to make us all proud."

She took both of my hands for a moment and all I could do was nod. It was a lie.

"You do not have to be nervous," she said.

And we walked out of the parlor.

Donning cloaks held for us by servants, the others chattered and laughed. A good-natured nervousness rippling through the air.

But even as they did, I wasn't nervous. I continued to be exactly as I was when Madam accused me of the same emotion.

I was trying not to cry.

CHAPTER 20
ARRIVAL

"Can you see it?" Jacquetta asked, her face pressed against the window

"Not yet," Gus said, shoved up against the other side.

"You've both seen it from the house," I said, leaning my head back against the seat, and kind of hoping it would ruin my hair.

"But we're *going* there now, not just looking at it," Gus said, her voice echoing strangely off the window.

"Maybe you should both just open the window and lean out," I said.

"Very funny. If I swung this window back, Mother would find out and kill me," Jacquetta said, turning toward me and rolling her eyes before gluing herself back to the window.

"Cinder, you have to be excited. You're going to be Queen," Gus yelled, her voice distorting as it bounced off the window until it was hard to tell what she said.

"Out of that whole conversation, that's what you took away?" I asked, but before she could answer me, or even react, Jacquetta squealed.

"I see it!"

Gus flung herself from one side of the carriage to the other, sending it rocking and me grabbing the edge of the seat so I didn't topple over.

"You have to see it," Gus said, glancing at me.

But I just shook my head. I couldn't tell them I had already been closer to the palace than we were now.

The tenor of the carriage rolling over the ground changed, turning from a general bumpiness to a rhythmic thumping, rising and falling over the wood of the bridge.

"We're crossing the bridge," Jacquetta yelled, and Gus grabbed her arm.

Crossing the bridge with no way to back out now.

I stared up at the quilted velvet of the carriage roof, tracing the lines of the tufting and shutting out the conversation swirling in the air around me.

Somehow, I needed to get away from them for a while tonight. I needed to find a place I could train without them watching and giving me away.

There were women in the palace guard.

Daughters of prominent and favored soldiers often followed in their father's footsteps. Maybe I could pass myself off as one of them. Even if all I could do was find a target for throwing knives, or find a bow and arrow. I had to do something.

Focusing on what I would be able to find, on the eventual release from some kind of training, at least kept the tremors at bay and gave me something to think about.

"Cinder, do you think King Tristan will greet us as we arrive?" Jacquetta asked, breaking into the too short respite.

I swallowed and shrugged, not trusting which words might pop out of my mouth, or even if they would be words. I might have just screamed and turned into a puddle of gelatinous muck.

No. I dug my fingernails into the seat cushion and forced my way back to the place I went to when a mission got hard: Survival.

The carriage was across the bridge, the sound of the wheels back to the irregular rumble of cobblestones beneath us.

But we had to travel up through the tunnels running under the walls of the palace to get to the interior courtyard.

Everyone in Onyx had heard about the marvel of the tunnel and the mighty palace running above and around it that created the tunnel.

All light streaming in the windows turned to blackness, not just dark. It was so devoid of light in the tunnel it seemed like the light within myself dimmed in reaction to it.

This was the Obsidian Palace. Formed by the first Dragon Kings of Onyx with their magic...

It didn't matter how long the tunnel was, or what the palace was made of, I still thought it was a combination of very skilled builders and a sorcerer or witch—maybe two—from the Protectorate Mountains.

People in some of the other kingdoms were rumored to have magic, and sometimes they had items people said were imbued with magic. But that was just propaganda the kingdoms put out to deter anyone from attacking them.

And, at least in the case of Corvid, the stories never made any sense anyway.

Corvid supposedly had magic. It was part of how most of their population fell under the slaver's knot in the first place. But if they had magic, they wouldn't need to have slaves. Unless they were so terrible that they actually thought it wasn't a horror and they were doing fine.

I shuddered and sat up.

The Amethyst kingdom was another one that people said had magic. It supposedly had some kind of magical item. But it didn't make sense either. If they did, would they really trade their people away to Corvid?

Even the Protectorate sorcerers and witches. Why would they lock themselves away, hidden deep within their mountain, rarely coming out if they were so powerful?

I blinked and widened my eyes, resisting the urge to rub them and destroy the careful makeup on my face.

Maybe I was right and there was no magic. Maybe others were right, and some people had it. But none of it mattered.

What mattered was pretending I was fine long enough to make it to the end of the day successfully so I could continue my mission.

Finally, the tunnel ended. Light poured in over Gus and Jacquetta's shoulders.

Jacquetta gasped and Gus's hands dropped from the edge of the window to fall limp in her lap.

"Cinder, you have to see this," Jacquetta said, and Gus nodded.

"I will when we get out of the carriage," I said, touching my hair as I sat forward, the off-the-shoulder strap of my dress making it impossible for me to even touch the back of my own head.

This dress was a cruel trick.

Our carriage slowed and Jacquetta sat back, pulling Gus away from the window. They both fidgeted and adjusted their dresses and touched their hair.

"You both look beautiful. There's no reason to be nervous," I said, which might have been more convincing if it didn't sound like I was scolding them.

"How are you so calm?" Gus asked, breathless.

"Because nothing will happen right now. The ball isn't even until tomorrow." And the only other option was for me to jump from the carriage, rip my dress apart, and find someone to stab.

"Nothing? The King may be waiting for us outside right now," Jacquetta said, her voice going all wistful on 'King.'

"I'm pretty sure King Tristan has better things to do than wait around all day while all the women roll up at different times." I looked out the window and the only thing I could see was that the visible area of the courtyard was empty, just cobblestones and the black obsidian wall of the palace.

"Look, if the King were waiting out there, way more guards would be posted," I said, gesturing outside.

"Oh."

Both of their faces fell as they turned to the window, but they brightened a second later as the door swung open, a footman stepping back to give us room to get out.

"Here we go," Jacquetta whispered.

Yes, here we went, into the real start of my mission.

CHAPTER 21
ALREADY HERE

I was the last of us to step from the carriage onto the portable wooden steps a footman placed in front of the door for us.

Jacquetta and Gus made no attempt to hide the fact they were struck as they took in the palace. They both had their heads tilted back as they slowly turned in a circle.

The courtyard wasn't empty, and was larger than I expected since the palace surrounded it completely. It was vast enough for the massive height of the obsidian walls not to block the sun from shining down on us.

One side of the ground floor of the palace seemed to be stables, and the rest had large arches set regularly in it exposing training grounds that made me want to ignore my assignment all together just to wander among them.

Grand steps that were as wide as Madam's large house led up to the next floor and doors flung open.

So far, we were the only carriage I saw in the courtyard, which made me want to drop into a crouch. Hiding in a crowd of women was a safer bet than heading into the lair of a king who was either the son of someone so incompetent that a war got out of hand and killed my parents, or so ruthless he didn't care if they died.

But I was right. There was no sign of the King among the people going about their day.

"Welcome to the Obsidian Palace," a woman in a military uniform said.

She had straight black hair that hung down her back in a wall as sleek as those of the palace. Her face was soft, but her expression as hard as a mountain. Even though she was short, she held herself so straight and tall it seemed like she should be taller than me.

This woman was a study in contrasts, and judging by the number of dragons on her sleeves, she was a general.

"Hello, General Pace," Jacquetta said with a single nod. "Thank you for greeting us."

Was that a careful recrimination of the King?

It took a conscious effort for me to keep my features schooled.

"Of course, Jacquetta. I trust Madam Valentin is well."

Jacquetta smiled and the General turned toward me.

"You must be Lady Cinder Ahmya of Lehar," General Pace said, with a small bow in my direction.

The combination of my full formal title with the General's bow made me feel like Ash must have been standing behind me.

"General," I said, with a tilt of my head, unable to say much else as my throat closed up. This wasn't normal. None of this was normal.

"Please, follow me and I will lead you to your rooms," she said.

Gus fell in behind her first, Jacquetta after her, and I took up the back of the line.

It was the way it was done, but it felt unnatural and wrong

not to walk alongside them. All titles, all royalty, all the formalities felt like a uniform that didn't fit.

But it didn't matter if I was comfortable being a Lady of Lehar as I walked through the doorway, the obsidian of the walls causing a reverberating hum through my bones. It was the skin I needed to live in. At least for a while.

General Pace led us through the grand front hall, across the stone floor that looked suspiciously like silver was embedded in it, toward one of the massive sets of stairs.

Jacquetta and Gus still had their heads on a swivel as they tried to see everything at once. All I focused on were the people we passed.

Most of the people around were guards or servants. Not a single courtier had appeared yet.

Although once we reached the top of the stairs, a man, probably near my brother's age, stood at the top of the other stairwell in the kind of sedate finery I associated with the Lords. It was a perfectly tailored suit, missing some of the gaudier adornments my brother would have worn. And he wasn't even wearing heels. He was far enough away it was hard to make out his features where he stood in the shadow of a pillar, but I was sure he was watching us as we passed.

How many people were going to be at the palace while we were here?

Did some of the young Lords and Dukes think it was a good time to find a wife if the King was doing the same? The idea that the King would be the catalyst for that kind of decision was more sycophantic than I could have imagined.

Our side of the upper story consisted of the longest hallway I had ever seen with so many doors I lost count. The two sets of steps led to different wings and didn't seem to connect at all.

The floors were still the strange stone, a kind I had never

seen before. It looked slick with a heavy shine, but it didn't feel like I was going to lose my footing or slide around on it.

So it wasn't only the thick, black, seamless obsidian that made up all the walls and the entire exterior. Even the interior of the building was strange.

We finally reached a door with my family sigil hanging on the wall beside it. They didn't have it just as a relief like the only representations of it left at home. They had the flames in bright green gems with the black drop of liquid on top made of obsidian. It reminded me of the tapestries we had hanging at home before the fires. As I passed it, I ran my fingertips across it and closed my eyes, sending up a prayer to Mother and Father.

My prayer, as it often was, wasn't even a real, fully formed idea. Just a call for help from the only people I knew beyond death itself wanted what was best for me.

Inside, I expected just a series of bedrooms, but it was more like a house.

Gus and Jacquetta headed through two of the doors off a large parlor area, complete with a desk and office supplies I couldn't imagine we had any need of, a dining table, and a small kitchen.

"When you said, 'rooms' for some reason I was just expecting bedrooms," I said, standing in the middle of the room and turning toward the General whose attention was fixed on me.

"Lady Cinder, we want you to be comfortable in the palace," she said, a slight emphasis on 'you' that made my stomach muscles tighten.

"Thank you. I am sure we will be more than comfortable here."

She smiled and bowed before she left the room, shutting the door behind her.

"Cinder, get in here," Jacquetta called.

I sighed and shook out my hands as I made my way to her.

The bedroom I walked into was twice the size of the one I had at Madam's house. The bed itself was twice the size a bed needed to be, and it still looked forlorn and sad trying to take up enough space in the room to have it all make sense.

But it was the glass doors and large balcony I found more interesting.

"This is your room," Jacquetta said, twirling in the middle of the space on a thick rug that took up most of the floor.

I looked past her to the doors to the outside, but she wanted my attention more than the balcony did.

"How do you know that?" I asked, stretching my back and settling into a less perfect posture.

"Because, it has the best view, and I think it's the biggest."

"Cinder, Jacquetta, you both need to see this," Gus called, and I was glad to focus on something other than who would sleep where. I didn't care as long as I got to sleep.

Gus stood next to the desk, a piece of thick paper in her hand, her head bent to read it.

"What's wrong?" I asked as Jacquetta came up behind me.

"You're invited to dinner," Gus said, holding the paper out to me.

Already. I wasn't just at the palace. I was already going to be put to work being who they wanted me to be.

CHAPTER 22
BELONG

"You know what that means," Jacquetta said, smiling at me.

"I don't." And I didn't care that much right at that second. The day was already too much as it was. Especially after the General's insinuation. Although, I tried not to think I knew what she meant, it still hung on me like even more heavy fabric.

"Cinder, as soon as the luggage is brought up, we need to get you ready," Jacquetta said, and Gus laughed.

"No. What I need right now is to see your rooms, then the balcony, get someone to bring us up food, and take a nap."

They laughed again, but I wasn't kidding.

Rolling my eyes, I went to each of the other rooms. They were still plenty spacious, but they weren't nearly as ridiculous. Which meant Jacquetta was probably right that the other room was meant for me.

It made me want to sleep on the sofa. Walking past them again as they huddled over the paper by the desk made me want to hide instead of going to dinner.

"Do you think King Tristan will have all of you there, or just a few?" Gus asked, holding the paper out to me.

Jacquetta took it, glanced at it, and then handed it to me, shaking her head.

"No. He's not going to want to look like he's playing favorites before it starts or risk causing even more political threats," Jacquetta said.

"Either way," I said, looking down at what I was sure was an invitation matched on every desk in every woman's room. "Tonight would be the only time we can say no because we're tired from travel."

"You're not saying no," Jacquetta and Gus said at the same time.

"And we're going to have you perfectly ready for tonight," Jacquetta went on, planting her hands on her hips.

"We need to get started right away," Gus agreed.

"But why can't I just take a nap until I need to get ready for dinner?" I asked, taking the piece of paper and setting it down on the desk.

"Cinder." Their matching exasperation with me almost made me laugh, but I was too frustrated by being the one trying to fight against their joint defense.

"Fine," I said, squeezing my hands together instead of rubbing my face like I wanted to, "But I need to eat. And I am going to check the balcony."

I walked away, but both of them followed me, smiles returning to their faces.

These two…If King Tristan really wanted to find someone who would help him scare the Corvids and anyone else threatening war, he should have picked one of them.

Opening the glass doors, they swung silently. And I finally smiled. Maybe tonight wouldn't be a complete loss.

"Wow," Gus said, coming up beside me on the balcony.

The obsidian of the walls made up the railing and the floor of the balcony as well, but there was a grid in the floor of the balcony that made it less slick.

Below us, there was a thin box with flowers in it along a window, and then nothing to the ground of the courtyard.

From up here, it was easier to see how the palace usually looked so dark at night from the outside. If they mostly used the rooms facing the courtyard, the whole thing could look darker and menacing from the outside.

Whether or not the builders intended it to be, it was a brilliant defensive use of part of the palace. And it made me want to look out a room on the other side to see if there were balconies and boxes there too. If there were, it was a mistake. They should have used all the aspects of the palace to their advantage, including the smooth sides of the building itself.

"Cinder, what are you thinking when you get that look on your face?" Gus asked.

I shook my head and focused on her.

"Gus, you wouldn't believe me if I told you," I said, and Jacquetta laughed.

"You look like you're planning a murder or a war. Leave that to General Pace. Come on," Jacquetta said, and Gus bit her lips like she was holding back laughter.

It took me a moment to swallow and bite my lip, collecting myself before I followed them inside.

"Let me order us some food, and then we can talk about strategy for dealing with the other women," Jacquetta said, darting out of my room.

"How is she going to order food?" I asked, sitting on the bed, the softness of it making me want to lie back even more than before.

"Madam said that the palace has a system in the walls of the kitchens that sends a piece of paper with a message on it to the main kitchen." Gus bounced up and down on the bed like she was testing it.

"Then why do we have a kitchen at all?"

Gus shrugged, but I thought it was likely they needed to fill up space in the oversized rooms.

"We have a kitchen for drinks and snacks," Jacquetta said, walking into the room with a pitcher, glasses, and three bowls of berries.

I reached out my hands, so hungry I didn't care that we were probably going to spill something on the bed.

"No, come over to the table," she said, heading back to the parlor.

"Making me wait even one more minute is cruel," I said, shoving myself up from the bed and stomping into the parlor.

And my friends—although I was starting to doubt they actually were that—laughed at me.

"Really not funny," I grumbled, taking a seat at the table.

The berries were sweet, and once my mouth was full, I closed my eyes and allowed the flavor to burst onto my taste-buds, basking in the sensation.

"Okay, so we have to focus on what the strategy will be with the other women now," Jacquetta said, and Gus nodded.

We spent the entire rest of the time we waited for the meal, the entire time eating the meal, and the entire time they pushed me around, tugging and painting, pinning and primping, talking about whether we should make some allies, and if so, who.

It didn't help.

By the time I was ready and waiting to be taken to dinner, all their tips and opinions swam in my brain as knotted as a nest of eels, leaving me wondering if I was going to be able to do this.

Maybe it was best not to stick my foot out just in case I was going to be the one to trip on it later.

The thought of deliberately calculating who I would find worth talking to made no sense to me.

Plus, their two options were to try and get close to the women I thought were the worst, most dangerous among them, or to get to know the women I thought weakest. And suggesting that in either case I should use it to my advantage made the food we ate curdle in my stomach.

Finally, a knock sounded on the door.

Gus ran to answer it and I folded my hands together in front of me, yelling at myself in my head to keep it together.

No matter what happened at dinner or what I thought of the women, I had to keep it together and not make a target out of myself.

"Lady Cinder," General Pace said with a bow. "I'm here to escort you to dinner. Jacquetta, this is also an invitation for the Ladies in Waiting to have a dinner of their own."

She handed over another thick paper and I had to smile.

Not only did she drop the overly formal language I hated, but the looks on Gus and Jacquetta's faces were a gift. They were so happy to be included in more than just attending me.

General Pace was watching me when I looked back her way, and when I smiled, one side of her mouth turned up.

"Have fun," I said, following the General into the hall. Then I turned to her because it didn't make sense. "I appreciate you taking the time out to escort me, but you are a general. You're very important and must have much to do that isn't walking me around."

"Every woman coming here has an advisor assigned to her," she said, and I raised my brows, "And I chose to be assigned to you. Madam Valentin spoke highly of you."

Ah. Madam and the General were friends. It made more sense. Although if I were the King, I would not have given the silly job to my advisors.

"Did every advisor get to choose?" I asked, feeling bad for the one assigned to Corvid.

"Well, I went first," she said, and I looked closely at her.

That was quite a limb to go out on for a friend's recommendation. And it was another person who would suffer when I finished my assignment.

If anyone discovered that I was the one who killed the King...

We came to the top of the massive staircase and a woman flanked by two men passed from one side of the grand foyer to the other.

General Pace's face narrowed. Her mouth pinched as she stared daggers at them.

Our own descent and walk had us trailing them to the threshold of large ravenwood doors, their engravings set off by gems of every conceivable color.

The images portrayed were of dragons in battle, the bright green of hellfire water pouring out of their mouths instead of flame.

No matter what happened with the other women in the room, I took the color on the doors as a reminder to act as if I belonged here.

And I walked inside.

CHAPTER 23
AMAZING

G eneral Pace came with me into an echoing ballroom
with a long slab of quartz sitting on obsidian plinths
acting as a table surrounded by white chairs sitting
in the center of the room.

"Subtle," I mumbled. The General smiled before managing to
repress it.

"Ah, so this is Lady Ahmya of Lehar," a short man with a
wide smile said, coming up to the General's side as we walked
across the floor toward the table.

"Please call me Lady Cinder," I said before the General could
correct him for me. I had the right to go by whatever name I
chose, even if they would never drop the Lady honorific.

His smile twitched and I offered him a small one back.
Whoever this man was, no matter how much he may not have
liked, nor been used to being corrected, if he thought I might
end up his queen then he couldn't afford to make an enemy of
me. And my smile wasn't kind. It was the type that told him I
knew that.

"Lady Cinder, please forgive me." He glanced at the General as if seeking permission for something.

"This is Chamberlain Rezan," she said, and I did a double take, wondering if I should have apologized for assuming the Chamberlain was a man.

Rezan was a common girl's name, but I felt stupid and didn't want to be rude.

"It is nice to meet you," I said, trying to get closer to a sincere smile.

"More the pleasure for me to meet you. I was so disappointed when you did not come to court. Although, I understand after your loss."

No matter how much I told myself not to, no matter how much I thought I prepared myself for this eventuality, my hands curled into fists at the mention of my parents.

"Come and meet some of the others who are here already. Some of our guests have not arrived yet. Some of them needed to travel a long distance." The Chamberlain laughed although I missed the humor.

"Marquessa Ziya, I would like for you to meet Lady Cinder and General Pace," Rezan said, gesturing between us and the violet-haired, painfully pale, woman from Amethyst in front of us.

"Very nice to meet you. Are you from Onyx as well?" she asked, looking between the General and me.

"Yes," the General said, leaving it at that, not adding anything else to the conversation, and leaving me to fill in the gap.

Ziya shrunk in front of me. It was probably my imagination, but I thought her hair became a duller shade.

"Have you been to Onyx before?" I asked instead, assuming she was going to say no. Few Amethystians ever came here.

"Oh, yes. My sister, the Queen, brought me with her contingent at the end of the last war. It is a beautiful country." She stood up taller, her hair was definitely brighter, and her grin massive.

Apparently, she missed that it was probably not a great reference to make mention of the last war. Least of all, her country's part in it, and therefore their part in my parents' deaths. It made me want to punch her in that purple head.

"Excuse us. We should take our seats," General Pace said, touching my white-knuckled fist with a finger and motioning to the table.

She didn't have to offer me an out from this conversation twice. I turned and walked stiffly to the table, flexing my fingers, sucking down deep breaths, and trying to force myself not to lash out.

Was that slave trading nightmare the Chamberlain's chosen?

"Is the Chamberlain the Marquessa's escort?" I asked in a low voice once the General was sitting next to me, keeping my eyes ahead.

"Yes. Chamberlain Rezan chose second," she said.

Long, slow breaths. My fists pressed together until my knuckles hurt under the table. It was my only outlet.

First to die after the King would be the Chamberlain and his chosen potential if I could find a way to not cause another war.

No matter who the royals installed after King Tristan was dead, I was going to make sure that no slave traders and no slavers ever got control over our country. Somehow, I had to kill the King before he could make an alliance with Amethyst or Corvid, and not get caught.

With people like the Chamberlain around, even with a different king, I didn't trust they would do right by the people of the country like Gus and her family.

Looking down at the dark place setting in front of me, I couldn't even focus on the pattern, let alone take in what was going on around me.

My assignment, never simple, got more complicated by the minute.

Finally, a servant set a plate in front of me, and I realized everyone was gathered around the table in their seats, ready to eat.

The conversation was introductions and carefully stilted comments of greeting, but I only partially paid attention.

I should have been hanging on their every word, and noting even the tiniest reaction someone had to something said or the presence of another person. But I was too busy trying to plan.

Until the General made a humph noise under her breath.

A large man with a thick beard and very little neck, with the adornments of a member of the high sect—the few members of the clergy who didn't hide in their huts next to the holy springs and trees and made themselves part of the world—waved a hand in the air.

"Shield Elio, please stop," the Chamberlain said and the General next to me went rigid while I almost choked on the food in my mouth.

"You have to admit, that even you want to know more about the sorcerers and witches up there. Why not have a fun exhibition of her power when she gets here?" Elio asked, his voice a deep bass rumble that was more felt than heard.

They continued to argue. The Chamberlain made it sound like the biggest negative about the idea wasn't that it would put the rest of us at a disadvantage assuming the woman had power, but that it was uncouth.

But a Shield…

Elio was more than just a member of the high sect—which was strange enough as far as I was concerned—but he was a Shield.

Shields had to accomplish two of four possible things according to the sect and the clergy, and they had to be witnessed: Perform a miracle; Discover a hidden holy site; Bring someone back from the dead; Or perform a spontaneous act of magic.

I didn't even know what it meant to perform a miracle, and I didn't think there were any living Shields. But I was looking right at one.

He was...not what I was expecting.

Most of the clergy I happened upon during my missions were thin, almost all aged, and many were so quiet it was hard to hear them speak at all.

This man's voice overtook what little space was left in the room after being occupied by his massive body.

Looking at the General, I wanted to ask what he had done to earn his title, but she was grinding her teeth and staring at the arguing dignitaries as if they personally offended her by being alive.

"Lehar, that is where you're from is it not?" A high whine of a voice with an accent and a nasal quality to it that made it hard not to cringe rose above the noise.

A woman with hair as white as the quartz of the table and eyes as dark as the obsidian walls sat down on the opposite side of the table from me, one black eyebrow arched high.

Corvid.

My chest tightened and I wanted to jump up into fighting stance even though it would ruin my dress.

"Yes, I am Lady Cinder Ahmya of Lehar," I said, my voice hard because what I wanted to say was, 'I thought you weren't coming, slaver.'

"Well, I am glad you are here. We arrived earlier than expected. When you have a moment, I would love a chance to speak with you about that amazing hellfire water I have heard so much about." She took a drink of her wine, paying no attention to my face or the faces of the people around the table.

The man next to her—so thin and fine-featured I would have placed him as younger than me if not for his head of thick gray hair—bent over his plate and didn't hide his face well enough for me not to see his horror.

So this was her escort, and he was none too thrilled with the job.

"Lehar does not trade with Corvid," I said and at least one person sucked in a breath.

But the Corvid, whoever she was, just looked up from her plate and narrowed her dark eyes at me. "I am a princess," she hissed.

"And I am not going to negotiate."

The General sat up a little straighter, her hands braced on the table in front of her and a cruel smile forming on her face as she stared at the Corvid princess.

Shield Elio burst out laughing and the Corvid princess' bone-white cheeks took on a tinge of red.

"Well, now that that's out of the way," Elio said, "Lady Cinder, I have never been to Lehar. Does it truly rain ashes there?"

Now we were in better territory.

"Yes, although it also rains, but our rain is black. It also snows, but that is gray. It is lovely," I said, to the amusement of Elio who grinned like I was the funniest person at the table.

"I love the stories of your home. They are all so amazing."

Amazing.

It was that, but not in the way Elio thought.

CHAPTER 24
OUT OF PRACTICE

After dinner we all said sedate goodbyes and returned to our rooms, a long line of escorts and potential brides traipsed up the staircase and toward our rooms.

Once we were safely behind the closed door to our suite, I stretched my neck and groaned.

"It went well, under the circumstances," Pace said, dropping into a military at ease stance.

Jacquetta and Gus ran out of their rooms, and I raised a hand at their eager expressions. I wanted to talk to the General before they peppered me with questions.

"The raven bitch wasn't supposed to be here until tomorrow, and I didn't think the snake was supposed to be here either," I said, Gus and Jacquetta's eyes went wide.

"Corvid and Amethyst are here?" They spoke in unison, but their question didn't need an answer.

"I was misinformed," the General said. By the look on her face, I suspected she thought that was deliberate.

"King Tristan can't really marry a slaver or a slave trader, can he?" Jacquetta asked, shaking her head and looking like she was about to vomit.

"One of them is a Marquessa and the other is a Princess," I said, rubbing my hands over my face. I had to get out of this dress.

"So what?" Gus asked, "Rank isn't everything."

Maybe rank wasn't everything to all of us, but to a king looking to strengthen his hold on the throne and make a powerful alliance...I wasn't sure.

"Can you explain to me why the Chamberlain is so pro-Amethyst?" I asked. The general took a moment to sit across from me.

"Amethyst is the wealthiest of all the countries."

Everyone knew that and we all nodded.

"Not just in monetary ways. It also has a huge cache of magical gems. Why do you think all the royals have purple hair?"

"Real magic?" I asked, even though I saw her hair change color. Magic was not real...just rumor to keep other kingdoms scared of old tales. If all their magic did was give them colorful hairstyles, then it was no more than a trick.

"We don't know what their magic can do, but we know they have it, yes," she said.

"But why would that make her a good choice, better than a Protectorate witch for example?" Gus asked, and Jacquetta looked just as confused.

"She's the confirmed magical user," I said, leaning back into the sofa and the General nodded. "No one really knows if the Protectorate witches all have power or just some of them. The Marquessa is the safe bet."

"Fine, but why the focus on magic?" Jacquetta asked.

"The Chamberlain wants the return of the Dragon Kings," I said, and the room fell silent.

Minutes ticked by with everyone in their own minds.

"How do we get King Tristan to see it like we do?" Gus asked, her voice was hushed but still seemed loud in the quiet of the room.

"However we can," the General said, pushing up from the other sofa, nodding to us, and leaving the room.

Jacquetta and Gus bombarded me with questions about everything from which escorts were assigned to which women, to what the food and the dresses were like.

I answered them all, but made them take the pins out of my hair as I did.

Once changed into a nightgown, all my jewelry set aside, and my hair undone, I begged exhaustion and went to bed.

Gus and Jacquetta remained in the parlor, talking. I could hear them with my ear to the bedroom door.

It only took me a few moments to discard the nightgown and don my old clothes.

The spike sat on my palms, wanting me to take it with. But if anyone caught me, it would be better if they didn't see it. A lot better.

And the only thing the dresses had over my pants was the ability to conceal my spike.

Swinging open the balcony doors, the chill of the night air rushed in all around me, carrying with it the scent of trees and hay. I wasn't sure where the trees were, but the hay reminded me there were stables down there which gave me a potential hiding place if it all went bad.

I pulled on a pair of gloves and stripped one of the sheets off the bed.

Out on the balcony, I wrapped the sheet around my waist and tucked my cloak around it, masking the color. The rest of me was covered in dark fabric except for my face. I hoped it would be good enough.

Scanning the courtyard, I watched some people who weren't aware I could see them. With no light from the room illuminating me from behind like they were lit in their windows, I was invisible to their eyes. I didn't see anyone looking toward my area of the palace at all.

Finally, I took a deep breath and climbed to the other side of the railing, my feet between the slats.

I slid my gloved hands down until they were touching the tops of my shoes.

Before I made the next move, I double-checked the distance to the thin box filled with flowers. In the dark it was hard to make out against the deep black of the palace wall with no light directly on it.

There was no point in waiting, I had as good an idea of how I needed to swing as I was going to get.

So I dropped my feet to dangle from the railing, moved my hands one by one onto the ledge of the balcony itself, and swung back and forth. On the second swing, I let go and twisted in the air.

I landed perched on the edge of the box, leaning down immediately to grab onto it.

Once I had a grip on the edge, I peered over the side down to the courtyard below.

No one was around and the archway right under me was dark as if no one was training in that section.

Good.

All over again, I gripped the edge tight and did a slow, controlled fall until I was stretched out and hanging from the box.

Only then did I let go.

The fall was longer than the ones I usually made, but I tucked and rolled with it, letting my momentum eat up the energy of the hit instead of absorbing it with my body.

At the end of the roll, crouched on the ground, I looked around and still didn't see anyone throwing up a flag of alarm, or even anyone around on the ground floor except for guards by the tunnel looking out.

Guys, the danger is inside.

I darted into the archway, ducking behind the pillar, and let my eyes adjust to this even fuller darkness.

The archery grounds ranged in front of me.

Unwrapping the sheet from around my waist, I tucked it behind the pillar and made my way through the edge of the dark underside of the palace, smiling the entire time.

Finally, I came to a section with the lights on.

Knife and axe throwing. Perfect.

Along one wall, all the weapons were hung in neat and defined spaces. I collected as many as I could carry, and took them back to a target lane.

I took five throwing knives into my hands, testing their weight and balance before choosing exactly how to place my hold.

Getting my hold set, feeling it was right, I spun and threw, hitting one entire ring outside the center.

"Out of practice," I muttered.

By the time I was done with the first five knives, I had marched the hits across the target in a line, only the first outside the spacing I wanted.

Moving over to the next lane, I took up three axes and did it all over again, happy when I got them all on the board because the axe wasn't my best weapon.

I was going to hit the last lane with another set of knives before I went down to the end of the lane and collected all of them, but I was interrupted by someone clapping behind me.

CHAPTER 25
KEEP CONTROL

I spun around into a crouch, one hand planted on the
ground where no more weapons sat waiting for me to
throw them.

"Sorry," the young man said, holding his hands up and smiling, "I didn't mean to startle you. I was just admiring your
work."

He had dark brown hair, almost black, with deep, rich, tan
skin as if he were in the sun a lot. There was even a touch of
what looked like a burn. People in my duchy never got that
same sun-touched look, even if they were naturally browner
than I was.

As much as the world slowed around me while I tried to
listen for others coming, for an alarm sounding, for someone to
act like I was caught, it didn't happen.

"What are you doing?" I asked, not sure what else to say.

The man's smile turned into a look like he wasn't sure I was
serious.

"Same as you. I'm here to train," he said, walking over to the line of targets, opening his cloak, and revealing a vest full of knives.

He took one in his hand, practiced in the weight of his own set. He turned to the side and threw, the knife flipping end over end. The light shining off it turned it into a blur. It hit right on the edge of the bullseye.

"Nice throw," I said, walking down to the end of the first lane and collecting my knives.

"You're new to the palace, I guess," he said, waiting until I looked his way to throw his next one so I would know where he aimed and where the knife went.

"I am," I said, which wasn't a lie. Not entirely anyway.

"Most of the guard prefer the other weapons."

After I collected the next cache of weapons from the next target, I turned back to him again, letting him have his turn to throw.

"The other weapons are good to train with too, but this was the bay that was lit and open." If he thought I didn't know my way around the rest, he was wrong.

"I am very glad I asked them to leave it open for me, then," he said, letting another one fly.

Each throw was well placed for the tight star he was creating. I moved to the last of the targets to clear my axes.

"You like to train late when no one is around," I said, turning back and making eye contact before giving him a nod, letting him know it was okay to throw while I was right here next to his target.

He smiled. It was warm and open, and it seemed like this guard and I had reached an understanding. Respect for skill, at least.

But the next throw went wrong. He overcompensated for my presence, probably without even realizing it. The knife twanged off the first one, sending them both flying along with pieces of wood like shrapnel.

I ducked, dropping the pile of weapons, keeping two axes so I could raise them and protect my face.

The wayward knife clattered at my feet, hitting my collected and discarded pile. I jumped back.

"Oh, no." He ran toward me, his eyes wide.

"Stop," I yelled, and took stock. "I'm not cut, but you can't choke up when someone is in range. What were you thinking?"

"I...I..." He stammered disconnected syllables, looking back and forth from me to the knife on the ground, to the target and shaking his head.

"How did you move so fast?" he finally asked, not even coming close to saying anything that sounded like he listened to what I said.

"Damn good thing I did, don't you think?" I picked up his knife, turning the handle out to him, taking a second to admire the Damascus pattern of flames on the blade, and thinking he didn't deserve a set so fine. Not if he was going to act stupid when someone was relying on him to get it right.

Snapping his head back like I slapped him, his face went slack.

"Yes. I am sorry," he said, stepping forward and taking the knife carefully from my hand.

I chose not to answer, just collected the weapons I was using and moved back to my starting place.

He watched me go, not pretending he wasn't, and it made me wonder what his rank in the guard was.

Just to prove a point, I walked down to the target right next to him and waited with a knife in my hand.

The man stood up straighter and nodded.

I let loose, throwing the first five knives in quick succession, whirling from side to side to get the perfect amount of momentum on them.

And just to prove my point, I didn't group them in a star with an open center. I grouped them in a tight cross pattern with the one in the middle going last.

Each one struck home seconds after the one before and his mouth dropped open.

Not bothering to wait until he processed that, I moved on to my next set of weapons and the next target.

Keeping my pace fast and moving from one to the next, I finished the round, breathing deeply.

He remained in the same place, his face painted in a kind of shock I usually only saw on injured people. But I needed to get back and get some sleep.

No matter what rank he was—which had to be higher than a first level with his formal speech and obvious wealth to buy his way in—I didn't have time to sit around and chat with a guard not quite ready for duty.

After I collected all my weapons from the targets again, I nodded to him, hung them all in their places, and left the training ground.

I ducked behind an arch, disappearing into the night, using darkness to cover my exit.

Watching him from here was too easy.

He collected his knives and moved onto a less destroyed target. His form wasn't bad. His hold was solid. The problem came in the release and sometimes in the move. It wasn't second nature to him. The knife wasn't an extension of his arm. This guard was probably better at the other disciplines and was picking up this one. That made sense.

Still, whichever rich family member bought him Damascus throwing knives should have waited until he was better at using them.

Making my way back to the arch under my window, I stayed in the shadows while I watched a team of guards switch with the ones at the gate before they walked out of the gate.

They were probably headed to the garrisons outside the palace walls, but they weren't in my way anymore. I focused on the distance between me and the flower box.

I recovered my sheet from its hiding place, tying the end into a loop, and finding a rock to twist into the looped end.

Not that my sheet contraption was the best option, but I nodded that it was the best I could do.

Winding the sheet loosely and hanging it on my arm. I swung the loop round and round until I had the right momentum, and then let it go, sending it at the box.

My first shot missed, just bumped against the bottom of the box.

Shit.

Trying again, I tossed the loop, this time slipping it over the corner of the box, the tail of the sheet hanging down to just out of my grasp.

Leaping into the air, I missed grabbing it.

More shit.

I launched myself onto the wall of the palace and used it to leap further up, snatching the sheet with one hand.

Waiting for a moment, letting the lurch on the sheet settle until I tried to move again, my entire body hung from one arm.

Once the sheet and I were still, I climbed.

Getting up onto the edge of the box was the easiest part so far.

The next leap was going to be even further, but at least for this one, I could use more of the sheet. If I got the throw right.

Retying the sheet, undoing the loop, and making a small knot in one corner at the end with the rock in it, I eyed the railing above me.

All I had to do…if I could just…

I flung the sheet, releasing the end and letting the rest trail after it.

With a small, hollow sound, it bounced off the rail.

Fuck.

Taking a quick look around the courtyard, none of the guards looked my way, but I was running out of time.

Again.

Another miss.

Fucking shit.

Once more, I wound up and hoped I knew where the gap between the rails was.

It caught and I let the sheet spool away from me, holding my breath that it would do what I needed it to. Because otherwise it would fall all the way to the ground, and I would have to start again.

'Please work,' I chanted in my mind, closing my eyes and asking Mother and Father to help me with this one.

Quickly crouching, bunching up my muscles, preparing my entire body, I shot up, launching myself into the air.

Every part of me was pointed and straight for a moment, suspended in the air.

But my hand caught the bottom corner of the sheet.

I snatched at it with my other hand, gripping it tightly, hanging still for a second, praying to Mother and Father that I wouldn't plummet to the ground.

Hand over hand, I scaled the sheet, as I got to the bottom of the balcony, the sheet tugged in my hand.

Was it slipping?

Another grab, this time at the edge of the balcony floor between the railings, instead of the sheet.

CHAPTER 26
TERRIBLE DAY

My hand clamped onto the edge just as the sheet gave.

I couldn't let it fall to the ground.

One hand screamed that the surface was too slick, I was going to lose my grip. I had to pull up the sheet with the other, and wrap it around my neck before I could take hold of the balcony with both hands.

By the time I had a grip, my breathing dragged in and out, my heart stampeded in my chest, and I scrambled, none too gracefully, over the rail to fall onto the balcony.

Laying there, I stared up at the stars, taking in the fact that I survived.

The sheet still hung over the rail, trailing off from around my neck.

I pulled it in as I tried to recover my ability to sit up, let alone stand.

Every muscle in my body shivered, the close call coursed through me.

Part of me wanted to just sleep there, under the stars who watched as I made my climb, with the sheet piled on top of me.

Somehow, I needed to find a better way to climb up and down this stupid obsidian.

Banging my head onto the balcony beneath me, the chill of the wind finally started to seep past the overheating of my body, the leftovers from my ill-advised training.

It was ill-advised, but it wasn't a bad decision.

Getting to my feet and dragging the sheet along with me into my room, I shut the doors behind me and climbed under the covers of my bed.

Sleep clawed at me, striking against the backs of my eyes and the inside of my mind. All I wanted was to lay there and pass out.

None of that would have been the case without the training, or more likely the trip back to my room. But it reinforced the idea that I needed to find a better way. At least I might be able to sleep soundly once in a while.

Besides, maybe finding my way around the palace would help us when we needed to get out without arousing suspicions.

First, though, I needed to get out of my clothes.

Dragging myself out of bed, I changed into my nightgown, shivering when the air hit the clammy sweat coating my body.

Forcing my eyes to focus in the dark, I shoved my clothes into one of my trunks and finally, finally got back under the covers.

Maybe I could ask the guard I met tonight. Maybe he would know of an easier way to get back out to the training grounds. But I would have to word my request carefully, and give nothing away.

Not that I had any reason to even seek him out and ask any questions yet.

The ball was tomorrow.

If King Tristan asked me to stay on, maybe everything would change too much for me to train, rendering a dangerous conversation a reckless risk.

And maybe he would send me home.

Everything really would change then. Not for the better.

Sleep still managed to taunt me, my body and mind exhausted, while it waited right outside my reach.

By the time the sun peered in through the glass doors, it didn't feel as if I slept at all.

Gus and Jacquetta bounded into the room, still in their nightgowns, Jacquetta with a matching cap over her hair.

"Wake up, Cinder," Jacquetta called, jumping onto my bed and then frowning down at me.

"Today's the big..." Gus started and stopped, planting her hands on her hips, "You look terrible. Big black circles under your eyes." She pointed to her own eyes as if I didn't know where she was talking about.

"Did you not sleep at all?" Jacquetta yelled, making me cringe.

"I slept," I mumbled, not lifting my head from the pillow, "Just not well."

And not as many hours as they thought.

"Shit, shit, shit, shit, shit," Gus paced back and forth.

"We can't send you to the ball looking like this." Jacquetta darted up from the bed and ran out of the room.

"That seems," I paused to yawn so large my jaw cracked, "ominous."

"Of course it's ominous. If we send you like this, no one will forgive us. We're supposed to help you. And instead, you're in here not sleeping and we didn't even know. Now you're going to go to the ball half dead." Gus threw her arms up and slumped down onto the bed.

I actually felt bad. As much as I needed the late-night training session, it put a huge wrench in our plans.

"You need to go back to sleep, get some more rest." Gus shoved herself up and pointed a finger at me, her mouth in a line.

"Easier said than done, I think." Although, it was hard to tell exactly what thoughts were running through my head. None of them were completely clear.

Jacquetta came back in with a mug of something pouring steam.

"No tea," Gus said, "That will only wake her up more."

"This kind will put her to sleep. Trust me. Mother gave it to me."

She motioned for me to sit up. I managed to do it, but I didn't want to.

Leaning back into the pillows, I took the mug from Jacquetta after she shoved it at me. I was more than willing to get a few more hours under the covers. Maybe I could avoid the getting ready process taking all damn day by sleeping through most of the daylight.

"Go on, drink it," Gus said, and Jacquetta pantomimed drinking like I forgot how.

But putting the mug up to my mouth let me whiff the concoction—which smelled as if someone had distilled dung and then added the sweet tang of hellfire water over top to mask it.

"This is disgusting." I turned my nose away and offered it back to Jacquetta. I would rather spend all day in a marathon of ball preparations than drink that.

"Next time you have trouble falling asleep, come and get me. The tea for that is better than this one. But now, you have no choice," Jacquetta said, staring down at me as she shoved the mug back toward my face.

I growled at her, but she just set her mouth to a firmer line.

"Fine." I closed my eyes and downed the entire noxious thing in two gulps, trying not to vomit or taste it.

Handing it back to her, the room spun.

"What in the hellfire was that shit?" I asked. Or at least I thought I asked.

Because my speech was slurred, and for a moment there were two of each of them standing there watching me struggle.

"No ball," I said, my eyes fluttering closed.

I forced them open again as they laughed.

"Already a terrible fucking day."

CHAPTER 27
REMADE

I was drugged. Not a little drought to help me sleep. That wasn't what I was given.

Not that I knew what Jacquetta gave me, but whatever it was, it was some kind of dark drug that stole control from me.

By the second time I awoke, Jacquetta and Gus were both dressed and darting around my room, yelling at each other.

Although, whatever they were saying, it didn't enter my brain properly.

My eyes slipped shut again.

The third time I woke, I sat up spluttering with cold water all over my face.

"What…shit…" I pawed at my face, trying to figure out what just happened and who I needed to slap.

"Get up," Madam Valentin said.

"Madam?" I blinked up at her where she stood over me with a large bowl in her hand and a scowl on her face. "But you're not allowed to be here."

It was a stupid comment, but it was true. I was only

supposed to have the help of my Ladies in Waiting and the palace staff.

"Stop acting stupid and get out of that bed. We barely have enough time." She turned and shoved the bowl into Jacquetta's hands.

Jacquetta looked like a kicked dog, her head hanging low.

Madam took a mug from Gus who wouldn't look up from the floor either.

"Here, drink this. It will help to wake you up. Then you are taking a bath," Madam said and twirled around to stomp out of the room.

"What happened?" I asked them, this time drinking a tea that tasted of sugar, chocolate, and berries. It was pretty good.

And it did send a zinging energy through my veins.

"I did the tea wrong, and you overslept," Jacquetta said, cringing and glancing up at me through her lashes for only a second before looking back at the ground.

"Did I miss the ball?" I asked, throwing the blankets off me.

"No," Gus said, shaking her head and looking over her shoulder at the parlor. "We just have less time than we wanted to get you ready. Madam Valentin is giving you about ten minutes to wake up, then she said we all need to run until you walk down the stairs."

"Run?" How was I supposed to run in a bath?

But I downed my tea and got out of bed.

"Even if you gave me the wrong amount, I needed to sleep. I feel much better now, so thank you," I said as I walked out to the parlor.

Jacquetta and Gus both finally looked up from the floor and took deep breaths.

"Oh," I said, spotting the spread of food waiting on the table, "Thank you, thank you, thank you."

I ran to the table, clutching my empty cup, sat down, and

shoveled food in my mouth, my stomach groaning in appreciation.

"Understand that only this one time am I going to let you eat like that," Madam said, standing by the settee with General Pace, staring daggers at me. "But, with the time constraints, hurry up."

Gus laughed and tried to turn it into a coughing fit.

Jacquetta looked like the sun had exploded.

And I choked on a bite, smiled, and did as I was told.

The second I finished, Jacquetta grabbed my hand and drug me after her to the fancy bathroom off my bedroom.

"Hurry up," she said, running around the room, gathering everything she thought we needed.

"What time is it?" I asked, slipping my nightgown off and climbing into the water.

"No," she yelled, stopping in the middle of the room with her arms full of things, staring down at my hands on the sides of the tub.

I turned my hands over and inspected them. Even though I wore gloves, there were scrapes and raw patches from climbing the night before. That alternative route to the training grounds couldn't get here fast enough.

"Mother," she yelled.

The bathroom filled with people, even General Pace came to see what her caterwauling was all about.

"How in world did you do that to yourself?" Madam asked, grabbing a valise from the corner and pouring things into my bath like she was concocting a spell and I was part of it.

"Accident," I mumbled, but the look on Pace's face made me think at least she knew better. Although I doubted she guessed at exactly what I did.

While they all ran around, getting things, washing my hair, scrubbing at my skin, rubbing things into my hands, I started to fume.

"None of you are going to answer my question? What time is it?" If we were that late, maybe we should alter our plans.

"It's two in the afternoon," Gus said, and Jacquetta blanched.

"That means we have six hours," I said.

"You are right. We need to move faster," Madam said, leaving the bathroom.

"Faster?" I asked, but no one was listening.

Six hours was more than enough time to get me ready for a ball, no matter how important it was. It wasn't like they had to remake me.

When they were done with my hair and doing what they could for my hands, Gus and Jacquetta got me out of the bath, wrapped each of my arms up to the elbow in pungent cloths, and marched me into the bedroom.

The dress was laid out across the bed, but I didn't have time to think about it before they sat me down on the stool in front of the vanity, and started in on my hair and makeup.

Not that I could do anything, but having my hands wrapped up made me feel even more helpless. It itched across my skin and made me long for a blade.

One at a time, Gus, and then Jacquetta disappeared into the rest of the apartment with Madam Valentin, and came back looking like queens themselves.

Gus wore a white gown that cinched her in at the waist and belled out at the skirt. It was a shiny satin with silver gems along the edge of the structured swoop of her neckline that made her breasts look like they could command their own orbit, and created a sort of off-the-shoulder sleeve.

It was breathtaking.

Jacquetta came back in an orangish red gown that no one but her could pull off. She made it look like a work of art. It was form-fitting until right above her knees where it swept out. The bodice had a low V and wrapped all the way around her neck with a collar that stuck up and out by a hand's width, framing her face in the brilliant fabric and setting off her dark skin.

She was a vision.

Both had hair piled on their heads with gems threaded through, and flawless makeup that set off all their best features.

Finally, they allowed me out of the bathing sheet and the hand bandages, wiping my arms down with a damp cloth, and got me into my dress.

Once I was done, I stood in front of the large mirror over the vanity and decided I was wrong.

They had remade me.

CHAPTER 28
OFFICIAL ANNOUNCEMENT

Standing between Jacquetta and Gus, we made perfect sense.

My dress was red and silver gray. It was a truer red than Jacquetta's, and my silver and gray were darker than Gus's. But we complimented each other. Even the shapes echoed each other.

There were two skirts on my dress—one was a close-fitting skirt with another slit in a red flame patterned lace so dark it was almost black covering gray satin. The other was a two-layered, gauzy, dark gray over red with the same dark lace encrusted with gems trailing down from my waist that started at my hips and swept around the back.

Something in the dress cinched me in, making my waist smaller, and me even happier I gorged myself earlier. But the bodice was covered in some kind of fabric that looked like all I wore on top was the same black-red lace with gems. It was cut so low it started at my waist and the lace trailed up my body, stopping just under my collar bone on one side while the other side swept all the up to my shoulder where it turned into a collar of lace standing up and out to look like knives. My mother's shoes were the perfect touch.

I loved it.

My hair was in long, loose curls, pinned over to one side so one of the tendrils fell down my bare shoulder.

"You are all magic," the vision of a girl more beautiful and more perfect than I would ever be said in the mirror.

"Not magic, just you," Gus said.

"Queen Cinder," Jacquetta said, and they all smiled while I tried to keep my face from falling.

Sometimes, it was easy to forget exactly why I was here. But I couldn't afford to get caught up in the fun of it, in the way it felt to have these friends who were so committed to doing what they thought would help me.

If I wanted to save them in the end, then I needed to keep my real goal in mind at all times.

"Do either of you have dresses in a different color palette, or are all yours coordinated with mine?" I asked, cocking my head to the side and running through the colors in my trunk.

"What do you mean color palette?" Gus asked.

"She is talking about the red, gray, and black we chose to represent Lehar," Madam said.

"You color coordinated to my lands?"

"Of course. It is a nice touch to be that thorough," Madam said with a decisive single nod of her head.

"But why red?" The black and gray I understood, but red didn't make any sense.

"To paint you in ashes and fire, black soot and flames."

"Hellfire water is bright green, like a chartreuse," I said, although her version sounded more poetic.

"It is?" Everyone except the general asked at once. Every set of eyes turned toward me.

"Yes, have you not seen it? You use it all the time." I saw their lights, even their heaters.

"Lady Cinder," Madam said, barely holding back her obvious irritation, "We have people who do that for us."

I nodded. Right. The only person who didn't look surprised was the General because they used hellfire water in warfare. Gus didn't have people to do that for her when she was growing up, but she probably didn't have the kind of house that used it either. Usually, the less well-to-do homes didn't have the luxury of hellfire fueled things.

"Now," Madam said, breaking into my thoughts, "I have helped Jacquetta and Augustina get ready, as I said I would. That is the only reason I was allowed to come, so I must go. I know you all will do me proud."

The General looked like she wanted to argue, but Madam was right. If someone found out she helped get me ready too, we would likely be disqualified.

Gus and Jacquetta said their goodbyes. So, too, did Pace, which left me standing in front of her, wondering what to say.

"Madam Valentin, thank you for…" I held a hand out to the room, because it was a lot more than a dress or even getting Jacquetta and Gus to focus. No one ever swooped in and saved me. Not anymore.

"You are welcome, and do not forget that if you can perform in my parlor, this ball is nothing." She gave me one of her rare smiles, and left.

She was more right than she knew. Barring some shocking development, I thought I had as good a chance as any of the better connected and more advantageous matches to make it through this first round.

"It's now eight. We should be going," General Pace said, gesturing to Gus and Jacquetta to stand on either side of me.

Jacquetta took the right side, Gus the left—which seemed correct somehow—and we set off.

Halfway down the hall, I realized I forgot my new spike.

I took a deep breath and reminded myself that I wasn't supposed to kill him tonight. Not when so many people were around, and the potential queens like me were going to be everyone's focus. It was fine. I wouldn't need a weapon.

But I felt naked without it as we descended the stairs, led by General Pace.

As we got to the end of the hall leading to the grand ball-room, the back of a black dress with feathers trailing the floor disappeared inside.

"Good." I spoke under my breath. The General nodded in front of me, and Jacquetta and Gus broke into smiles.

The Corvid Princess probably arrived a few minutes late intending to be last, to make her big splash of an entrance.

No matter how different my mission from hers, I took joy in thwarting the raven bitch's plan.

"When we walk inside, let me have a moment to introduce you properly," General Pace said.

Guards stood outside the two-story doors. At the general's nod, they swung them open enough for her to slip through.

Her voice reverberated off the surface of the obsidian walls and floated through the air as if she was announcing us to the palace itself, to the Dragon Kings who formed it, and to every citizen of Onyx.

"The Ladies in Waiting to my Candidate Potential for Queen of Onyx."

A deep breath, only that and the sound of her voice moved through the space.

"From Onyx, the maiden Augustina Rivers."

Gus left my side with her head held high and a smile on her face, although she had a tremor in her hand.

"From Onyx, the maiden Jacquetta Valentin."

Jacquetta turned into a younger version of her mother—just as perfect, just as intimidating—and walked in.

"And my Candidate Potential for future Queen of Onyx, the Lady Cinder Ahmya of Lehar."

Deep breath, I reminded myself, and tried to find the place in my mind where Madam's parlor existed.

The guards opened the doors wider, and I stepped forward.

By the time I walked through into the grand ballroom, a small smile was on my face and my heart was at a steady pace.

She was right.

Even as the entire ballroom looked my way, stopping their hushed conversations to take me in, nothing was as scary as facing Madam Valentin's judgement.

I waited, letting the people get their fill of me, until the General stepped to the side and gestured for us to follow her.

We passed the Corvid Princess, in her black dress with feathers along the bottom, thin straps at the top, and black metal wrapped around her upper arms with huge black feathers sticking up from them like my lace flame knives.

Her mouth was a sneer, her brow lowered, and she held her hands at her sides in fists and watched us.

First win of the day was already on the board, and it was points to me.

Pace led us to one side of a dais set up at the end of the room with a throne and an opulent chair on it.

"King Tristan is not here, yet?" Gus asked, slipping perfectly into the formal speech patterns.

"He is," the General said, shaking her head, "I already saw him in the crowd, but he is not dressed as the King yet. He does this. It is irritating."

"Wait..." Jacquetta stood on her toes and scanned the room, "Where is he?"

"Right there, heading into the antechamber."

Pace tilted her head to the doorway on our side of the dais, just at the back of the platform.

The back of what looked like a guard, with dark brown almost black hair disappeared through the door.

"But why does he do that?" I asked, my curiosity getting the better of me.

"The advisors are not supposed to treat him as a king when he does it, even though that makes it more dangerous from a security and protection standpoint. He does this at events especially because he wants to see the arrivals, but does not want to add to the stress with his presence."

She shook her head again, and I understood that it was far less safe for him if he was not afforded the same protection in order to blend in. But I found the rest of it relatable in a way that made my stomach hurt.

I didn't need to find King Tristan relatable. I didn't want to.

For the benefit of my own sanity and my mission, I shoved it all far away from me and accepted a glass from a passing server.

"Thank you," I said, and the server turned bright red.

"You are going to have to stop talking to people for the night," Gus said, smiling after the server walked away.

"Why would I do that?"

"Because, with the way you look, one of them might pass out," Jacquetta said and laughed.

My companions laughed together, but all I could do was shake my head and smile.

The beauty in the room was beyond measure, all around me, it was hard to take it all in. I wasn't special.

Chances were the server had a strong accent and hadn't mastered the formal speech accepted at the palace. Many struggled with it. Even I did sometimes at Madam Valentin's house, and I was taught while Mother and Father were alive.

We shouldn't tease someone for that.

Just beyond the door the King disappeared through, a herald climbed the steps of the dais with their traditional horn and came out to the center.

He blew the horn, the low haunting sound shaking through my entire body.

"Presenting, His Majesty, King Tristan Sweven, the Dragon King of Onyx."

Dragon King in name only, I thought while I clapped politely, trying not to roll my eyes, and watched the door he went into.

It opened and a young man, a little older than Ash, in high court finery, except for boots instead of heels, walked out upon the dais.

He...looked familiar.

My hands stilled as he smiled and looked directly at me.

King Tristan was the young man in the training yard with the Damascus blades.

CHAPTER 29
BEFORE IT BEGAN

I t was all over.

Before it even began, it was over.

I couldn't catch my breath.

While King Tristan spoke, while he welcomed everyone to the palace, to Onyx, and to the ball, the blood drained from my head.

My feet felt like they were weighed down by the rush of blood, like they were too heavy, and I was never going to be able to move again. I would never be able to run from that place, as if it held me hostage.

All our work, Ash's expectations, my mission…all of it was dead and worthless because I wanted to train and doing it in my room wasn't good enough. Because I had a moment where I let my feelings matter more than my assignment. More than my parents.

Of all the things I never wanted my brother to be right about —the times I questioned him and he called me a selfish, unserious girl who wouldn't do what needed done for our parents because I didn't love them as he did—was I everything he accused me of being?

King Tristan said something that caused everyone to cheer, and he scanned the room. I didn't know what it was. It remained noise just beyond the ability of my brain to comprehend while all I really heard was the thundering sound of my regret-filled heart.

He climbed down from the dais and made a straight line for me.

Jacquetta and Gus grinned widely and performed perfect curtsies when he reached me. I dropped into a curtsy a moment later than they did. Another mistake.

But he just smiled and laughed. It finally broke into my mind, although it sounded distorted. As if the enjoyment in it was shocking to my system and couldn't be properly processed.

"Please, stand," King Tristan said.

I swallowed and followed his direction.

He bowed in turn.

Was he toying with me? Or was the bow a formality he couldn't help but perform?

Bracing myself to be humiliated in front of everyone, for him to dismiss me right that second, I wasn't sure what to do when he held his out to me.

"May I have the first dance?" He asked.

Dance?

No one denied the King. Not even me.

So, with the rhythmic sound of my blood pumping loud in my ears, I placed my hand on his.

He led me out to the middle of the dance floor as the other guests parted in front of us and clustered into small groups along the edge of the room.

All of them watched us, their eyes focused and hard.

"Valz, please," King Tristan called to the musicians.

With my hand in his, he placed his other one on my waist and I put my other hand barely on his shoulder.

The music started up, beautiful and haunting. It was an old tune from before my parents were born.

It didn't matter how well I managed the dance—I didn't put a step out of place—but it all felt wrong. Like I was dancing toward the moment when Ash found out, when I should have been doing everything I could to change the ending.

My spike was in my room, tucked in my trunk because I was fool. Again.

"Forgive me for not telling you who I was," King Tristan said.

"No, I should apologize," I said, a tremor in my voice and no idea how to even do that, let alone how to get him not to punish me for it.

"I think we were both just nervous for today and looking for a way to work through it." He nodded and, like an idiot, I did too.

"So, what I really want to know is how often you train to get that good?" he asked, laughing when I snapped my eyes to his, even though it wasn't the right part of the song to do it.

Correcting my head placement, I started to think he was serious.

"You are not…mad?"

"Mad? Why would I be? If anything, you showed me that one guard up and down the floor was not enough."

His answer didn't dispel all my doubts, but it did help me take a breath, if only for a moment.

"If your majesty would like, I would be honored to show him some of the techniques my brother taught me," I said, trying for something that might make him keep me around. Ash didn't teach me, but I couldn't explain Jocelyn. My voice hitched on the word brother, making old scars and bruises ache.

"That would be lovely, and please call me Tristan. I feel as if I know you a little, and I know none of the women here." His voice sounded melancholy. As if we weren't all here for him.

Well, I was here for him, but not in the way the others were.

"I have no doubt that they would all love to know you better."

Stupid. It was stupid to say that, to talk about the other women in a positive light increased my risk of not getting my chance.

Maybe he would want to train with me. Maybe that was how I would get down to the grounds and back every night. With his blessing. And maybe, it would be how I would kill him.

A terrible training accident…the idea had merit.

"Possibly," he said and laughed, a sad sound for something that should have brought him joy.

"You do not think so?" It was a risk to ask such a bold question, but it was the only advantage I had, the crack in his happy-to-be-fawned-over-enough-to-have-this-strange-competition image.

"Unfortunately, not everyone is direct. Especially when they are dealing with a king. And sometimes people do things for terrible reasons." He shook his head and performed an advance turn not always included in the valz. It sent me spinning around him to end up bent backward over his arm.

But he righted me in a moment, and I chalked it up to getting too familiar too fast.

"Do you mind me asking who the craftsman was who made your throwing knives?" I asked, trying to get us back on a positive track. "They are beautiful."

Then he did laugh, a full, real laugh, rich and surprising.

"Of course you noticed them. They are a work of art. I am sorry to say that the craftsman was one of my father's dear friends and he was taken in the last war."

He was taken in the last war…I swallowed and took in a deep breath, forcing my heart to slow.

"I am sorry for your loss." It was an empty platitude, and I knew how very little it did to stem the tide of grief. But it was what people said in those moments when there was nothing else to say.

The song ended and applause erupted from the onlookers. But King Tristan didn't let me go.

"Lady Cinder, if I may, I would very much like to dance with you again."

He looked and sounded so earnest, so sure.

"Anything Your Majes—" the look on his face stopped me from using the honorific and I smiled, "anything you want, Tristan."

His eyes searched mine, a small grin formed on his face, and he ran his thumb over the back of my hand.

"Your Majesty," Chamberlain Rezan said, coming up to the side of us.

The King didn't look away from me, but he did release me and stepped back.

"Save me another dance soon, Lady Cinder," he said, and turned to walk away with the Chamberlain.

I was left in the middle of the dance floor with the fact that it seemed I was wrong, trying to breathe. He wasn't going to send me home. Yet.

And I just found a perfect avenue to go down that might give me a chance to kill the King.

CHAPTER 30
INTERNATIONAL INCIDENT

"Lady Cinder, may I have a word," General Pace asked, her eyes bright as she came to me with Jacquetta and Gus almost bouncing out of their shoes.

"Of course." I tipped my head to her, and on weak knees started to walk away.

"Maiden Jacquetta, Maiden Augustina, will you please go and see what the other Ladies in Waiting think about what just happened. And maybe put in a word…" She gave them a pointed look and lowered her voice on word.

"Yes, General." Jacquetta bit her smiling lip, one brow raised, and I realized they had formed some kind of plan I wasn't privy to.

"This is going to be fun," Gus said before she stood up so straight it looked like a salute, and walked away, she and Jacquetta heading in opposite directions.

Secrets upon secrets, and hidden agendas on top of hidden agendas. What kind of a sword arm was I that I didn't see any of it coming, and didn't know what their plans were?

While I followed Pace, I looked over my shoulder as my

friends disappeared into the people gathered around the dance floor as it filled with people taking positions for the next dance.

General Pace led me to the side of the room and a thin door almost hidden by two of the pillars that ran all the way to the ceiling lining the room.

It was a small room, but it was probably my favorite so far in the Obsidian Palace. While everything else about the place seemed too large and too opulent, this room was like a small parlor in a cozy home.

There were a couple plush chairs with foot stools, the walls were lined with books, and there was even a fireplace in one wall.

"If only the rest of the palace looked like this," I said, my voice reverent.

Pace smiled, but it was soft. She looked down at the floor as if remembering something she was fond of.

"Queen Tanith would have agreed with you," the General said, looking up from the floor to scan the walls.

"Why are we in here?" The place suddenly felt less welcoming once I knew it belonged to the mother of the man I was supposed to kill.

"I didn't think you ever came to court." It wasn't what I was expecting, nor was the way she said it like a question.

"That's because I haven't been to court." And I didn't understand what she was talking about.

"King Tristan never acts like that with strangers, though," she turned around and shook her head, staring as if the books would give her an answer that made sense.

Books weren't going to, but neither was I. Not entirely.

"We spoke of training. He heard I had some skill, and I suggested we train together sometime." That couldn't get me in too much trouble.

Her mouth dropped open.

"You spoke of training? You're supposed to be a Lady trying to become Queen."

"Queen to a country facing the possibility of war." That shut her up. Queen Tanith was a warrior herself. She and King Duman led the war efforts at the front of the line. It was why King Tristan was on the throne. It was a risk they paid for...just like my parents.

"Well, at least it seems as if we may be able to use this success. Whatever you're doing to make him smile that way, I guess you should just keep doing it. And I will play our hand." She quirked a brow, gave me a small smile, and opened the door, gesturing for me to go back to the ball.

I didn't know what to make of our very small time away from the ball, or the strange pronouncement of a hand to play. But I shook my head and followed her directions, too happy to not have to strangle the King in front of the entire party and put all my friends at risk to worry about her machinations.

Besides, maybe I could find a way to make the Corvid Princess even more angry. She must have been about to burst into flames after watching the King pick me to dance with first.

And I couldn't wait to see it.

Out in the ballroom, it was impossible for me to spot Jacquetta and Gus. Even with Gus's height and Jacquetta's bright dress.

People whirled and spun, pranced and meandered all through the room.

It was dazzling with the black walls reflecting the hellfire water lights and the colors of the clothes. But in a way that made me long for the ease of the tiny parlor.

I wandered over to the wall where towers of delicacies almost outdid the guests in their finery, and picked up a drink from a passing server.

Standing near the table with a drink in hand—whether or

not I dared to eat in my tight bodice—at least made me look less like the single stalk of wheat that had escaped the scythe.

"Lady Cinder," the Amethyst snake said, coming to my side with the Chamberlain nowhere near.

"I see, you managed to give your retinue the slip," I said. "How fitting."

Maybe I should have kept the last bit to myself because she wilted before me.

"Is this how this entire trip will go? All of us sniping at one another over a man?" she asked, curling her nose up at the word 'man.'

"Do…" I couldn't ask the question in my head, it wasn't wise, but…"Forgive me, Marquessa. I should not blame you entirely for the way your country conducts business."

There, that was fair. Although it made my stomach hurt just to say it, and I wasn't sure if I would ever mean it.

She smiled, bright and open, while she took a deep breath and reached for my hand.

I froze. If she grabbed my hand, I wasn't sure what my reaction would be or if I could suppress it. Her country was on the other side of the war that killed my parents, and they traded slaves. I didn't want her to touch me.

For weeks I prepared for the idea of King Tristan's hands on me. Now I had seconds.

But all she did was tap my hand and pull hers back to her side.

"You don't know how much I appreciate that. I have so few friends here."

She didn't gain another because I said something not awful to her. What was wrong with her? No one was that naive. Were they?

"Well done, Lady Cinder," the Corvid Princess's caustic voice broke into our conversation.

Marquessa Ziya's eyes went wide, and she cringed.

A terrible person from a terrible place made me question myself because she made a good point with her look. Everything about Corvid and the Princess was gross and definitely worthy of that look.

"You like my dancing that much? I am sure there is some slave you can buy that can teach you how to dance." Raven bitch.

Ziya's face pinched like she was holding in a laugh, although I didn't think it was funny.

The Princess cocked her head to the side with that fake smile.

"Why so stabby, Cindy?" she asked.

I stepped to within a finger width of her face, staring into her eyes as she tried, and failed, to not lean away from me.

"My name is not Cindy." I couldn't hold back my sneer, or the wicked grin that took over my face when she looked around for a way out only to realize she was backed up against the table. "But if you really want to see stabby, that I can do."

I turned and walked away, flexing my hands so I didn't ball them into fists and punch a random passerby.

King Tristan was somewhere in this mass of people, and I needed to find him.

For once I didn't want to get a hold of my target to kill them, but instead to set up training time for me so I wouldn't kill someone else.

Besides, I should probably ask him if it would be considered an international incident if one of the Potentials ended up dead. Just in case.

CHAPTER 31
FINE

"Oh, I'm so glad I found you," Jacquetta said, grabbing onto my arm.

It took a genuine effort as I stiffened under her hand, not to lash out automatically because of the mental space I was in.

"You've been looking for me?" My voice was still hard like I was talking to the Corvid Princess.

"Have you been with the General this whole time?" She turned like she was looking for someone, but at least it gave me a minute to try and focus on her instead of the run-in with the raven bitch.

"No. I went and got a drink." There was no reason to explain the entire conversation. Not yet anyway.

"There she is, Gu—" Jacquetta started to yell Gus, shook her head, and nabbed a server walking by. "Do you see that tall young woman in the gray and silver gown? Can you bring her to me, please?"

He ran off to do her bidding, and I tried not to laugh.

If this wasn't the palace, if so much didn't rely on what we did here, the idea of her screaming Gus across a room full of royals would have doubled me over with laughter.

Madam Valentin was going to call me a bad influence if Jacquetta kept on doing—or almost doing—things like that.

Finally, Gus joined us, biting her lip to hold back a smile and failing.

"Come on," Jacquetta said, pulling us around the back of the dais, next to a wall.

"Are you trying to get us privacy?" I asked, looking around at the servers and others who passed by our little corner.

"Yes, but…" a server walked by, and Jacquetta paused, eyes wide and staring at me as if his presence finished her sentence.

"Follow me." How I found myself leading my friends to the small secret room the General brought me to, as if I knew the palace well enough to know where all the best parts were, I didn't understand. This place was as foreign to me as it was to Marquessa Ziya, but I was sure she wouldn't know of the room.

I opened the little door and ushered them through, closing it behind us.

"How in the world?" Gus asked, turning in a circle, taking it all in.

"The General. Now tell me what's going on," I said, putting my hands on my hips and relaxing my back for the first time since I put on my dress.

"Well, first, the Ladies in Waiting from Corvid and Amethyst are a tough stone to polish. I don't know if we'll get any good information from them," Jacquetta said.

"Right, but," Gus said, making the word but last longer than was necessary as she looked at Jacquetta and bit her lip on her huge grin again.

"But we have a plan with the Ladies in Waiting from the other Potentials from Onyx." Jacquetta did a little dance, and

Gus joined her, like whatever those words meant was far more important than they sounded like.

"What kind of plan?" It would have been nice to know what they thought was dance worthy.

"So, the Ladies in Waiting from the other Onyx Potentials are going to help us, and we'll help them," Jacquetta said, still dancing.

"And, even better, we're all going to sabotage Corvid and Amethyst," Gus said with a twirl.

"That's a good idea. But…why are they doing this? And can we trust them?" I asked, still not feeling like dancing.

Gus and Jacquetta stopped at the same time, the smiles falling from their faces as they looked at each other. I ruined it for them.

"Well, all we can do is hope they'll stand by their word," Jacquetta said, and Gus nodded.

"So, how was dancing with the King?" Gus asked, putting her hands together like she was a little kid begging for a cookie.

"Um…" I didn't know how to answer that. And it went so fast from talking about strategy to focusing on the King and the fake reason I was here, that it made me want to run out the door.

"Cinder, come on. You can tell us. Was his hand sweaty? Was he beautiful up close?" Jacquetta asked, wiggling her eyebrows.

I rolled my eyes and laughed.

"He was fine. His hand wasn't sweaty, and he was fine looking," I said. There was no way I was going into detail about what I thought of his looks. It did me no good to admire him. I had a job to do. He was pretty, and he needed to die.

"Fine." Gus nodded with her lips pushed together. "I like that as a euphemism for pretty."

"Oh for…" I threw my hands in the air and they cracked up laughing which made me smile and shake my head.

"I'm kidding. Let's get back out there before the King tries to find you and you're missing," Gus said, slipping her elbow through mine.

We smiled at each other and looked back to Jacquetta whose eyes were wide and mouth hung open.

"Jacquetta, are you okay?" I asked, slipping my arm from Gus and stepping toward her.

"The King already found us," she said, pointing toward the door behind me.

"Very funny. Come on," I said, shaking my head and turning toward the door.

But she wasn't kidding. King Tristan stood in the doorway, leaning against the jamb, with his arms crossed and a grin on his face.

"It's amazing. You find your way around a strange place better than anyone I've ever met," he said, his overly formal speech pattern slipping, which sent my heart hammering in my chest as if I thought Madam would come around the corner and chastise us both.

"Your Majesty," I said, and curtsied.

"Cinder, please, we talked about this." He grinned and shook his head.

Gus and Jacquetta snapped their eyes toward me and then back to the King.

"If you're going to come into my hiding place," he said, "you should really call me by my name."

"Sorry, Tristan," I said, and Jacquetta made a little high-pitched squeak, probably thinking that Madam was going to show up and drag me away for my breaking decorum. "General Pace brought me in here for a minute when the ball got too much for me."

"That's the same reason I come in here sometimes." His smile was soft, and a tiny pang of guilt ran through me for lying and making him think we had that in common.

"Well, then we should leave you to have your moment away." I gestured to my friends as he straightened in the doorway.

"No, no. Stay. This is nice. I would like a chance to talk to you more." He looked from me to Gus and Jacquetta, blinking as if he just realized they were there. "Your Ladies in Waiting, too."

"Pardon us, Sire," Jacquetta said, "Lady Cinder can stay, but we have duties. Very kind of you to offer."

She grabbed Gus's elbow and steered her out of the room, shutting the door behind them.

"Your Ladies are subtle," Tristan said, and I couldn't help laughing.

"They really are wonderful, the best friend's I've ever had, but you're right. Subtle, they are not."

"Best friends…" He walked over to one of the chairs and sat down, gesturing to the other one with his eyebrows up, as if he thought I was going to say no to the King. I perched on the end of the chair. "It's nice you have them."

"It is." I smiled and looked over to the fireplace, wishing it was lit.

"How long have you known them? Are they from Lehar?"

Looking back at him, I found him staring at me, but in a way that seemed interested instead of calculating like Ash always was.

"No, they aren't from home. I've only known them a month."

His eyebrows shot up, but he didn't comment.

And I realized that my answers weren't careful enough. I should have friends. Ones I knew all my life.

"You don't have anyone you're close to at home?"

"My brother, Duke Ash, and I are close." I was his sword arm. That made us close.

"Duke Ash," he said, looking away from me and shaking his head before he looked back. "He's a shrewd negotiator."

I shrugged, not knowing what he meant by that.

"Siblings, yet so different," he mumbled, looking deep into my eyes.

Ash and I were different, but the King didn't know how much.

The door to the room opened, and a server came in with a mug and a plate on a tray.

I smiled and stood.

"Forgive me, but I must take my leave. And you should take the time to eat in peace." I turned and walked away, not waiting to be dismissed.

Being alone with the King without my weapon felt like a betrayal of my mission. Of my brother.

Talking about Ash with him was too much.

Maybe I could hide in the bathroom until the ball was over. Maybe.

CHAPTER 32
LAST DANCE

I spent most of the night after that standing near the food table, and pretending to be busy.

Gus and Jacquetta found more fun in dancing with the guards and trying to get more information from the other Ladies in Waiting.

But I was more than fine being on my own.

One of the other Potentials from Onyx and I exchanged pleasantries, but I couldn't remember her name or even which area she was from. My mind was back forth between thinking about home, about my parents and Ash's expectations, and the little anteroom.

Finally, I took the last sip of my glass and felt a tap on my elbow.

I turned around to find Tristan smiling at me.

"Now that I've done what I was supposed to, and danced with everyone, would you give me the honor of another dance?"

The way he said 'supposed to' made me think he wasn't completely happy about this situation.

"Of course," I said, and then whispered, "Tristan."

His smile was brilliant as he took my hand and led me to dance floor, the crowd parting for us. But unlike last time, when the valz started other couples stayed out on the floor and all the people in the ballroom kept talking loudly.

It was much better to dance when the people around had other things to focus on.

"You know," he said, his voice low, "I prefer it this way. It almost feels like we blend in."

There was no way at that second for me to see his face without breaking my movement, but it was probably better that I not see him. Not when I was thinking the same thing.

"Well, it certainly is less pressure when fewer people are staring."

He laughed again, loud and full.

General Pace may not have seen him laugh this way with people he didn't know well, but I couldn't imagine him laughing any other way.

"Cinder, you have no idea how many years Mother made me take dance lessons because I just couldn't get the steps, but you're so right."

It took me a second to say anything, my tongue tripping over the words.

"No one would ever know you struggled."

Was that why he always picked the valz when he had the chance?

Like I did when I was at Madam's.

The music changed and he stopped, still holding my hand.

"I'm not going to make an announcement tonight, but I want you to know I would like you to stay on. And I hope that tomorrow, when a knock comes on your door, you'll go with me to train again." He looked like a teenager asking someone if they liked them for the first time, even though he was closer to thirty than thirteen.

"You have no idea how happy I will be to train again."

He laughed, but this time it was small and intimate in a way that made me want to run away.

"For me," I went on, because that seemed a little too eager, "training is an outlet. One I have greatly missed recently."

"Perfect. Because I feel the same." He let go of my hand and bowed low to me, too low for a king to a duchess, let alone a Lady.

My answering curtsy was deep and low, with a bowed head.

When I stood up again, he smiled and disappeared behind the dais.

Did that mean I was his first *and* last dances of the night, or was he coming back?

A moment later, Gus, Jacquetta, and the General found me and peppered me with questions.

"I will spend all night telling you all about everything, but first I need to get back to the room, out of these clothes, and order some food."

They looked at me like I grew another head and told them I named it Raymond.

"You can stay longer. I did not say you needed to follow me right now. But I need to go." My stomach was going to start eating itself soon if I didn't give it room and get some food.

"Lady Cinder, what about the King?" Jacquetta asked.

"Oh, he left." I turned and headed back to my rooms. The weight of standing up straight and being perfectly proper all night was heavier than it had been before I knew the end of my duty was coming.

I didn't check that they were behind me, but I heard their footsteps hustling across the hall after we left the general hum of the ballroom.

"General Pace is talking to a server, having food sent up to the room," Gus said as she got to my shoulder.

"She'll catch up to us in the room," Jacquetta said once she was with me, too.

"Really, if you two want to go back and dance some more, do it." The last thing I wanted was for them to feel cheated of any part of the night because I was a killjoy.

"Cinder, I am more than ready to take off these shoes and put my feet up," Gus said.

Her shoes weren't like mine, well-worn and aged to be soft as air. Hers were a gift from Madam for the ball alone, and probably tight and stiff.

"And I am more than done pretending some of those people have interesting things to say," Jacquetta said with a laugh.

There was a story in that laugh, and I got the impression that someone in particular was a great disappointment to her.

Jacquetta and Gus would have plenty of stories of their own to catch me up on, and I was shocked to find I looked forward to it.

When did I became a person who wanted to just sit and chat?

But if it was spending time with them, it was fun. It wasn't just because they were the only real friends I had known since the war. It was because I would have chosen them as friends even before that.

Somehow, against the odds and my own history, I had two very good people on my side.

The fact that I was likely to let them down made me slump the minute we got inside the apartment, my shoulders heavy.

We helped each other out of our dresses and complicated hairdos and sat in the parlor in our nightgowns.

Gus even dragged a blanket out of her room.

"You know, we can turn up the heat," I said, laughing and pointing to the hellfire fireplace, one of the automatic fancy ones that turned on with a button.

"I know, but this is cozier."

The door opened and the General entered with a servant pushing a cart piled high with food.

"Oh, thank you," Jacquetta said.

After the servant left and I had a large, full plate in front of me, they started in on the questions.

"So, tell us everything," General Pace summed it up after the volley of questions from my friends finally slowed.

I laughed, and told them almost everything. Only holding back the fact that I thought the training session would be a good opportunity to kill him and we might have to run from the palace afterward.

Not that I knew how, but I wanted to stop it from coming down on them.

To do that, it was possible my mission was about to get a lot more dangerous for me.

CHAPTER 33

OBSESSION

"**A**re you sure we shouldn't go with you?" Gus asked as I threw on my cloak.

"Do you want to train in throwing knives?" I asked.

Gus's face lit up, but before she could say anything Jacquetta interrupted and said, "Ew. No."

I thought back to the Gus I first met, and decided that I was going to have to manufacture a way to get her down there to train with us. A way that wouldn't scandalize Jacquetta.

"Well then. I better get down there. Don't want to keep the King waiting." I grinned and walked out of my room, but they followed me.

"You mean Tristan, right?" Jacquetta asked, her voice heavy with a taunting tone.

"Very funny." I shook my head and they laughed as I walked out the door of the apartment.

General Pace was walking toward me in the hall.

"Hello, General. I didn't expect to see you tonight," I said as she fell into step beside me.

"I am supposed to be your escort, and that includes not-well-thought-out trips to the training grounds." Her face was rigid and still.

"Am I in trouble? Because I thought you approved of me training with him."

"You should train with him, but you're going to be training with him on a discipline he is not yet very good at."

"General, you're underestimating him. He is actually very good. But if you're talking about me being better, then, yes, I am. I also probably practice more often than he does in knives."

Understatement, but I couldn't exactly tell her why I practiced knives so much or that they weren't the only thing I was good at.

"Are you sure you want to show him how good you are?"

I stopped in my tracks and stared at her, sure I didn't hear what I thought I did.

"You…you think I should downplay my own ability with someone to…what? Make him feel better?"

"No." She looked me in the eye, and even though I couldn't make any kind of sense out of her words besides what I guessed, she looked sincere.

"What I mean is," she said, "you should also work on something he can teach you. If you are equals, it's better for you." She tipped her head, and I tried to think of a world in which a king and someone trying to 'win' his hand, up against others doing the same, was in any stretch equal.

Instead of saying anything, I nodded and kept walking. It still sounded suspicious to me, but the general did know more people than I did. Maybe it would be wise to listen to her. Although anyone being so fragile about learning from someone didn't make sense to me.

Not that I was going to hold back in the things I was good at. I wasn't sure I knew how to pretend not to know the proper way to throw a knife. But it was possible he would want to try something I didn't know or wasn't as practiced at.

"How did you, a lady, get so accomplished in the war arts?" she asked as we walked down the stairs.

"My parents taught me some, and after," I chose not to say their deaths, she understood, "I kept up with the practice, using it as an escape."

She turned to look at me as we walked through the front doors into the courtyard.

But I didn't have time to try and decipher the look on her face. King Tristan waited at the bottom of the stairs, his face turned up and smiling at me standing high above him.

"Hello," he said. I walked down to join him, until our height difference forced me to look up at him slightly.

"Good evening, training partner," I said.

"Oh, I like that." He grinned and squinted his eyes, looking into the sky. "To just be someone's training partner…"

"Do you struggle to find time to train?" I asked, not wanting the conversation to be centered around him being someone's partner.

"Let me put it this way," he said, tipping his head toward mine as we walked, "we'll probably be interrupted today while we train by one of my secretaries for me to sign a paper that I'm expecting them to finish."

So, no assassination today.

I smiled at him, hoping none of the disappointment I felt showed on my face and knowing some of it got through.

But his smile grew soft as he looked at me.

Why me being disappointed caused him to look that way I didn't…I did know.

He thought I was sad we might be interrupted at any moment.

King Tristan surprised me. Again and again, he turned out not to be what I expected him to be.

Still, the faster I killed him and forgot about him, the better. Not just for Ash and the mission he charged me with. Not even just for Mother and Father and the revenge their deaths deserved and called for.

In a perfect world, I would have been able to kill the King right away, before even leaving the training grounds.

But I was in Onyx, and it wasn't perfect.

I wanted King Tristan dead right away because he made me uncomfortable.

"What's your usual training schedule?" he asked as we came to the edge of the grounds. He scanned the area.

Unlike last time, lights were on in every arena, every discipline was available to us, and guards wandered everywhere.

Even if I didn't know someone was going to interrupt us, now was not the time to kill him if I had any hope of getting away. And I had to get away. Jacquetta and Gus made that true.

"I don't usually have a schedule so much as a current obsession that I work on until I improve enough to be satisfied."

"You…" He furrowed his brow as he studied me, as if he could make more sense out of my words if he looked hard enough. "You just work on one thing at a time?"

"For me it works best. Besides running through some of the forms I know as a warmup and to stay limber, that's what I do."

Well, that and use my skills in real world scenarios that forced me to be better than I might have been otherwise just so I could do my assignment and get home again.

"So that's how you're so good at throwing knives."

"Must be," I said with a shrug, growing uncomfortable with the fact that he now knew my level of proficiency in one discipline. Maybe General Pace had a point. But how was I going to be able to keep a wrap on some of my skills? The idea of deliberately being bad at things I was actually good at made me want to puke.

"Have you done much archery?" he asked.

The archery grounds were next to the knife throwing, and I breathed a little easier looking at them.

"I've been wanting to improve on my archery skills." My smile covered my lie. I never bothered to work on archery beyond the basics. My assignments required me to get up close. Archery wasn't the tool of an assassin who wanted to cover their tracks.

"Perfect, because it was the first thing I learned. So how about we start with archery, and then move to throwing where you can show me how it's done. Do you want to keep this routine until we both become proficient?"

He was so excited that his words came too fast, like this was the best plan he had thought of in a long time.

I didn't miss that the way he said it made me think he wanted me to stick around through more than this next round for the potentials.

"Sounds like a great plan."

We moved to the bows hung on the wall next to the archery range. I realized I already passed through most of the trials set out for the women at the palace, and I didn't do it with the rules Madam grilled into me. I did it in the years of single-minded work I put into my own training before King Tristan ever thought about taking a bride.

CHAPTER 34
SHARP LESSONS

"Here, try this bow. I think it will fit you well," Tristan said, handing me one while he slung the one that he wanted to use over his shoulder.

Tristan knew his way around the archery course. He even moved with more ease, as if he were more comfortable in that space than he was when we threw knives.

Our range at home was one lane with targets placed at different distances, but this one was multiple lanes like the knife range and every other one had two targets, one halfway down and the other at the far end.

He stationed us next to each other, with my lane being one of the double targets. Which was probably good since I wasn't positive that I would even be able to hit the closer of the two.

"You know the basics?" he asked, standing next to me at the end of the range as if he was going to notch the arrow for me.

"I think I have the basics," I said, trying not to laugh.

He stepped back with a self-deprecating grin on his face and tipped his head.

My turn to not be good at something.

Nocking the arrow was fine, pulling it back was fine, even anchoring it and setting myself to release it was all fine. But somehow, the chances of me hitting the target or the arrow going so far afield as to be embarrassing was still half and half.

I took a deep breath and let go.

The arrow hooked so far it slammed sideways into a target on a different course.

"Damn it," I said, and looked wide-eyed at Tristan who just raised his brows at me before he stepped closer.

"You're not giving the arrow time," he said, nocking his own and leaning close so I could watch as he faked a shot.

"When you release, you're moving a split second later to look and see where it lands. But the arrow hasn't cleared your bow yet, so you're turning it in the process."

He went through the motions of releasing an arrow without actually letting go of the one in his hand.

But the second time he did it, in slow motion, he moved a fraction as if he was getting a better look down range.

"I do that?" I asked, trying to run through my movements, even the micro adjustments I made while shooting.

"You do, but it's an easy thing to fix. Just wait a beat. Count it out even." He smiled and stepped back into his own lane.

An easy fix. The concept of having anything to do with a training of any discipline be easy was so odd to me I stood dumbfounded as he prepared to shoot.

He had impeccable form, like my mother had when she was working with her own bow and arrows before they were lost with her. There was a relaxed air to the way he held himself when he was shooting, even though it was strong and steady, as if his body mimicked the qualities of the bow and arrow.

Tristan made eye contact with me just before he loosed his arrow. I got the impression he was checking that I was watching.

I was. And I watched as he made a perfect shot that hit the target right in the center.

"Wow," I said, honest in my surprise and appreciation for his ability.

His smile was brilliant. And then he showed off a little, taking shots with three arrows nocked at a time, trick shots, the whole while grinning like he was having the time of his life. When he aimed deliberately at my target, and made a perfect shot from an angle, I laughed outright.

"After last time we were down here, I deserve that display," I said.

It was his turn to laugh, and with one more shot he had emptied three quivers. Arrows stuck up all over the targets in most of the lanes, turning them into porcupines.

"Okay, let's collect your arrows, and then it's my turn to not be as good," I said, shaking my head.

"Cinder, I have a feeling that if you knew archery was my favorite discipline you would have spent six months working nonstop to be able to outshoot me," he said.

There was a smile on his face and joy in the sound of his voice, but mine was fake as we pulled the arrows from the targets.

Maybe General Pace was right. I wondered if Tristan would send me home if he thought I was too good. Attempting to be lousy at things I was good at nauseated me.

In all my years of training in all manner of weapons, Ash never suggested I should be worried about the fact that I got very good at it. He wanted me to excel at being a killer while he spent his time in his office or running his errands. I was his sword arm, so he didn't have to be.

Now, I was faced with the reality that being someone's sword arm in our world might have come with more costs than just the way Ash treated me or the risks.

Sure, I wanted to be deadly and enjoyed training, but someday I hoped to get my revenge and have some life not dipped in blood. One where I trained just for fun.

But would anyone ever accept me in that someday?

General Pace was alone, and she was much older than me. Her entire life still amounted to her duty. Would I also always be only that?

"Cinder," Tristan said, his voice low and soft.

"I'm sorry, what?" I blinked, trying to remember if he was speaking to me a moment ago or not, and failing to picture anything but my own worries.

"Are you okay?"

"Yes, I'm fine. I was just thinking..." I couldn't tell him exactly what I was thinking, and the tremulous smile on my face fell as I tried to find something else to say.

"Thinking..."

He looked worried, and that wasn't what I wanted to happen today.

"My mom used to have a beautiful bow. But, come on, I want to see if your suggestions helped." There, that was true, even if it was only a tiny part of what was running through my head.

A small smile and a twitch of his brow were my only clues as to whether he believed me, but I gathered the rest of the arrows on my side of the range and tried to be the woman Madam wanted me to be, to put her on like a cloak. At least for the moment.

While I collected the arrows, I glanced up regularly at Tristan. And every time, he was already looking at me.

I flashed him a shaky smile and went back to what I was doing. Over and over again.

Finally, we finished and placed the arrows in the collection of quivers.

"Okay, so I just try not to move at all?" I nocked the first arrow and looked over at Tristan who just nodded in response.

There was no more stalling. I was out of time to avoid embarrassing myself.

Nocking the arrow and pulling it into position, anchoring my hand on my chin, I stared down the line to the target.

Deep breath.

Release.

It hit the upper edge of the target. But it hit.

I whooped and jumped in the air.

"Well done," Tristan yelled. "You barely even twitched. You keep practicing and you'll be better than I am in no time."

"Thank you," I said, grinning and enjoying the way he seemed proud of me because I was proud of me too.

"Keep going. Start your practice by going through all of these," he said, gesturing to the quivers at our feet.

He didn't have to ask me twice.

Only two shots went as wild as before, which meant my percentage was so much better it was amazing. But I had a long way to go still to be anywhere near as good as him.

After the last arrow flew through the air, hitting just inside the first one I shot, I picked up his bow and mine and carried them to the wall.

"Now we work on your knife throwing form," I said over my shoulder.

When I turned around, he was collecting the arrows and whistling.

The tune was the same as the valz we danced to right before he left the ball.

Collecting the arrows with him while being serenaded by a whistled version of a valz was not at all on the list of things I thought would happen when I came to the palace. But…it was nice. Being able to train was nice, and the tune was pretty—even if it was out of place. Then again, I was out of place, too.

"Are you ready to be lethal?" Tristan asked when we put the full quivers away. I choked on air.

"Excuse me?" I asked, my voice like a strangled croak.

"You ready to show me how to get as good as you are with those knives?" he asked again, raising his brows at me like he was trying not to laugh.

"Of course, come on," I said, my smile tight as I turned and almost fled to the knife range.

I collected a set of knives from the wall, and Tristan opened his cloak to expose his own set, pulling one of them out.

"First," I said, balancing the blade I had to use on my finger, "find the balance of your blade."

He followed my lead, doing the same with one of his.

Of course, mine was just a tad blade-heavy because it was likely a set for beginner guards to practice with, but his were perfectly balanced. He tried at first to put his finger in the same spot on his blade as I had on mine, but adjusted when he realized what was happening, that it was tipping and would fall off his hand.

"Good, see your set is perfect. The balance is exquisite." I allowed myself another moment to look at the Damascus, its shine mesmerizing.

"Now, you need to find which grip is most comfortable for you. Do you want to hold it in the middle?" I asked, demonstrating the standard grip, holding it in at the balance point.

He tried it, but by his stiff back and furrowed brow, I guessed this was the problem.

"You're not comfortable holding the knife like that. Which is fine, but you shouldn't try and force your hand to do it that way if something else would work better for you."

I stepped over to him, wrapped his hand into a fist, and slipped the knife into the space between the knuckle of his pointer finger and his thumb.

"This is a pinch grip. How does it feel?" I didn't really need to ask because the surprise and ease throughout his entire body was so obvious.

"Most people can't throw like this and never bother to even try it, but I want you to throw a few like this and see if it isn't better," I said, stepping back and crossing my arms in front of me.

He smiled and stepped into the loose and relaxed throwing stance he wasn't as comfortable in the last time.

While before he was far too stiff, now he was fluid and looked like he was about to dance.

The first throw was near perfect, and the knife hit just the right spot on the edge of the inner most ring.

"Now *that* was a throw," I yelled.

Tristan smiled at me, threw his arms around me and lifted me into the air, my body going rigid.

I yelped and he put me down, laughing and so happy he looked like he was going to run around hugging everyone.

"Do you know how long I've been trying to make that other grip work right for me?" he asked, shaking his head and getting back into position.

"You going to throw them all?" I asked, standing back and grinning.

He did throw them all, making a decent, if slightly messy, grouping.

"Okay, now you show me how it's done," Tristan said, his grin still massive as he stepped back.

It was probably wise to let it go and pretend I wasn't interested in doing it so I could keep this session on a high note.

But even if it was wise, it wasn't possible for me.

So I threw my knives, and celebrated with the person I was supposed to stab after every one of the blades struck home.

CHAPTER 35
FLIRTING WITH EDGES

"How did he say goodbye?" Jacquetta asked, placing the last pin in my hair the next day before brunch with all the Potentials.

"Just goodbye. General Pace was standing right there to walk me back to the room, and we haven't known each other very long." Did they really expect great declarations of love in front of the General after training?

"You need to find a way to know him pretty fast because you can bet some of the others are trying to get to know other things about him," Gus said with a wicked grin and a wink.

"Do you really think someone is going to hunt down where his room is and pop up in his bed naked?" I asked, trying not to blush at the idea of a bunch of naked people just roaming the halls trying to find Tristan.

"Very funny. I'm just saying, some of the Ladies in Waiting were talking about how 'alluring' their potentials were." Gus rolled her eyes at me, but I was still stuck on the idea of how someone would find their way to Tristan's chambers without risking being labeled a spy.

"So…what exactly am I supposed to do with this knowledge?" I asked, shaking my head which made Gus point at me with her lips in a thin line before she got back to work on my makeup.

"Act like you want to be the one in his bed," Jacquetta yelled.

I opened my eyes wide, looking at Gus who couldn't keep the stern look on her face, and we both broke down into laughter.

"Fine, laugh," she said, planting her hands on her hips, "But you could afford to turn up the flirt."

"Maybe the next time we train, I should just rip his clothes off, throw him up against a target, and have my way with him," I said which sent Gus toppling over to lay flat on the bed.

"Oh, what? Stop." Jacquetta was laughing too, but also looked like she thought I was a lost soul, "You spend entirely too much time around guards."

But I didn't. I spent entirely too much time around no one.

"Jacquetta," I said, my voice low and my eyes on the floor. "I don't know how to flirt. I know bawdy jokes and how it all works, but I've never tried to flirt with anyone."

"What are you talking about?" Gus asked, sitting up, all the laughter gone from her face.

"All I've done since my parents died is train and spend time with my brother," and be his sword arm. "The last time I flirted, even unintentionally, was when I was fifteen. And I don't actually remember what it felt like."

I also didn't remember what it felt like to want to.

My brother was my brother. The other people around were his gross friends. And the only other people I got close to were the ones I killed. Not a lot of people to even remotely consider romantically.

"Cinder," Jacquetta said, her voice soft as she sat on the bed next to Gus, facing where I was parked on the vanity stool.

"When you were training with the King, did he touch you for no reason?"

"No…" I didn't think he had, but there were so many times he looked at me in a way that felt like a touch.

"But he did something that seemed close, intimate in some way that was more than just training, right?" she asked, Gus nodding along with her.

"Yes, but that's just him I think." Why did I feel like I knew him well enough to say that, to weigh in at all on what he was or wasn't?

"That's not just him. That's him around you," Gus said, and this time it was Jacquetta's turn to nod along.

"We just met. There's no way he could like me enough already to flirt." No way. He couldn't. Could he?

"Oh, Cinder," Jacquetta said, looking at me like I was a child who just asked if the Dragon King would burn me if I got too close.

"Neither of you know him any more than I do. It's just as likely that he's acting the same with all the potentials. I'm not special."

"All of the Ladies in Waiting keep trying to make a big deal of the way he writes an invitation to their potentials." Gus's voice was flat, like I was supposed to take something obvious from that.

But the only thing I got from that was that he wasn't spending much time with the other…

"Shit," I said, the blood draining from my head.

"Exactly. It's a big deal," Jacquetta said, smiling. "So now you need to capitalize on it by flirting back."

"What does that mean?" My voice was edged with hysteria, because even if I knew, even if it made sense to press my advantage to get closer to him and make an opportunity for his assassination, the idea of doing it made me lightheaded.

"Next time you're together, touch him when it isn't strictly warranted. Just on the hand, no big thing."

"And look at him a lot when you probably should be looking at other things."

"If he touches you, or is close to you, hold your position a second too long."

"Those are just the first little things, but they'll help."

Just the first little things sounded like a lot, and they sounded terrible. Did everyone calculate the way they interacted with someone on purpose down to how long they touched their hand?

"How does anyone get to the point of loving someone? How do they ever trust it isn't all just a game of things designed to trick them?" My question was a whisper, one that Jacquetta and Gus didn't answer. They just shook their heads and finished my make up.

"When you find yourself at the next step, we'll plan it out. But for now, you don't want to be too late to brunch," Jacquetta said, and Gus smiled.

"Go let them all know why the King chose you," Gus said.

I shook my head and wandered out of my bedroom. Tristan had not chosen me. He had lots of time to choose whomever his advisors wanted him to, and I still didn't think that would end up being me.

Besides, he was going to be dead long before he could decide anyway.

The general waited on the other side of my door to walk me to the formal brunch with all the others.

"You did well with King Tristan last night," she said by way of hello.

I tipped my head to her because I wasn't sure if I was supposed to thank her or not.

"He asked me to tell you that he won't be able to train tonight, but he would like to train tomorrow."

For the first time since the flirting conversation started with Jacquetta and Gus, I felt like I was finally on more solid footing. And my answering smile was real.

"Eventually he's going to get better at knife throwing than I expect to be at archery, and then he might not want to train with me," I said, proud that he improved so much with my suggested grip change.

"You and I both know he will just find a different discipline to work on with you. It was never about the skill improvement," she said.

It was...my feet stuttered on the floor, and I took a breath to get back on track.

"General, why does everyone seem to think that except me?"

"Because the people inside of what's happening are always the last to know."

CHAPTER 36
ALLIES AND LIES

I t was a unique feeling to walk into a brunch full of people I knew without them saying a word, didn't want what was best for me, and would gladly stab me if they knew how and could get away with it.

And I kept having to do it.

"Lady Cinder," sneered the raven bitch in another black-feathered disaster of a dress. "How nice of you to join us. Did you sleep in after entertaining the King all night long?"

Every set of eyes in the room focused on me, some with obvious hate raging in them.

"Well, if you knew your way around a bow and arrow or how to throw a knife, you could have trained with us," I said, pretending the looks on all their faces didn't bother me.

"Please," she muttered as I made my way to my seat. A servant placed a plate and drink in front of me in seconds.

The General sat to my right, the same thing repeating for her.

Marquessa Ziya was missing for this meal, but I assumed she

was tired of constantly being forced to talk to the raven bitch while every Onyxian avoided them both.

Sitting next to me on the left side was a young woman, younger than my twenty-two years, in a beautiful blue dress. She had pale blonde hair in long ringlets down her golden brown back and eyes the exact same shade of turquoise as the lace collar on her dress.

"I have always wanted to visit Lehar. Is it as interesting as I am told?" the girl said, and I was sure she was a girl.

This wasn't just a very young-looking woman. This was a teenager. A child, sent to be part of a very adult affair.

Leaning to see past her to the official acting as her escort, I realized that the escort was so old we probably all looked like babies to them. And I had no idea who the escort was or what their official role was. But it didn't matter, someone in this girl's life should have cared more about her being a child than their possible connection to power through her.

"It is interesting," I said, choosing not to elaborate on the reasons I thought she shouldn't come to my home. "Where are you from? I am sorry I do not remember meeting you at the last get together."

"No, we did not meet then. I do not tend to talk to many people until I know my way around a little more." She opened her eyes wide and shook her head, staring up at the sweeping ceilings.

"Makes sense. This is a lot." I couldn't help smiling at her. I liked her. Thrown into a shit situation way too young and still managing to be smart about it. Good for her.

"I'm from Breakwater," she said, dropping the formal language and blinking those eyes that looked so much like the sea she lived next to. "My name is Duchess Inara."

"Duchess? You're so young. I apologize for asking that. You probably get it all the time, and it's irritating."

She smiled at me and nodded.

"Normally, it is irritating, but you recognized it so fast. I appreciate it. Being made Duchess two years ago was not what I was expecting for sure."

Two years? She had to have been under fifteen when she was made Duchess. And I thought I had a difficult time after my parents were killed.

Part of me wanted to know how her parents passed, as if morbid curiosity was a good enough reason to ask such a thing. But the rest of me more than understood what it did to have to explain over and over.

"And now you're here."

She must have heard a question in my tone because she leaned closer to me and in a whisper said, "With no intention of marrying. But Breakwater needs the King to station some navy ships on our coast."

Her eyes cut to the raven bitch, and I understood.

Duchess Inara came to the Obsidian Palace for her people, to protect them from Corvids along the coast who she either had trouble with already, or thought she was going to have trouble with.

"You know, the raven bitch and I should have a chat," I said.

Inara laughed but shook her head.

"Something funny little girl?" the raven bitch asked.

"Oh, leave her alone," I said, narrowly avoiding calling her a raven bitch to her face. What was her name? Something that sounded like the noise a cat made when it barfed. Princess Fiachra. That was it.

"You probably can't even throw a knife," she said, her nasal voice grating on my last nerve.

I snatched a knife off the table and threw it over her shoulder to bury itself in the chair right next to her head.

"What the fuck?" she screeched. I smiled.

"That is what it looks like when you know exactly how to throw a knife, Princess Fiachra. If I was a bad shot, you would be dead right now. Maybe you would not be shocked enough by it to swear in front of all these people if you ever bothered to learn about anything that was not you."

I turned back to Inara.

Princess Raven Bitch slammed her chair back and stomped out of the room, which earned me more than one smile from the other potentials, and a sigh from her escort who followed in her wake.

Duchess Inara bit her lip to keep from laughing and I just waved a hand as if we should get back to our conversation.

She let herself smile, but shook her head.

"My Ladies in Waiting told me about your training with King Tristan, but don't ruin your chances over her. One accident with a knife slipping is one thing, but maybe just ignore her now." Inara grinned.

"I hope my Ladies were good to yours," I said, picturing Jacquetta and Gus haranguing them to drop out at the right time to give me more of a chance.

"They're wonderful. And I want you to know that as soon as my business is finished, I intend to see the sea again." She winked at me, and I squeezed my eyes shut.

"So they did strong arm your Ladies."

"No, no. It was always my intention. I'm on a mission," she leaned close again, with her tiny whisper, "And I am in full support of an Onyx throne."

Scanning the other Onyx potentials around the table, it was easy to see which ones were part of Gus and Jacquetta's plan, and which ones still wanted the crown for themselves.

But sitting next to me, the Duchess was no small ally.

Her Breakwater duchy ran the entire coastline and made up for most of the international trade of our kingdom. It was smaller in size than the Thirteen Rivers Valley and the duchy of Astrea it belonged to, but it was strategically important.

"Maybe I can talk to Tri— the King on your behalf when we train together again," I said, my voice low and stumbling over his title.

"That would be amazing," she said, her eyes shining and then a sweet smile formed on her face. "Did you just almost call him by his name?"

It didn't matter that it didn't mean anything. Everyone thought it did and I couldn't correct them.

"Yes." There was no point in lying about it.

She nodded and sat up straighter, pride beaming from her.

"Good." She took a bite of her food and I laughed.

We passed the meal in companionable chat while eating the rich foods.

The whole time I grew to like her more and wish we could be real friends, but I couldn't shake the fact that I was lying to her.

Or that all her faith in me was misplaced.

Did it matter if I talked to Tristan about sending naval support to protect Breakwater if I just killed him right after? And after he was gone, who exactly was set to take over the throne? And what were they likely to do for her people? Or mine?

Maybe it was time I found out.

CHAPTER 37
LEGEND

"Can someone please pass me a tart?" I asked, snuggling further into the blanket wrapped around me where I sat on my bed, facing the window in the dark.

"Do you mean *another* tart?" Jacquetta asked, giggling while Gus handed me one.

Our backs were all propped up by every pillow we could drag from the other rooms. We ate deserts while we looked at the stars peeking over the towers on the other side of the palace.

I nibbled off a bit of the sweet treat and closed my eyes, relishing in the tastes of the berries mixing with the flaky soft crust.

"This is the best part so far," I said, and Gus sighed like she agreed with me.

"You only say that now because you and King Tristan haven't kissed yet," Jacquetta said, and I threw my napkin at her. "Hey."

I laughed, and Gus choked on her own giggles.

"Come on, Jacquetta, none of that tonight," I said, just wanting to spend some time with my friends without the pressure of the bizarre place I found myself in.

"No, Cinder. I know you want to ignore it and pretend we're all back at Mom's just having fun together. But we really do need to try and make this work." Jacquetta was so sincere, so urgent sounding, it made me feel the weight of her plans for me all over again.

"Why? Why does it have to work?" I asked, aware that I sounded whiny, but unable to stop that tone from leeching into my voice like a poison.

Every muscle in my body went from relaxed and comfortable to tight and braced as if expecting an impact.

"Because we need an Onyx throne and King Tristan needs a queen, someone he can rely on and form a family with," Gus said, her voice patient in the dark, floating to me on sounds like the ones my father had used when he was trying to help me understand an important point.

"What's the worst that could happen? Someone else in Tristan's family takes over the throne?" I asked, swallowing because I was close to treason out loud, in front of them, by just suggesting the possibility. And I waited for Jacquetta and Gus to scream at me in response.

"There is no one else in his family, Cinder. If King Tristan's line fails, then the line of succession is broken, and the rule of the Dragon Kings is ended. Other royals would fight to take the throne for themselves, plunging us into civil war. And none of them have the magic—even the lore of it—like the Dragon Kings." Jacquetta's voice had all the horror it deserved floating through the darkness, making it take on an edge of pain and fear it didn't have before.

"And if the Dragon Kings are no more, Onyx is just waiting for other kingdoms to come and tear us apart, claiming each shattered part they can rip from the whole for themselves." Gus's voice was like a eulogy at a funeral, dimming even the shine of the stars, making the black of the palace walls across from us a deeper shade of sorrow.

Gus fell silent and Jacquetta didn't add anything else, leaving me to fight the ghosts of my parents and the voice of my brother.

Shades of my parent's deaths, using Ash's words, spoke in my mind as loud as if they were in the room. But more than that. As if they were the room itself and seared into the walls of the palace by the same heat and magic that created them in the first place.

In the patch of sky visible out the window, the flames of the volcano constellation were the only part of one complete enough to identify, the rest hidden by the palace around me.

Flames and ghosts. Around me, in my mind, in my heart, and burning like a river of hellfire water through my memories.

How was it possible to be all the things to all the people they needed me to be?

Kill Tristan, avenge my parents, make Ash happy…it was my mission, but it might mean risk to my friends, risk to my life, and near certain destruction of my country.

Spare Tristan, save my friends, save myself, and save Onyx itself, but in the process lose the only purpose my life ever had, destroy my brother, and ruin the chance to mete out justice for my parents.

My options were irreconcilable. They had no happy medium, no halfway. The only thing I could do was pick one… and that was impossible.

"Do you think he would prefer to not marry at all if he didn't need an heir?" I asked, my voice as low as if I was afraid the moon itself was listening, and as shadowed as the room around me. "Because I'm sure that some woman, or many, in Onyx would be more than willing to give the King a child."

"If it wasn't for the legend, maybe he would let that happen," Jacquetta said.

"But he doesn't seem like the kind of person who wants a connection that transactional," Gus answered.

"Wait," I sat up, and even though I couldn't see her as anything more than a deeper shadow, I leaned forward and looked toward Jacquetta. "Are you talking about the Dragon King legend? Because he doesn't have any magic. We already know that. Even if he had a child, we would only be able hope the baby would have it."

Shuffling sounds floated to me, and I thought I could make out her sitting up too.

"A legend within the history of the Dragon Kings says that they don't get their magic until their true love unlocks it."

I laughed. I couldn't help it. It just burst out of me in ugly staccato barks.

"Cinder," Jacquetta yelled, and a pillow slammed into my head, which only made me laugh harder.

"You really shouldn't have told her. I told you she would act this way," Gus said, and my laughter finally died down.

"Hold on, you two talked about this? You knew about this the whole time and you're only telling me now? If he's trying to make some kind of real love connection with someone here, that's something I should probably know about."

"Maybe if you didn't guffaw like a donkey when you hear the words 'true love,' we would have told you," Jacquetta yelled.

"I mean…" Was she serious?

"See?" Gus asked, and air flying past my face made me think I narrowly avoided her flying arms. "You don't believe this situation is anything other than a craven political tool, and it doesn't matter that the rest of us think it's more. You're too damn stubborn."

"But…I…come on…he…"

While my mouth didn't work, and fully formed sentences remained beyond my ability, Tristan flashed in my mind.

Tristan in his mother's anteroom. Tristan with his head back and laughing. Tristan with that pride on his face when I shot the bow well. Tristan as he rubbed a thumb on my hand.

"Oh, no," I said.

"Do you see it now?" Jacquetta asked, her voice soft.

"Because we do," Gus said.

I buried my head in my blanket, stretching it across my face tight with my hands, gripping it like I was going to use it as a garrote, and I screamed.

The blanket got hot, shoving all my frustration and confusion back at me in heat and pressure.

Finally, I raised my head and sucked in a breath of the crisp night air floating in through the open window.

"I was always told that Dragon King got his power when the country needed it." I shook my head, my voice barely a whisper.

"Everyone hears that, and it's part of the same story. The love unlocks it, they only use it for the country." Gus's voice was as soft as mine, but hers sounded like a lullaby.

"Why are all of his advisors making this into something that's just as bad as I thought it was if he's really wanting to find love?" I asked, although the way I said love still sounded like I was allergic to the word.

"Because they're all hedging their bets," Gus said with a humph, as if she wanted to shove them all into the river.

"Mother said that the General said that the King made a deal with the advisors. If he finds love, he gets to pick, no matter who it is. But if he doesn't, he will pick the one most of them want him to," Jacquetta said in a voice so grave it was impossible to laugh at how silly her trail of sources was.

"So, if Tristan finds love, he might become a real Dragon King and Onyx would never have to worry about going to war again. But if he doesn't, he will marry whoever his advisors want him to even if it's the raven bitch," I said. And if I killed him, Onyx would be plunged into war among the royals for the throne and attacked by the other kingdoms from the outside at the same time.

Avenging my parents' deaths was more than just one thing up against so many others. It was the only thing. It was the entire focus of my life since the moment Ash told me they were gone. And it might destroy my world to get it.

CHAPTER 38
PRIZE

"Cinder," Jacquetta yelled from the parlor as I was taking a bath the next day.

"Still in the bath," I yelled back. It was the third time someone had something vital to tell me since I got in the water, and I seriously contemplated asking Tristan if I could train twice. Once with him later, and once right after I got done washing up.

But Jacquetta slammed the door open this time instead of yelling through it to ask me what I wanted to wear to brunch with the other potentials.

Her eyes were wide, and somehow she looked harried even though not a hair was out of place on her head and her makeup and clothes were flawless.

I sat up and braced myself to jump out.

"No, don't move. We have to plan," she said, thrusting a letter into my face.

Wiping a hand on the towel at the edge of the tub, I eyed her and took the letter.

"The King wants to have brunch with the potentials today," Jacquetta said, rendering the letter useless.

"Okay." No matter how blasé I sounded, my heart sped up. If I wasn't in the bath, I would have been sweating.

"It's not okay, we don't have enough time to get you ready for a brunch with the King. You have to hurry up, and we have to rethink what you were going to wear." She snatched the letter from me, tossing it aside, and dumped a glass of water over my head.

Spluttering, I didn't put up a fight, just let her wash my hair and shove me around as she got me ready.

For the first time since the ball, the idea of being near Tristan made me want to run and hide.

"You know he's seen me in the regular clothes I wore to train in. Why are we worrying so much about how I'm going to look this time?" I asked as she pulled me out of the tub, wrapped a bathing sheet around me, and rubbed my hair with another one.

"Because you know now what he really wants to find." She made me hang my head toward the floor so she could brush it out and continue drying it.

"And because some of the advisors and potentials want you thrown out after the last brunch," Gus said, stomping into the bathroom with her hands on her hips and the General in tow.

"Princess Fiachra," General Pace said, "and a few others who are jealous of the connection you already have with the King want him to get rid of you. It's why he's coming today."

"Shit." I squeezed my eyes shut while the blood rushed to my head, and they kept working on my hair.

"Yeah, shit," Jacquetta muttered.

"What were you thinking?" Gus asked, with a yank on a section of my hair that made me suck a breath in through my teeth.

"I was thinking that the raven bitch was too used to threatening everyone around her and needed to be taught which country she was in. But fine, I won't throw anymore knives when she's around."

"Maybe you shouldn't throw anymore knives at all," Jacquetta said.

"A much better plan," Gus said, agreeing with Jacquetta even though they both had to know it was a stupid suggestion.

"Training with Tristan involves throwing knives," I said. And it was my best advantage against the other potentials.

For a second, I didn't hear them scolding me, and I was no longer aware of how uncomfortable I was bent over while they brushed out my hair.

Inside my own mind, not when I was playing the part, and not when I was talking to my friends, I thought about my position as a potential before my position as Ash's sword arm.

Somehow, I had to snap out of it, and focus on what I came here for.

Ash had to know all the threats to Onyx if Tristan died, he must have had a plan. That was the only explanation, and he was too smart for it not to be true.

Thinking it through—at least enough to remind myself of my faith in my brother—allowed me to breathe deeply and actually help prepare for the brunch.

It didn't take long before I was standing in my underwear, my hair pinned on one side with combs that blended into my brown hair, and cascading down the other in loose waves, looking at my dresses.

"Why not wear the black one?" Gus asked, touching her favorite of the daytime dresses.

"Because the raven bitch will be in black," I said, looking past all the dresses only in that color.

"I like the gray one," Jacquetta said, smiling at one that was actually silver, completely bedecked in gems, and anything but a day dress.

"This one," I said, pulling down a deep, rich red one so dark it looked like blood, and simple in its cut, if not in what it did for my body when I put it on.

"But that one is…" Jacquetta said, raising her brows and widening her eyes.

"A lot," Gus said, wiggling her brows up and down.

"You guys." I rolled my eyes. "First of all, we don't have time to argue about this. Second, it's a sexy color, but it's simple. And not an evening gown. Third, I like it."

"Okay," they said in unison and giggled as they helped me put it on.

When I walked out into the parlor, the General almost looked like she was going to fall over.

"Is it that bad?" I whispered to Jacquetta and Gus.

"No." Jacquetta said with a laugh.

"Nothing about it is bad," Gus said and nudged me to get going.

Trying to figure out what was wrong with all of them did me no good, and I decided that I really did need to get to the brunch. As it was, I was going to be late.

General Pace and I walked at a steady clip down to the grand ballroom where we always dined.

She reached out a hand to pull back the door, the guards standing back to either side, and I touched my hand to hers, stopping her for a moment.

I took a deep breath, but no matter how hard I tried, knowing Tristan was behind the door made it hard to focus.

"Come on. No different than any other day," General Pace said, swinging the door open.

But she was wrong.

And stepping into the room with everyone else already

seated and Tristan at the far end of the table, proved she was so wrong it was as if we were in another world entirely.

Most of the other women were in some kind of gold dress.

Gold on blue, gold on purple, gold on white.

Even the raven bitch was wearing gold on black.

Somehow the memo went out to everyone but me that when we were having brunch with the King, we were supposed to wear gold.

The raven bitch sneered at me, barely suppressing her glee.

Others in the room hid their reactions better. And most looked to Tristan, as if wondering what his reaction would be.

I did the same as I made my way to the one empty seat at the foot of the table, as far from him as it was possible to be.

He leapt to stand and bowed to me.

Curtsying in return, the red dress spun out from me, turning my small movement into a dance of air and fabric.

Tristan smiled as I stood up. His smile was soft while his eyes held a hint of the same pride he had in training. Like I passed a test I didn't know I was taking.

I took my seat, and he took his, never taking his eyes off me.

General Pace sat to my right, and nodded to me.

Whatever the others thought this was, and whatever I thought was going on before I came to this little brunch, I was starting to believe we were all wrong. This was a lot more than a mid-morning meal with the king.

CHAPTER 39
MORE

When the brunch was over, Tristan arose from his seat, bid everyone farewell and walked out a door at the back of the ballroom. He didn't pass me on his way out and I wanted to run after him.

To do what, I didn't know. And I knew the longer I stayed in the company of the others, the more trouble I was likely to land myself in.

So I took the opportunity to tap the General on the arm and make my way out of the ballroom.

I wasn't done with my food. I was more than a little hungry still, but I could eat in my rooms.

By the time I got to the room, I was chewing on my bottom lip like it was the rest of my meal. At the door, General Pace stood back.

"Aren't you coming?" I asked, trying to make my brain focus on her instead of back on the ballroom.

"Lady Cinder, I'm sorry, but I have other duties. They're calling me." She looked over my shoulder for a second and smiled before she walked past me back toward the stairs.

Opening the door to my rooms, the silence was heavy inside. Jacquetta and Gus must have been with the other Ladies in Waiting, which was fine with me. Even though I couldn't get out of my dress without their help, at least it gave me a moment to try and understand what was happening.

First, though, I had to order food. I couldn't think through much while still hungry. The only way I functioned without food when on a mission was by having a single focus. Here, nothing was singular. Nothing was simple.

But I didn't get a moment to think. Seconds after I sent the paper with my order on it, a knock sounded on my door.

"That was fast," I muttered, running across the room to fling the door wide, my mouth watering at the thought.

It wasn't a servant with a tray.

Tristan stood in the hall, glancing down toward the stairs. As soon as I opened the door, his gaze swung to me, a grin forming on his face. He stepped inside, shutting the door behind him.

He was so close to me, the warmth of his skin radiated out to me as he looked me up and down and ran a hand along my arm, sending goosebumps rising in the wake of his fingers.

"Listen," he said, his voice a low rumbling, "I know that I shouldn't be here. Especially since the General isn't."

No, the General saw him coming down the hallway and created this moment for him. That look over my shoulder as she begged her leave...it suddenly made sense.

"But you *are* here," I said, my voice breathless and the air not coming fully into my lungs anymore.

Tristan smiled, giving me that soft look that didn't make sense to me again. He took his hand from my arm, making my heart jump into my throat as he played with my hair trailing down one side.

"I..." He looked into my eyes, like he could find an answer to some question I didn't know before he took a deep breath and said, "This dress…is a very good color on you. I wanted you to know…"

His eyes didn't leave mine, but every bit of movement in him stopped. His breath came in sharp bursts.

"Are you okay?" I asked, leaning closer, checking him to see that he wasn't sick somehow.

"Yes, I'm sorry," he said, smiling and shaking his head as he stepped back from me, curling his hands into fists he held back against the wall behind him on either side of his hips like he was bracing himself for a blow.

I stepped back too and looked at the floor. My head spun and my stomach ached while my heart hammered away. I didn't know anymore what I should do at this moment.

"We're training tonight," he said, like he was reminding himself of something, but what he did was give me a rope to hang onto instead of free falling.

"Maybe tonight, you'll beat me with your new grip." I grinned at him and stepped away from the wall, cocking my head to the side.

For the first time since we met, the widening of his eyes, tremor in his lip, and white knuckles on his hands while his breathing hitched and dragged made him look like one of my targets when they realized why I was there.

All the blood drained from my head and the smile fell from my face.

"Tristan?" I whispered.

His face crumpled and he shoved himself from the wall, wrapping his arms around me while I gripped the front of his shirt in my hands. The heat of his body through the fabric brought my blood flow back with a vengeance.

"Cinder," he whispered, looking down at me as he touched the tip of a finger to my chin and tilted it up to look at him.

A knock came on the door. We sprang apart, both of us

pressing against the walls of the short entryway into the apartment.

We stared at each other, and I wasn't sure where I was anymore, what just happened, what it meant, or even if I should get the door.

Tristan didn't move. His eyes didn't leave mine, and the blank look on his face didn't twitch.

They knocked again, and I jumped to the door, swinging it wide open.

A servant on the other side with a tray full of the many foods I ordered, bowed and wheeled the cart past me, not seeming to register the King was right there.

I nodded to the server unable to trust my words, and with another bow to us both, he left, pulling the door shut behind him.

"You, um, I mean," Tristan stammered, and shook his head, looking at the cart instead of at me. "You weren't done eating brunch?"

"No," I smiled. "But there was no reason to stay after you left, and I wanted to eat up here. Although it turns out Jacquetta and Gus aren't here anyway."

"Gus?" I got the feeling he was going to say something else, but when I said her name, he furrowed his brow and asked.

"Augustina." I shrugged and smiled. There was no point in pretending it wasn't what I called her.

He grinned, and it was like magic was real. All his confusing looks and strange reactions of moments before turned into the same version of Tristan he was when we were training.

"I should let you eat. I'm sure your friends will be back soon. Don't worry, I won't call her Gus." He came close to me, took my hand in his and kissed the back of it, sending ripples up and down my arm.

But before I could say anything, react in anyway, or even

begin to try and figure out if I should, he was gone. And the room, in his absence, was cold enough for a shiver to run down my back.

The door opened a moment later, and I stood up straight, a smile blooming on my own face.

It was only Jacquetta and Gus.

"Was that the King?" Jacquetta asked as I deflated and slumped my way to sit on the sofa.

"Yes."

"Why do you look like that? What did he say?" Gus asked.

"He…" What did he say? "He told me he liked my dress and we're training tonight."

"That's it?"

And it was. But it was more than that. I didn't know how to explain it, because what more it was, I didn't have a clue.

CHAPTER 40
MINE

"I f he likes that color on you, then you should wear this cloak," Jacquetta thrust the deep red garment at me as I held my old one in a limp hand.

"But this one is mine," I said, knowing it didn't entirely make sense that I would be so attached to these few old clothes.

"Cinder," Gus said, taking mine from my hand, "They're all yours."

She was right, but a pang hit me when she folded up my old cloak and put it back in the trunk.

"Okay." I took the new one from her, the fabric of it softer and thicker than my previous one, and draped it around my shoulders.

"He's right. It is a good color on you," Jacquetta said, looking me up and down.

"I still think the black is better on her," Gus said with a shake of her head like the idea anyone could have a different opinion was ludicrous.

Smiling, I turned toward the parlor, but pulled up short as the General stepped into the doorway.

"General," I said, not sure how to ask what I wanted to.

"Lady Cinder, before you wear that cloak to training, I should prepare you for how distracted it will make the King," she said.

My whole body went rigid. I wanted to drag her around to the table, sit down, and shut everyone out until she explained it all.

"The color of the Dragon Kings is the same green as hellfire water."

I knew that much. It made sense according to the artwork on the doors that showed their fabled fire was the same bright green. But I couldn't figure out how that had any connection to my very not green dress and Tristan's visceral reaction.

"But his mother's color—the one she wore to marry his father, and the one she wore to almost every important event— was crimson."

Jacquetta and Gus sucked in their breath, but I couldn't breathe at all.

Somehow, without ever meaning to, and even as a mistaken assumption of Madam's about what colors would match Lehar, I invoked his dead mother.

The pain that shot through my heart, as thoughts of my own mother, and the idea that anyone would inadvertently conjure her so thoroughly for me, was enough for my knees to be weak. How did he treat me kindly when he must have been in pain?

"Queen Tanith always said that her color was his color. You wore his color today."

I wore his color today. The one his mother was married in. Oh, gods, he thought it was a sign.

"Oh." I didn't have any other words. I couldn't even form coherent thoughts.

"Does he know it wasn't planned?" Jacquetta asked, and it

snapped me back to the room, to the reality of the careful calculations running through everyone's mind in this twisted game.

"Believe me, he asked me after he spoke with you. He seemed to think you made it clear you didn't know, but I made sure he understood that it was not something I told Madam Velentin or you."

No, she had not told me. If they had asked me, I would have been wearing green. As it was, if the raven bitch didn't always wear black, I would have been in black.

My friends and the General all seemed more than pleased with the happy accident that led to such a connection forming in Tristan's mind, but I was still worried he thought I meant to do it.

And the look he had on his face right before he wrapped me in his arms, like the ones I saw before someone died by my hand, gave me enough of a precursor to how gutted he would be if I killed him now that a knot formed in my weapons hand.

It cramped and ached, making me rub my weapons hand with my less dominant one, just begging it to stop.

Finally, the General decided it was time for her to bring me to the training grounds.

Even without the cramp in my hand, the idea of seeing Tristan again made me want to run in the other direction.

Being here, in the palace with Tristan, and around my friends, and even the other potentials, turned everything around in my mind.

I am his sword arm, I reminded myself on a loop.

His sword arm didn't falter. His sword swung true and swift, delivering the killing blow so efficiently no one bothered to ask if it was assassination and assumed it wasn't. Complications from a fall off a horse. A bad heart problem. A reaction to food gone bad. The shock of a bad turn of events being too much.

Of all the reasons people formed to explain away the deaths

of the people I killed, none of them thought it was the silent girl in black who stole into town late in the night and no one saw approach anywhere near their target.

I needed Ash.

I needed my brother so many times since our parents died, and he was rarely there when I did. If he was, he even more rarely gave me what I wanted. But he always gave me what I needed to keep being his sword arm.

Now, though, I was alone.

Alone, surrounded by supporters, and going to meet the King. Again.

His sword arm should strike before it got worse. His sword arm shouldn't allow room for feelings to block their strike.

But as I reached the edge of the pool of light where Tristan was picking the bow I used from the wall with a smile on his face, I missed a step and almost fell.

The General grasped my arm and helped me upright.

Our shuffling alerted Tristan, who turned around. His eyes softened as he took in the red cloak on my shoulders.

"Cinder," he said, his voice so low it was more a part of the wind than words.

General Pace nodded and left, but a guard ran up to her not far from the edge of the range.

"Tristan," I said, biting my lip, unsure now how I was supposed to act with him while we were supposed to focus on training. My hands shook and I gripped them together in front of me.

He walked toward me, something in his step as unsure as my hands were.

"I know this is a ridiculous request because we're supposed to be working on your archery skills, but can I shoot first tonight?" he asked, grinning.

"Sure." How was I supposed to answer that? It wasn't a

ridiculous request. It was fine. But he seemed so sure it was going to be a problem that I almost laughed at him.

"Good," he said with a whoosh of breath. "I need a turn on the range."

He handed me a bow and a quiver and made his way into position at a lane.

The first shot he tried to take didn't set properly and it landed in the dirt to the side of the target.

"Fuck," he muttered, and I bit my lip, covering my mouth with my hand as I giggled.

His next shot managed to hit, but barely. The ones that followed grew progressively better until halfway through the quiver, he looked at me.

The next shot he took struck right by the second, sticking out on the edge of the target.

I walked closer to him, his hands too tight on the bow and the next arrow not yet nocked.

Once I got to him, I put a hand on his. It shook under mine where he held the bow.

"Don't be nervous," I said, my voice low. "It's just me."

"Just you," he said, but in his mouth the words meant something very different, and my hand shook more than his.

"King Tristan," General Pace called, her voice clipped and urgent, every bit the general in a moment far more consequential than training.

"Speak freely General," Tristan said, unslinging the bow and quiver from his shoulders.

General Pace glanced at me, but she said, "Sir, there has been an attack."

"Cinder, I am sorry, I have to go."

I took the bow and quiver from his hands and nodded.

"Go, King Tristan." My voice sounded like the General's and

my hands didn't shake anymore, even as he bent and kissed my forehead, the heat from his lips like a scalding drop of water.

He turned and marched along with the General, long strides and a bent head as he listened to the details of whatever terrible thing had happened.

Part of me wanted to know what was going on, and part of me wanted to drag him back and have him look at me like that again.

But, instead, I did what had always worked before, I trained.

My shots were lousy and my focus imperfect, but I kept going until the only thing in my mind was the way it felt to pull back the arrow and release, without checking my aim.

CHAPTER 41
LETTERS

I got back to the apartment to find Jacquetta and Gus asleep on my bed, wrapped in the blankets from their own rooms, the lights still on.

Turning everything off, I grabbed my nightgown and went into the bathroom to change.

Instead of getting ready for bed, I leaned back against the shut door and slid down to the floor, holding the nightgown to my face as I tried not to think about what was happening wherever Tristan was.

General Pace said there was an attack.

By whom?

On what?

How many more orphans were created tonight as I worried about dresses and cloaks? How many more girls were left as wards of their brother whom they loved as much as they loved their parents, but whose hands would forge them into tools of vengeance?

Or, worse, how many were stolen and dragged to Amethyst or Corvid as slaves?

And who would avenge them?

Tristan and General Pace had to be trying to get to them, to get some troops to wherever it happened and save as many Onyx citizens as possible. But what could they really do?

Especially with the raven bitch and the snake in the palace?

Could they afford an international incident while everyone was here?

And what could I do about any of it?

Some sword arm. I was as useless as a sword arm without a sword.

No amount of training would make me someone who knew what group was attacking us, or enough about the other countries to know how to get to them and cause pain.

Pain was all I was good at. To not know how to mete it out when it needed to be, to be trapped in a black castle of beautiful, useless things, choked me with my own inaction.

And how was I supposed to kill the King while attacks were happening and the threats circled, when the fallout might cause more casualties like me?

I pressed the nightgown harder to my face as I cried.

My tears didn't want to stop when I ran out of patience with them.

They fell for all the times I didn't cry for my parents, all the times I didn't cry for my own loss, all the times Ash forged me into something so hard the tears wouldn't come.

More than that, I cried for the girls like I was, and the one I would become when I plunged my country into chaos by killing a king who seemed like someone other than the monster my brother said he was.

Since the day my parents died, Ash told me Tristan was callous and cruel. That he didn't care about any of the people of Onyx, he only cared about his own power.

This stupid search for a queen seemed to be part of that.

J. DARLENE EVERLY

But now...

Now I cried myself to sleep on the cold bathroom floor with the King's colors wrapped around me to keep me warm.

In the morning my shoulder ached, and my eyes felt like after the early days when Ash was upset with me doing poorly in training.

Getting up, my hand tingled as the feeling came back to it. My throat was dry and aching.

Jacquetta and Gus still slept in my bed even though sunlight poured in through the window. Walking out to the parlor, I saw a letter on the table that wasn't there the night before.

The outside of the folded letter bore the Dragon King's seal.

I took a deep breath and rubbed some of the remaining fuzziness out of my puffy, sore eyes.

My Dear Cinder,

Last night I wanted to stay with you. I wish I could be with you today as well.

But the situation here requires my presence.

I wanted you to be aware that this happened in a small town in Thirteen Rivers Valley, so that you do not worry over much for your people.

Lady Solaria and her daughter are safe.

I am here with my troops trying to determine what I can in the aftermath and find a way to stop this from happening again.

This will not turn into another war if I can help it. No matter how much I would rather be there, this must be my first priority.

When I return, I hope you will agree to continue training with me.

Until then, General Pace will stay on at the palace to ensure the safety of everyone there.

Sincerely, Tristan

He didn't sign it King, and he didn't address it to Lady Cinder. This was a letter from someone who thought he was writing to a trusted friend.

Whatever unlocked in me the night before, attacked me again.

Tears sprang to my eyes, making the words of his letter, the careful script of his writing, blur in front of me.

How was this king, this man, son of the one who killed my parents? And how was he such a terrible king that cared nothing of his people like Ash said?

Going out of his way, taking the time when he was in the middle of a crisis to write a quick note to me, to reassure me of the safety of those who mattered most to me when he could have just sent a message through the General, was an act of kindness I couldn't square with the person Ash painted of him.

But my brother wouldn't lie to me. He had no reason to.

Somehow, he didn't know something.

That was the only answer.

As soon as I made sense out of it, my tears dried up.

Maybe I could find a way to talk to my brother. While Tristan was gone would be the best chance I had.

I ran into the bedroom and swiped the last tears from my face as I shook Jacquetta awake.

"Cinder?" she asked, sleep heavy in her voice until she really looked at me and shot upright in bed, grabbing my face in her hands. "What in the world happened to you?"

"It doesn't matter. I didn't sleep well last night. Listen, I need to talk to my brother." I was talking too fast, the words pouring out of me, but this was too important to worry about how strange I sounded.

"Why?" Gus asked, her head still on the pillow, and no sign of the same panic on her face as Jacquetta had.

"Because I need to talk to him. As soon as possible. Before Tristan gets back to the palace."

"King Tristan is gone?" Gus sat up at that.

"Yes. There was an attack in Thirteen Rivers Valley that he's dealing with. It'll be fine, but I have to talk to Ash before he gets back." Why weren't they listening to me?

"Oh, you're going to tell him you're going to be Queen, aren't you?" Jacquetta asked, bouncing up and down on the bed.

"Jacquetta."

"Duke Ash sent you here. He's going to say it's more than okay." Gus said, a huge grin on her face.

"Please. Can Madam get a letter to him?" Maybe I didn't need to talk directly to him. Maybe I just needed to write him a carefully worded letter explaining that we were wrong.

Once he understood, he would have to call off the mission. He would call me home and end this thing. I just knew it.

"Write him the letter. General Pace will take it to Mom," Jacquetta said, and I took a deep breath as I nodded and smiled.

Ash would understand the risk to Onyx. He would know Tristan couldn't have been who we thought. There was no way he would make me do something that would hurt the country and the people. After all the worry and the tears, it was going to be okay. All I had to do was wait for him to write me back and hope he called me home before Tristan returned.

I just needed to find a way to tell him what I needed without making it so obvious that if it was intercepted it would be a risk. No problem.

CHAPTER 42
LEGENDS AND MAGIC

A week later, Tristan wasn't back yet, and Ash had not responded. But I knew it was only a matter of time before I could go back home, and go back to a life where I didn't worry about the safety of my friends or the fate of my country.

Everyone would be better off if Tristan chose one of the other potentials from Onyx. Between General Pace, Jacquetta, and Gus, they would find the perfect person and steer everything in her favor.

It was for the best that it didn't come down to me.

Most of me was at peace and more than happy to go, but part of me was sad. I didn't want to think about that part.

So, instead, I learned how to play card games with Jacquetta and Gus, and trained at night after the General brought me down to the range.

Around midday, after a lazy morning, we sat around the table, dealing another hand.

"Cinder, if I didn't know better, I would swear you're cheating," Jacquetta said, and Gus laughed.

"No need to cheat when you two are so easy to read when you're lying," I said, which stopped Gus's laughter, but made me smile.

"That's it? You're able to tell when we lie?" Gus asked, dropping her hand onto the table.

"Well, I don't need to when you lay them out like that." I gestured to her cards, displayed for all of us to see. "We need to re-deal."

"First, I think we should get lunch," Jacquetta said, shaking her head at me like she wasn't sure she ever wanted to play again.

I just smiled and wrapped my arm around my knee where it was raised so my foot could rest on the seat while the other rested on the cross brace of the chair under me.

"You are trouble," Gus said, but she laughed.

The door to the apartment swung open and the General darted in before shutting it behind her.

"Get a dress on. He's coming up," General Pace said.

Jacquetta flung the ordering notebook away from herself and grabbed me. The chair almost toppled over as she dragged me into my room, Gus fast on our heels.

"What's the big deal? He's seen me dressed like this before," I said, looking down at my training clothes.

"Not after a long time away," Gus said, yanking on my hair.

In a flurry of hands, they had me in another red dress, this one more suited to a picnic in the middle of the summer than some kind of important meeting with the King like they seemed to think this was.

"But this one is…" Nothing special.

"Perfect," Jacquetta said, applying a touch of makeup.

"We're just brushing the hair, right?" Gus asked, yanking on it again.

"Yes, no time for anything else." General Pace stood in the

doorway, glancing between me and the door to the apartment. "Hurry, get back to the table. I'm going to make myself scarce."

She disappeared and Gus and Jacquetta pulled me into the parlor, back to the table.

I still didn't understand why we had to pretend like we didn't know he was coming. The second he got here the other advisors were probably running around just like General Pace did.

We sat around the table again, Gus collecting all the cards and shuffling them only once before she started to deal.

A knock came from the door, and Jacquetta ran a hand over her dress before she went to answer it.

When she opened it, swinging it wide, Tristan stood on the other side, still dust- and dirt-stained from his travel in a cloak so coated in grime it made me think he only brought one.

I smiled and stood up, he closed his eyes and took a deep breath. When he opened them again, weariness had fallen away like it didn't belong on him.

"Cinder," he said.

My name, simple and unadorned.

Jacquetta and Gus retreated to my room, leaving the door open, as I made my way across the parlor to him.

"Are you alright?" I asked when I got closer.

"Better now. For some reason I was sure that by the time I got back, you would be gone." He reached out a hand, but looked at the layer of dirt coating his skin and pulled it back to rest at his side.

I took his hand in mine, his skin heating upon contact.

"You're making sure no one killed each other while you were gone?" I asked, with a laugh because I was the only one likely to do that, and I kept to myself the whole time.

"The thought had crossed my mind." His smile was soft, but

there was a guard up in his eyes that had not been there before. "I came here first."

Of all the things he could have said, that wasn't what I expected.

Did he know I wrote to Ash? Had someone intercepted my letter and been able to decipher what it meant?

"Your cousin and the baby are still safe. I want you to know that."

I nodded. He was still trying to reassure me. If he only knew what Solaria had lived through already, he would know I had no doubt she would have been formidable if attackers came after her or Liberty.

"Any word on who attacked?" My voice was hushed, I wasn't sure if someone from the Corvids or the Amethysts were in the hall, listening.

"No. And I need to make an announcement to send some people home today." His voice was ominous, low and dark, like there was danger in the task I didn't see.

"You're worried about it," I said, not sure what else he wanted me to notice.

"I am. But more worried about the potentials I have to keep on for now." He searched my face, his eyes imploring me to understand.

Finally, I did.

"Princess Fiachra and Marquessa Ziya are staying." I bit my bottom lip, knowing that in this, at least, he was being the consummate politician. By keeping them on, when there was a threat of attack, he was hoping to forgo more violence.

He nodded and I swallowed, looking down at our joined hands.

Tristan stepped closer and lifted my chin with his finger.

"You need to do what's best for Onyx," I said, and he sighed, a small, sad smile forming on his face before he let me go and stepped away.

"Everyone will be invited to dinner tonight. I'm afraid it will be a big formal thing." He waved a dismissive hand in the air, and I laughed.

"It's probably best to have it be public to avoid a scene," I said, and it was his turn to laugh.

"After the dinner tonight, I want to talk to you. If I give the General instructions to somewhere in the palace, will you come to see me?"

The look on his face was so worried, it was as if he thought I would really say no.

"Of course."

His smile was brilliant, and he bowed to me before he started down the hall.

I shut the door, not wanting to see him go from room to room, telling everyone else he was back and inviting them as well. For a minute, I wanted to pretend the dinner was private too.

Even though I knew I wasn't right for the kingdom, and I needed to go home soon, I wanted to enjoy it for now.

Gus and Jacquetta came out to the parlor at the same time General Pace appeared from wherever she had hidden herself.

"So, we're all going to a big dinner tonight. I suppose you're going to torture me for hours to get me ready?" I rolled my eyes when Gus and Jacquetta both clapped and grinned, more than a hint of maniacal glee coming from them.

"He's trying to find a way to get rid of the Corvid and Amethyst women, but he's stuck, isn't he?" General Pace asked.

The smile fell from my face, and I glanced back at the door Tristan disappeared through.

"Yes. I think, no matter how much we all want an Onyx throne, he's going to be forced to pick one of them."

"Not if we have anything to say about it," Jacquetta said.

"And not as long as you keep getting private invitations," Gus said.

I shook my head. It wasn't that simple.

"What we need is for the legend to be true, and for him to come into the Dragon King magic," the General said.

They nodded and waved me forward to start getting ready, but I was back in the parlor with the General and the impossible need for magic.

Relying on a mythical legend and magic wasn't a battle plan. No matter how smart the General was on the battlefield, I needed to come up with something else.

I just didn't know what I could do yet that would help this situation. It was going to take more than my spike to fix this.

CHAPTER 43
STILL HERE

"What is this?" I asked, my voice reverent as I ran a hand down the chartreuse satin gown in Gus's arms.

"Mom told the dressmakers about the color of hellfire water, and they sent over more gowns," Jacquetta said, the smile on her face told me she understood how much this color meant to me.

"It's beautiful."

"You haven't even seen it on yet," Gus said, grinning as she helped me step into it and wrangle though the complicated neck that included a gold chain I didn't understand until it was on.

The dress skimmed along my body until right below my hips. The bodice was so deep cut down the front my navel showed, but it went all the way up to my neck where a strap wrapped around and connected at the back of my neck, leaving the rest of the back open. The gold chain was part of the dress somehow although it looked like a necklace that hung a gold dragon sigil like Tristan's between my breasts, went under the straps of the gown and then reappeared again to hang the flame sigil of Lehar into the small of my back.

With my hair pulled tight into a high ponytail that hung in one huge curl, it was my favorite formal dress I had ever seen.

"Please tell Madam, this is the most perfect dress I could ever imagine," I said, staring at myself and wondering if I could just wear it over and over again.

"It's gorgeous," Gus said, her head to the side like she was swooning, which was so funny I couldn't help laughing.

"Gus, we should make you a green dress. With your hair, you would look better in this than I do," I said.

"Oh," she chirped, the dreamy look in her eyes turning to glee, "Madam had a couple made for me and Jacquetta too."

"Why aren't you two wearing them now?" I asked, turning to shoo them out.

"Because we aren't going to a fancy dinner tonight. We're saving those dresses for the next ball," Jacquetta said, a hungry look in her eyes.

"Are there going to be more balls?" My voice sounded tired, but Jacquetta and Gus just laughed at me and tugged on my hands.

Leaving the apartment next to the general, I felt like I was going to be the best dressed in the room. But that didn't mean my stomach wasn't doing a training exercise all by itself while I got closer to seeing how this was all going to go.

"King Tristan will love that gown, don't worry," the General said, and I smiled at her with a nod of thanks.

Maybe he wouldn't. That wasn't what I was worried about, and I couldn't tell the General that.

The hardest part of suddenly having friends was navigating the distance I had to keep from them. And no matter what my brother said when he returned my letter, that wasn't going to change. They could never know what I was any more than they already did.

We reached the ball room and walked inside. This time

people were still milling about, but as sure as Tristan said, there was the massive dining table in the middle of the room as before.

It made me wonder if after tonight, when there were fewer of us, we would move to a smaller dining room and a more intimate table.

Depending on who was left, I hoped not.

"Lady Cinder," Duchess Inara said, coming to my side in a bright blue gown that made her rich brown skin glow and her pale hair stand out even more.

"Good evening, Duchess," I said, with a curtsy.

She dipped a small one back to me, but her eyes were on the gold chain on my chest as she smiled and shook her head.

"Whoever your dressmakers are, they have outdone themselves. I never thought the color of hellfire water could be so beautiful." She met my eyes. I was struck again by how young she was, and reminded that I had not yet brought up Breakwater's needs to Tristan.

"Thank you, Duchess. I do love it, but I must admit I envy your blues. A gorgeous color on you." I smiled and leaned closer, dropping my voice and meaning my concern when I asked, "How are you?"

"It seems our trouble unfortunately migrated," she said, and I nodded. "But with the robust response to that, I have hope for Breakwater."

"Good." Although I meant it, I wanted the same thing she wanted for her people. I wrote the appeal to Tristan in red in the front of my brain. If I could do something to help her and her people, maybe I could make up for what I almost did to the country.

"After this time at the palace, and the troubles are done, I hope you come to Breakwater. I think we may have something to help with your..." She looked into the air like she could pluck the words she needed from the dust motes. "With Lehar's air quality concerns."

I raised my brow and my mouth popped open before I schooled my features again, "Really?"

"Yes. I think you will find many," she waved a hand as if it was finding the words for her now, "surprises in my duchy."

"Duchess, I would love to see you, Breakwater, *and* any surprises you may have for my people." I took her hand in mine. The thought that she might have a way to help clear up the ashes raining down on Lehar—or even make it easier on the lungs of the people—made me want to run with her to Breakwater that second and find out what she was talking about.

"Perfect." She leaned in closer, her voice barely even a whisper, "Anything I can do for our Queen."

"Inara," I said, pulling back and not sorry I didn't use her honorific as I should have.

"Listen, I want it to be you. But whether it is or not, I mean it. Come to Breakwater, and I will help your people."

She was so sincere, her face so caring and open, I smiled and nodded.

"No matter what happens, I do want to see it," I said, and she let go of my hand with a nod before she turned to find her seat.

"We have assigned seats tonight," General Pace said, gesturing for me to find mine as well.

Moving down the table, I found the one labeled Lady Cinder Ahmya of Lehar. It was to the right of the head of the table.

Tristan sat me next to him.

Everyone made their way to their seats and stood behind them, waiting on Tristan to arrive.

He did just a moment later, clean and dressed in his less ostentatious version of court finery. It made me smile to see him refuse to wear the heels, as if he didn't want to be stuck hobbling around in the case of an attack. It was the reason none of the soldiers ever wore them no matter the occasion.

"Good evening, everyone. Thank you for coming to dinner on such short notice," he said when he got to the table, smiling around and making eye contact with everyone, his gaze lingering on me for a moment too long.

"As you know, I have been dealing with the issues of the kingdom, and I want to thank you all for staying on in my absence."

He took a deep breath, and put a hand to the medal of the king that hung low and skimmed the top of his stomach.

"I would like to have dinner with all of you, and enjoy your company for as long as I can. Getting to know you all has been a joy and a gift. But I do not want to keep you waiting if you would like to know what the plan is going forward. While I am doing this with the sincere intent to find a queen. I hope you will understand the complications involved in that pursuit and forgive me if this next part may be painful to some of you. I spoke to some of you earlier and know your wishes. I have attempted to align this with them."

What wishes? Was he talking about the potentials who told Jacquetta and Gus they were going to bow out? Was that still happening?

No. I didn't want that to happen. I wanted an Onyx queen, and it couldn't be me no matter how much they plotted.

"Under the domed dessert covers, you will find either a green plate or a gold one. If you find a green plate, I would like to invite you to stay on with us for a while longer. If you find a gold plate, I will greatly enjoy your company for dinner, and I will see you off tomorrow to continue on in your own great endeavors." He gestured for us to look and see what color we each had.

Inara had a gold plate, but she smiled at me when she realized I was watching her. I smiled back.

The raven bitch had a green plate, and her grin was smug and wicked, as pointed as the feathers on her gown.

Lifting my own cloche, the handle was cold on my sweaty palm, and the color of my plate was green.

The same green as my dress. I had to suppress a laugh.

Madam Valentin outdid herself. Again.

CHAPTER 44
INVITATION

After dinner was over, more potentials than I thought
would ever talk to me cornered me on my way out
the door.

"Congratulations, Lady Cinder," one of them said, looking
over her shoulder as the raven bitch and the Marquessa left.

Once they were gone, the women crowded around me
relaxed, the visible tension in their shoulders and the way they
held themselves releasing.

"Thank you," I said, unsure what else there was for me to say.

"We're all hoping to call you something other than Lady one
day," one of them said and the others nodded.

I smiled and looked at the floor, the need to run as far away
from their expectations as possible making me shuffle my feet.

"Should you need anything, if there is any way we can help,
let us know," a woman with dark brown skin, black hair, and
purple eyes said as she took my hand.

The lady must have had a royal Amethyst ancestor at some
point, but she was rooting for an Onyx throne.

I squeezed her hand back and smiled at her.

No matter how much I didn't think I should be the queen, we both wanted what was best for Onyx.

"Whatever is best for the country is the most important thing, but I want you all to know how much I appreciate that we all want the same kind of queen," I said, trying to find the right words and biting my lip when they grinned and giggled as if I said something other than what I meant.

"My Lady," they said, one by one, curtsying and making their exits. Each curtsy made my stomach roil more, the lovely dinner no longer sitting well.

By the time the General and I were the last ones in the room, I could barely breathe.

"They all want..." I couldn't even say it out loud.

"You have made powerful allies." The General tapped my elbow, and we made our way out into the grand foyer, a trail of beautiful, well-placed women ahead of us, closing themselves into their own rooms before they went home.

"No matter what you thought you had when you got here," the General said, her voice low so only I could hear, "You now have much more on your side as far as the cold calculations of what's politically best for the country."

"It's not me, though. It's all Jacquetta and Gus."

"How do you think any of these connections and alliances are made?" She opened the door to my apartment for me, but I was leagues away, thinking back to my days with the governess and my mother, learning about the complicated web of the royals and their connections to each other.

When did I become one of them, one of the ones in the books that had lines connecting them to others that needed to be studied in order to understand them at all?

"So?" Jacquetta asked, running out of her room in her night-gown with her sleep bonnet on already.

"Tell me, quick," Gus said, her hands over her face where she was ensconced in blankets on the sofa.

"I'm staying, but so is the raven bitch and the Marquessa." I went to stand by the window while they talked to the general about what happened at dinner.

Outside, in the courtyard, carriages were already lined up.

"Are some leaving tonight?" I asked, interrupting a story about the offers of aid I got at the end.

"Some of the potentials have lands of their own that they want to get back to right away," the General said.

Duchess Inara. She must have been one of the people leaving.

To be so young and yet so much wiser than I was. In a perfect world we would have a queen like her.

Knocking sounded on the door, and I turned to see who would be here now. Tristan must have been saying goodbye. There was no way he would shirk his duties to console the others to steal me away to talk.

General Pace opened the door, and Inara was on the other side in a cloak.

I ran to the door and smiled, "What are you doing here?"

"Lady Cinder, before I leave, I want you to have this," she said, handing me a ring and a letter.

"But what is this? Are you leaving right now?" I asked, looking at the silver sigil ring with waves on it from Breakwater.

"I packed before the dinner." Inara waved it away like it was nothing, and focused intently on me. "No matter where you find yourself in Onyx—or even in some other kingdom near a wharf— this ring will get you help and even bring you to Breakwater should you need it. But that paper is where you should send any correspondence to me." She smiled and I took her hand in my free one.

"This means a lot to me, and I will do whatever I can for Breakwater, and for you." Outside of becoming Queen, I would do anything to help this young Duchess and her people.

"You already have, my friend." She squeezed my hand and let go, tipping her head before she hurried down the hall toward her waiting carriage.

I shut the door, looking down at the gifts in my palm and slipped the ring on my finger.

"When did you help Breakwater?" Jacquetta asked, and I could only shake my head.

"Honestly, I have no idea." I looked back at my friends who were still here and smiled. "Unless just being someone to talk to a couple times is something."

"She wants you to be Queen, and to have a queen from Lehar wear the waves will mean a powerful alliance to anyone who sees you wear that." The general raised a brow at the ring, a small smile playing on her face.

It made me want to take it off, but having a symbol to reflect a friend—someone I wanted to know better and who wanted to know me—was more important than some implication that eventually wouldn't matter.

But, as Jacquetta, Gus, and the General talked more about the dinner, I was left wondering what the General meant by Lehar being powerful.

Lehar was just a poor duchy dependent upon hellfire water for everything. Why did people assume that meant we had any connections or assets?

I shook my head and watched out the window again as potentials and their retinues loaded up.

The first carriage was ready, the trunks loaded on the back, the Ladies in Waiting climbing inside, with Inara right behind them.

She stopped before she stepped inside the carriage, looked up at the palace, her eyes searching until they found mine.

I smiled and raised a hand in goodbye, the Breakwater ring on my finger.

With a wave and a smile, she climbed in herself.

After the three carriages in the courtyard were gone, my friends behind me still talked of details and reactions and what we were supposed to do next.

Knocking on the door interrupted their conversation again. But this time, I knew who it was.

General Pace opened the door as I moved across the room to Tristan standing in the hall.

"I'll be back soon," I told Jacquetta and Gus, although the General fell into step behind us as we walked down the hall.

"How did they take it?" I asked, taking in the haggard expression on his face and the lines at the corners of his eyes where they pinched.

"Everyone was fine, but this is…more complicated than I ever thought it was when I agreed to do this," he said.

Although I wanted to ask how, I waited, letting him relax into telling me whatever he brought me out to say.

We wound down the hall, and down the stairs. Instead of turning into the grand foyer, we crossed to the stairs that went up in the other direction to the other side of the palace's second floor.

"I've never been on this side of the palace," I said, looking at the paintings of monarchs past lining the walls.

"This is the royal wing, where I spend most of my time when others aren't here," he said, glancing back at the General who had fallen far enough behind she couldn't hear our conversation.

Ahead of us was another set of massive doors engraved like the ones to the ballroom, but these included a giant red heart behind the image of the dragon breathing green fire and a woman standing in the flames.

He paused with his hand on the door, looking at me. The lines in the corners of his eyes lessened as he pulled the door open.

"No one usually comes past here," he said, and I swallowed.

One more thing I had no business knowing, what the private quarters of the royal family looked like.

The door opened onto another hall, this one short and clogged with doors.

He took me to the first one on the right, a simple door of metal, shining in the hellfire-powered light overhead.

Inside was a room even smaller than the anteroom we hid in during the ball. This one was like being inside a bookshelf.

One small window was in the far wall, but the shelves wrapped all the way around it and soared into the air far above where a ladder led to catwalks circumnavigating the room at regular intervals.

"Are we in one of the towers?" I asked, leaning back and trying and see the top.

"This is my private office," he said, walking to the window, stepping around the desk in the middle of the room littered with papers, books, and so many things it gave me a headache.

I made my way to him at the window, looking out on the side of the palace that ended on rocks at the edge of the water.

"Your view is beautiful," I said, wondering if he ever spent time looking out into the courtyard, if he could see my rooms from his own.

"Cinder, I want to ask you something," he said.

"Tristan, can I ask you something first? Before I lose my nerve or get distracted and forget only to beat myself up about it later?" I turned to him, fidgeting with the Breakwater ring.

"Of course." He raised his eyebrows and smiled, leaning against the bookshelf around the window.

"Duchess Inara of Breakwater is a friend. She told me about threats from the water and her concern about her people. I wasn't sure if you knew about it or not, but I wanted to let you know."

His smile fell, his face grew grave and serious as he nodded, looking out the window for a moment before he turned back to me. His face softened again.

"I spoke to the Duchess about this and assured her I would help—and I will—but you wanted to bring this to me?"

Even trying to explain myself made my focus scatter, looking at him as I attempted it didn't help.

"Thank you for helping her." There was so much more to say, but how I was going to say it, I wasn't sure. And how he would take it, I had no idea.

"When I was at home," I said, looking out the window, "There were times I wanted something to change, something to be made better for my people. But taking my concerns to Ash wasn't an option. He always knew more than I did, understood all the aspects of what was going on and sheltered me from it. I guess, I hoped I could bring this to you, and you would help because I don't know how."

And I didn't. I knew how to kill. Ash reminded me so often it was burned into my mind. The only thing I really knew was how to kill. He knew more than me about everything else.

"Do you really think you don't know how to help people? Because telling me that Breakwater needs help—with their young Duchess who is doing remarkably well on her own and had to swallow a lot of pride to reach out—is doing something."

Snapping my eyes to his, I found him looking at me, studying me as if he was seeing me for the first time.

Whether he liked what he saw wasn't clear, just that whatever it was grew obvious to him as we stood there.

He reached out a hand and rested it on my cheek, his palm growing so warm it sent heat radiating through me.

"Tristan," I said. My voice didn't sound like my own. It was wavering and unsure, but I was anchored in place, unable to step back or even raise a hand.

General Pace, at the doorway, cleared her throat and he stepped back, his hand dropped to his side, allowing me to breathe again.

I needed him to send me home soon, before this got any more complicated and I became an even larger impediment to him finding the right queen.

Leaning close to me, his eyes focused out the window as mine were, he said, "Tomorrow night, I want to take you somewhere away from the palace. But we need to ditch your escort."

Smiling, because this was much closer to something I was actually good at, I nodded.

"Done. I'll meet you on the other side of the bridge."

"Perfect. I'll send word on the time," he said, turning to look at me, a grin on his face and a twitch to his brow betraying a hint of disbelief.

He held his arm out for me. I set my hand in the crook of his elbow, and he led me back toward my rooms.

All of that lead up must have been for his invitation, although it seemed like there was something I was missing.

CHAPTER 45
TRUTH

"**D**id he propose?" Gus yelled as soon as I walked back into my rooms. Tristan was right outside, standing next to the General and the door was still open.

"Not funny," I yelled back, my face painted with murder. She shrank back. I turned to Tristan and General Pace where they wore matching looks of suppressing a fit of laughter. "Sorry about that, good night."

After I shut the door, not giving anyone time to say anything else, I turned around and Gus and Jacquetta cracked up laughing.

Through the door I heard the guffaws from Tristan and the General.

"Good night," I muttered, stomping into my room where I stopped in the middle of the floor, staring at the bed as I realized I couldn't get out of my own dress.

"Shit."

Jacquetta and Gus, barely holding it together, their lips pressed into thin-lined smiles, followed moments later and helped me undress.

"You two are going to kill me," I said as they made their way out, the laughter they were suppressing bubbling out of them.

The only good thing about getting embarrassed so completely, was that they forgot to interrogate me about my little trip with Tristan. Which was something I wasn't prepared to talk about at all.

Every moment I spent with him, every day I spent in the palace, my mission grew more complicated, and my allegiances stretched further.

While I played with the Breakwater ring on my finger, I prayed to my parents for Ash to send me word soon.

"Bring me home, Ash," I whispered into the dark of my empty room.

At least at home, I always knew what to do.

In the morning, Jacquetta and Gus were sitting on my bed, a tray of food in front of them, their eyes bright.

"So? What happened?" Jacquetta asked.

Burying my face back in my pillow, I groaned.

"You can't give me time to even wake up? Last night wasn't enough?" My voice was muffled by the fabric, the heat from my breath making the pillow remind me enough of Tristan's hand on my face that I sat up.

"No. I'm sorry I said that, but I do want to know what's going on," Gus said, handing me a muffin.

I closed my eyes and dropped my head, rubbing my face with my free hand.

"Fine. He brought me to his private study. We looked at the view. I asked him to help Breakwater. That was it." And it was…sort of.

"Damn it, Cinder." Gus threw her hands in the air, and I raised a brow.

What was she so upset about?

"You should kiss him," Jacquetta said with a nod, and I choked on air.

"Excuse me?"

"It's so obvious. He keeps spending time with just you. You finally learned how to flirt." Gus pointed at me like she thought I needed to shut up even though I didn't say anything.

"He came to you first after he got back. And you enjoy being with him. So, what's the hold up?" The look in Jacquetta's eyes was her version of Gus's pointing and all I could do was open and close my mouth.

"Sometimes it seems like the rest of the world wants you to figure it out and marry the King more than you want to make it happen." Gus shook her head.

"Any time you could make this happen." Jacquetta slumped to the side like I was sapping all her ability to stay upright just by being.

"Chances are he's spending a lot more time with the raven bitch and the Marquessa than we know."

They scoffed, but I knew the favoritism we saw was only part of the story.

"Amethyst and Corvid are both threats. There was just an attack. You can't tell me that he isn't seriously considering an alliance with one of them to help the kingdom," I said.

"Right, but that's exactly why you need to make a move," Gus said, her voice almost a yell.

"You could make all of that unimportant. I've seen the way he looks at you. You could end this tomorrow. All you have to do is let him know," Jacquetta said, leaning toward me.

I pulled back and took a bite of the muffin.

They were putting their hopes on the wrong person, and I couldn't even tell them to stop.

"Fine." Gus shook her head and grabbed a scone, taking a huge bite.

"Go at your own pace, but if he gets too close to Corvid or Amethyst, you're going to have to stab it home." Jacquetta pointed at me, looking just like Madam Valentin, before she grabbed a muffin too.

Stab it home.

Her choice of words stabbed something. They stabbed me in the stomach with enough force to make me put down my muffin and struggle to swallow the bite in my mouth.

"Tonight, I'm training by myself. Tristan has something he needs to do," I said, laying back into my pillows. "But he said he would send a note about tomorrow."

"Let's hope that what he needs to do is send more people home," Gus said, and Jacquetta nodded, eyes wide.

"I'm going to have a bath. I'm not hungry yet," I said, climbing from the bed, careful not to topple their tray of breakfast.

Gus went to move, probably to help me, but I waved her away.

"No. Eat. You don't need to help me today." I shut the bathroom door behind me and did what I needed to.

There was no real reason for me to have a bath, not when I was planning what I was for tonight. But there was a very real reason for me to get away from my friends.

Ash really did know more than I did.

He kept me isolated, away from forming bonds of any kind with the people who lived near us, let alone forging friendships.

Now I knew why.

As the bath filled, the steam billowing around me, reminding me of the pools beneath my home. I thought about Meg.

She was probably the person who knew me best besides Ash, and we weren't friends. My brother made sure of that. Whether he wrote me to tell me to come home or not, these women would be in my heart forever.

But I was a lie to them.

My love for them, my care for my friends, was real.

Yet I was not.

Would they ever speak to me again if they found out what I really was?

They certainly wouldn't want me to be Queen.

If all else failed, I had that. If there was no other way to get out of being Queen, of making them move on from the disappointment and their hopes for me, I would tell them the truth.

A queen I was not, but a killer I could be, even if what I was killing was their dreams and plans.

Sinking beneath the stinging heat of the water, I hoped Ash would call me home and I wouldn't have to psychologically attack my friends.

CHAPTER 46
COMMUNICATIONS

At dinner, we sat around the table eating the decadent food Jacquetta ordered. She kept glancing at me. A knock came at the door.

"I'll get it," I said, jumping up and trying not to run.

On the other side of the door a servant stood holding a tray with a letter on it.

"Thank you," I said.

He tipped his head, smiled, and walked away without a word.

Knowing Tristan was going to send word didn't dim the rush that flooded my system just looking at the letter in my hands with his seal on it.

I shut the door and turned back to my friends at the table, their focus solely on me. Raising the letter in the air I smiled before I tore it open.

My Dear Cinder,

I am sorry to delay training. My meeting tonight will probably run as late as ten, and I do not want to interrupt your sleep that much.

Please meet me when we have the time again. There is a tree I want to show you. It is a marvel that it is standing as it was struck by lightning once.

And there are some people I wish to introduce you to. Although, I think a gown would be too formal for that visit, and training clothes too informal. If you brought something you think suitable, it would be a great personal joy of mine for you to meet them.

Sincerely, Tristan

He wrote it in code.

Of all the things he did, understanding to write the note in a way that wouldn't worry or tip off Jacquetta and Gus should they read it, made a shard of my heart less sharp at the edges.

I folded the letter and held it to my chest, smiling.

"See?" Jacquetta said.

"You should kiss him for sure," Gus said.

Even their pressure couldn't upset me right now. Nor could it steal my appetite.

I sat down and ate my fill for the first time all day.

At the end of the meal, faking a yawn and about to excuse myself, another knock sounded from the door.

"Do you think he got done early?" Gus asked, jumping up before I could get it.

No, because it was a fake meeting. But what if he was calling off our excursion? What if something had come up?

She thanked the person at the door and turned around with another letter in her hand. But by her wide eyes and raised brows, it didn't seem like what she was expecting.

"What is it?" I asked, my stomach in my throat.

"This letter is for you, Cinder, but it has your sigil on it."

"My sigil?" I got up and took the letter from her.

It was the flames of Lehar on the seal.

Ash wrote me back.

Opening this letter made me want to hide, not run out into the courtyard and across the bridge on an adventure.

Lady Cinder,

We are doing well here, very ready for word of your successful endeavor.

I have no doubt, sister, you will make Mother and Father proud in your dealings with the King.

Please let me know if there is anything I can do to help you. Until then, I don't expect to hear from you much as you must be very busy, and focused on what you need to do there.

Duke Ash

He wanted me to kill Tristan. Still.

It didn't matter what I said, how clear it was that I shouldn't do it. Ash still thought it was for the best.

And I didn't know enough to be sure if he was wrong or right. What if there were factors I didn't know about?

My breathing was shallow and uneven. My dinner threatened to make a return appearance. And I couldn't make out the words on the page anymore through the haze of my vision.

"Cinder? Are you okay?" Jacquetta asked.

"Fine. I..." I didn't know what to say. I didn't know what to do. I didn't know what I was. "I just need to go lie down."

She looked to Gus who shook her head. I bolted from the room, shutting my bedroom door behind me, and flinging myself on the bed.

Why didn't Ash listen? Did he really want me to risk my life to kill Tristan? Did he really want Onyx plunged into chaos?

He couldn't want that. He had to understand something I didn't.

But...I didn't know how to be his sword arm now.

Every other time I killed who he told me to, I didn't question my mission.

Now...just thinking of driving my spike into Tristan's side, of finding that perfect place between his ribs, and ripping apart his aorta in a single thrust made every part of me rebel.

I jumped from the bed and ran into the bathroom, losing my dinner in the latrine.

Tristan couldn't die. Not now. The country needed him. And I…couldn't be the one to do it.

Ash wanted me to, though.

Not once in the seven years since our parents died and left us with nothing but each other had I ever gone against his will. Not one time did I ever tell him no.

Besides, if I did told him no, he would have made me pay for it. He would have showed me that he knew better and questioning him would only lead to pain.

Pain was always the way he taught me.

Trouble with training? Pain helped me focus and motivated me to get better.

Wanting to take a break from killing to rest? Pain reminded me how few people could do what I did and that I needed to stop their pain by ending the lives of people causing it.

Questioning one of Ash's decisions? Pain told me all the ways he was in charge as Duke and knew more about everything than I did.

But killing was what I knew best.

And I knew, no matter how much it cost me, killing Tristan was what I needed to do.

I just didn't know if I would be able to do it.

But if I was going to then this trip, away from the guards and all the people likely to catch me and punish me, was my best shot.

Hours went by. The small sounds that managed to make their way through the door to me settled into perfect silence.

Finally, I got up, checked the time, and peeked out into the parlor.

Jacquetta and Gus must have been in their rooms. The parlor was dark, and they weren't out there.

Tristan made it clear that I was to wear a plain dress, which made my way to get out of the palace more challenging, but I knew I could make it work.

All I had to do was make the rest of the plan work. And kill the King.

CHAPTER 47
LIKE YOU

With my bundle under one arm and my training clothes on, I made my way down the hall, walking like I had a reason to be there.

I only passed one servant and they were so accustomed to me coming and going from the training grounds now, they didn't even blink.

Crossing from our wing of the second floor to the royal wing was the worst part.

But the guards in the grand foyer watched toward the front doors, not once turning around to see me steal into the wrong side by myself.

Once I was on the other side, I ran through the doors and into Tristan's study.

It was the only room I knew how to get to that had easy access to the outside of the palace instead of the courtyard.

Besides, it was better than the rooms—whichever they were —that would have dumped me out on the lane around the other side where I knew guards were watching.

Here, I had time to hang my tied-together black dresses and

my black cloak out the window, using Tristan's chair braced across the open window as an anchor.

I shoved my other bundle into my shirt, hoping the color wouldn't be too bright in the moonlight, and that no one was watching if it were.

Climbing out the window, through the narrow gap that the braced chair left for me, I gripped my makeshift rope and sent a prayer to Mother and Father that I wouldn't fall to my death.

But as I repelled down toward the rocky coastline of the river, I questioned if maybe it would be for the best.

Maybe my death, no matter how it came about, would have been better than Tristan's.

No matter how macabre my thoughts, my grip on the fabric didn't ease, and my movements didn't falter.

Finally, my toes hit the ground, my hands just at the bottom edge of the fabric I tied together.

I took a deep breath and pulled my other bundle, shoved into an empty pillowcase, from my shirt before I took off my shoes and placed them next to the wall of obsidian.

My first toe in the water, the chill ran all the way up my body. But it wasn't until I waded up to my chest that the shivering started, and my teeth chattered.

Swimming with one hand holding the full pillowcase above the waterline, I drifted closer to the bridge as I made my way across the river, the current dragging at me.

Getting too close to the bridge would probably mean being spotted. The pillowcase above my head was like the white flag of a stupid idea.

But my feet hit the ground, a rock knocking into my numb toe in a way that made me wonder if I broke it.

With little time left before the icy water of the river left me ill, I made my way, ungraceful and loud, out of the water to the shoreline.

Once on land, the wind hit my sodden clothes, and it felt like ice formed all over me in a thin layer. I managed to stop making so much noise, and found my way to a dip before the hill that led to a building.

The dip was the best I was going to be able to do under the circumstances, I was too cold to look for a better spot.

I stripped my clothes off, the fabric sticking to me like a magnet, and the wind an all-out assault against my skin as I exposed it.

But I laid the clothes out in the dip, hoping I would be able to find them again. I pulled the red dress out of the pillowcase along with my red cloak and another pair of shoes.

Once I got it all on, the cloak wrapped tight around me, shivers wracked my body.

I shoved the pillowcase into the interior pocket of the cloak, and made my way up the hill, trying to force the muscles in my body past their chill so they could warm again.

At the wall of the building, I made my way toward the bridge.

Tristan's letter said to find the tree that had been struck by lightning. And he said that he would meet me on the other side of the bridge when we were in his study.

Making my way through the edge of the city at night, with the strap of my new spike wet and stiff against my leg, every step reminded me why I was here.

But before I could even think about carrying out my mission, I needed to find the place I was supposed to meet him. And I needed to get warmer, because my muscles ached with the cold while I willed them not to seize completely.

Finally, a break between buildings led me to the road that ran along the waterfront.

A park across the street, four buildings down from the bridge, held a lot of trees, the first I saw in my trek.

There, the second tree into the park looked charred on one side, and below its branches, a man in black, in the shadows and waiting.

He ran to me, and I didn't brace myself, my arms too closely locked around my body.

"Cinder, I was so worried," he said, wrapping his arms around me.

I let out a whimper as his warmth enveloped me, a tendril of my hair that had escaped the pins dripped frigid water on my cheek.

"Are you okay?" he asked, pulling away from me to look at me.

"Too cold," I said through my chattering teeth. I gripped the front of his cloak and pulled him back to me.

With his arms around me, the heat of his hands running up and down my back, the edges of the cold cocoon I was trapped in started to fall away.

"Is part of your hair wet?" He sounded dumbfounded as he touched the back of my neck.

"Yes. It was the only way to get out of the palace without getting caught," I said.

"Don't tell me you swam across the river," he yelled.

"Shhh. Fine, then I won't tell you."

"We don't have to be quiet, I'm the King. The worst that would happen is we were returned to the palace and some guards would get a bonus."

No. The worst that could happen was that an assassin would take the chance he gave them, by believing no one would want to hurt him, and kill the King.

"Tristan," I whispered, burrowing my face into his chest.

His hands on my back grew tender and he put his cheek to mine, the warmth of him, the higher temperature he seemed to run at, chased away the last of the cold wisps running through my veins.

I sighed and he held me a fraction tighter.

"Are you warmer now?" he asked, his voice low and soft.

"Yes. Thank you."

His cheek on mine, I felt his smile before he pulled back from me.

Even as he started to walk with me, he kept his arm around my shoulders and my body tucked close to his side.

"I'll get you inside in just a few minutes," he said, although he didn't push me to hurry my steps too much.

"Now it's much better." And it was. Maybe the magic of the Dragon Kings was just that they were warmer-blooded than the rest of us, and that was enough to cause all kinds of lore.

"Good." He kissed the side of my forehead and I swallowed.

Not because the kiss stung, hot though it was, because it didn't. But because the spike strapped to my leg was suddenly the only cold thing left about me and it sang a song of pain up my leg with every step.

"So," I said, smiling at him, "Are you going to tell me where we're going?"

"Do you know how many times I've wanted to tell you about this place?"

"You have?" I cocked my head to the side to see him better. He was smiling.

"I come here as often as I can get away. I don't want it to become a big thing that the advisors try to shut down, so I use my personal account to pay for it. I know some of them would appreciate it, but others would rather I leave it to the Dukes and Duchesses to handle."

No matter how hard I tried, I still couldn't figure out what he was talking about.

"But I wanted you to see it. I thought you would understand better than anyone else."

"What would I understand?"

Ahead of us loomed a large brick building. We were on the edge of one of the expensive neighborhoods in Bridgeton. This home was grand, with a large yard around it and high gates.

The sign on the front gate, which opened with a key Tristan pulled from his pocket, said Shield Home.

"Is this a place where only Shields live?" I asked, not believing there were enough in the entire country to fill such a large place.

"No, I named it that for protection. No one from any country, no matter what happens, would dare to threaten a place protected by Shields."

"But it isn't protected by them?" I asked as he unwrapped his arm from me and fiddled with the key in his hands.

"I can only hope it is."

What he meant was still a mystery, but I followed him up to the front door which opened without a sound.

Inside, the hellfire-powered lights were turned down low, but music emanated from a room off the foyer.

Outside, the building seemed grand, but inside it looked like a place children decorated. The stairs and the floor were all wood, but the walls were bright colors covered in shapes, letters, and numbers.

Tristan led me into the room with the music where a group of children, huddled together under blankets on the floor instead of on the sofas and setees, listened with different levels of attention to someone playing a lullaby on a stringed instrument that I knew was from Amethyst, but I didn't know the name of.

"King Tristan," one child yelled.

Children jumped up from their huddle and ran to him. The

music stopped, and they landed on him with hugs and smiles that seemed tinged in sadness.

"Hello, everyone. I hope you're not still having trouble sleeping," he said, placing a hand on one child's head, and hugging another that was wrapped around his leg.

"Yes, your majesty," a young man said, setting aside the instrument. "But the music seems to help."

"I'm glad the music is helping. Since you're all up, I want to introduce you to someone who is a lot like you." He held a hand out to where I stood to the side, unsure what I was doing here or how these children and I could be alike.

"This is Lady Cinder," he said.

"Hello, thank you for letting me come visit," I said, crouching down so I could look the littlest ones in the eyes.

"Are you an orphan too?" asked a pre-teen girl with a braid down her back and a bandage on her hand.

I stilled my face, trying not to let the horror of her words show.

"Yes," I said.

The children all looked to me then, their tiny faces open in wonder. Somehow, I felt like I needed to explain. "My parents were taken in the last war."

"Our parents were just taken," the little girl said.

"Mine were taken two years ago," a little boy offered.

"How old were you?" another little voice asked.

"I was fifteen. My brother and I were left with just each other." Two little boys who looked exactly alike wrapped their arms around each other.

Looking at all the little faces as they made their way from Tristan to me, their hands light as they touched my shoulders, my hands, my cheek, and my hair, for the first time in a long time the thought of losing my parents didn't make me angry. At least I had them as long as I did.

"And you're a Lady?"

"Yes." I smiled. "My brother is a Duke. We were lucky."

They nodded, but they seemed to grow taller looking at me.

"But you're doing okay now?" the young girl asked, tugging on her braid.

I smiled, trying to will all the encouragement I could into it.

"What's your name?" I asked.

"Angeline."

"That's a beautiful name. And I know you may not believe me right now, but yes. I am doing okay."

Some of the kids sat down, looking at me with rapt attention. I joined them, sitting on the bare wood floor.

"You see, it took a while. There were times afterward that I would even laugh at something, and feel guilty for being happy."

Nods, and a sniff from someone.

"But after a while, I started to pray to my parents. I asked them to look out for babies I met. I asked them to protect me when I was scared. And now, I think they're watching out for me like they did when they were here."

So many of the little faces all turned up to look at me had tears swimming in their eyes. But slowly, one by one, they closed their eyes, their mouths moving on silent words.

It was everything I could do to keep my own tears at bay, to remain strong for these small people who had more strength than I ever would.

After a few moments, some of them started to open their eyes, sad smiles blooming on their faces.

The sound of a baby crying upstairs and footsteps on the floor above broke the spell.

"Are you all ready for bed now?" the young man asked.

Children nodded. They got up from their places on the floor, coming to me and holding me tight.

I tried to hug each of them in their orderly line with the

same level of comfort and love my mother imbued her embraces with.

One little boy sucked in his breath when I hugged him, and squeezed me so tight it hurt. But it was the best pain I ever felt.

When he let go, he went to Tristan and hugged him, too, before heading up the stairs like all of them did.

Eventually the group all went to bed, the young man trailing after them up the stairs. I stood up from the floor.

"How long has this place been here?" I asked, my voice a whisper.

"Since the last war. There were so many children who needed someone to take care of them and someone to love them," Tristan said, his voice low too.

"Did your parents set this place up?"

"No, this was me. While they were on the front lines of the war, I was here at the palace doing what I could to run the country. And when children were collected after terrible things happened to their families, I kept them at the palace. But that place is too much for scared little kids. So, just after the war was done, I set this up."

"Why wasn't I sent here?" I turned from the stairs to look at Tristan whose smile was sad.

"Your brother wanted you to stay with him. If there is any family left for the children, I ask them if they will take them in first."

"Did you meet with my brother?" I couldn't imagine how that meeting went.

"I didn't then. We only corresponded by letter. I've never been to Lehar. But I've since met Duke Ash many times."

Although I knew he had met Ash, I didn't know he wasn't part of the last war at all. Tristan wasn't at any of the battles that took the parents of any children, let alone mine.

"You brought me here for the kids," I said, finally understanding why he would put me through the sadness of being face to face with younger versions of what I went through.

"I tried to tell you. To explain. But…" he rubbed a hand along the back of his neck, "I couldn't find the right words. I'm sorry to spring this on you. They need someone right now, though. And you gave them a gift tonight."

That look he got, the one that looked like pride beamed out of him and I smiled.

"Maybe they gave me one, too."

And they gave him a gift. His life.

No one was going to die tonight. There was already too much death, and I wouldn't add to the count. Tonight at least.

CHAPTER 48
RETURN

"How are you getting back to the palace?" I asked after we left the home.

"I bribe the guards. And you should come with me. I don't want you trying to swim back," he said.

"But if I go with you, someone in the palace will find out. It could cause all kinds of problems." I shook my head, Princess Fiachra would accuse us of all kinds of things.

"Cinder, please come with me. I don't care what anyone thinks. I want you to be safe and warm." He raised his brows at me, and held his face close to mine, looking into my eyes.

"Tristan, trust me right now. I know what I'm doing and I'm fine." I looked away from him, not wanting to betray how much I wanted to do what he asked of me.

He tugged me back into his chest, one warm hand cupping my cheek.

"I don't know how you do all you do, but tonight…" He bit his lip and looked down at the ground, touching his forehead to mine before he looked me in the eye again in the scant lights on the road. "Tonight, you were even more amazing than you usually are."

"Thank you for taking care of the children in there."

"Why does it sometimes seem like when you say nice things, you're saying goodbye?" He shook his head, searching my gaze.

"Right now, it's because I need to make my way back to the palace. It takes me a little longer than it does you." I smiled. He laughed, his hand trailing through the short damp hairs along my neck.

"Please come with me, Cinder. If anything happens to you…"

If anything happened to me, he would marry the right queen, and not have the threat of an assassin inside his home anymore.

"Go, Tristan. Get home. I'll be inside in no time."

"How, exactly, are you getting back in? No one can climb the obsidian walls. They're too slick."

"That's going to remain my little secret." I stepped out of his arms too fast for him to pull me back. I needed to use the heat he poured into me to my advantage and get through the water before it wore off.

"Be careful," he said, his hands in fists at his sides.

"I'll see you in a little bit." I turned around and ran through the night, keeping my body temperature up as high as I could, my cloak clenched tight around me.

Finding my clothes turned out to be easier than I thought it would be, but putting on the cold, soaked garments was almost impossible. The pants got stuck halfway up my legs, and the shirt rolled up on itself in the back and didn't want to untangle even as I yanked on it.

Eventually, I was ready to take another plunge. I ran up the riverbank until I was past the tower I was aiming for, hoping that this time I could let the current work for me.

Getting in the water again made me instantly regret my

decision not to go with Tristan, whether or not it would have caused a scandal, and whether or not it would have given away how I got out here in the first place.

Using the current turned out to be the best idea I had all night, but I was still shivering by the time I landed just down river from my target.

I picked my way across the rocks and put my dry shoes back on where I left them beneath my makeshift rope.

The hardest part wasn't holding the pillowcase in my teeth so my wet shirt didn't soak my dry clothes. And it wasn't pulling myself up once I had a hold on the end of the fabric.

No, the most difficult part of the whole process was getting my shaking hands to extend high above me and grab on tight to the fabric in the first place.

But once I had it in my grip, I pulled myself all the way up. Hanging on tight, with the end wrapped through my feet, I made quick work of getting up the makeshift rope.

Part of the reason I went so fast was to get out of the cold. Part of it was the need to get out of Tristan's study before he got back and decided to work late in there.

Most of it, though, was that I didn't trust the tied-together dresses to hold.

Finally, I reached the window and hauled myself over the ledge. Shivers running through my entire body made it hard to squeeze through the gap.

Before I did anything to undo the flag of the dresses tied out the window, or even pry the chair from its place wedged into the window frame, I stripped out of my freezing and sodden clothes and put the red dress and cloak back on.

The shivers didn't stop as I pulled the chair out of the way, reeled in the long bundle of fabric, and shut the window.

And they didn't stop as I untied the string of dresses from

the chair, shoving it all in the pillowcase along with my wet clothes.

Even after I snuck out of the private part of the royal wing, shivers still roamed up and down my body as I clutched the stuffed pillowcase to my chest under my red cloak.

But the closer I got to the grand foyer, the more the shivers were replaced by dread and the kind of tingles that presaged the arrival of something terrible.

For some reason—and I couldn't place why—nothing felt right.

I was gone for three hours at most. Nothing horrible could have happened in that short amount of time.

On a breeze that shouldn't have been there, the smell of smoke and the metal tang of blood wafted toward me.

Pulling my spike from its holster, gripping my skirts in my other hand, pressing the pillowcase against me like a shield, I moved slowly down the rest of the hallway.

Just past the opening to the stairs, the bodies of guards littered the steps.

The doors to the palace yawned open into the night where wailing echoed into the grand foyer.

"Gus. Jacquetta," I said, my voice swallowed by the horror around me.

I ran down the stairs, leaping over the bodies, and up the other side.

Our hallway leading to our apartment had even more bodies piled along the walls. Guards, servants, and people in finery were everywhere, crumpled in heaps, alone and in small groups. My blood ran as cold as the river water.

Blood pooled where the bodies lay, but I didn't see Gus's bright red hair. And none of the women with dark skin were as dark as Jacquetta.

"Please," I said, to whom I wasn't sure. Maybe to my parents. Maybe to the palace itself.

It didn't matter as I approached our door and saw it hanging open, a panel smashed out of it, the wood splintered.

I threw the full pillowcase into the room, and nothing happened. I followed it at a run into a parlor of turned-over furniture. There was a smear of blood, bright and garish along a wall.

All the doors to the bedrooms were closed.

Crouching outside Jacquetta's, I thrust the door open and rolled inside.

No one was there. The only damage was the bedding torn apart, shredded and dragging onto the floor.

Gus's door didn't open when I tried it. The lock was engaged. I stood up and kicked it in, sending it slamming back against the wall before I crouched and entered, one arm up as a block, the other holding my spike at the ready.

Just like Jacquetta's room, this one was empty.

But in here the bedclothes weren't shredded, just mussed like someone sleeping had been interrupted.

I looked back across the parlor to my room, the door shut, a cracked panel near the doorknob.

The few steps across the room to my door was enough for me to imagine Jacquetta and Gus in their night clothes, being attacked by faceless people, fighting back as best they knew how. And dying in the process.

Standing at my door, off to the side, with a hand on the knob and the other gripping my spike, I set all the images in my head aside.

If anyone hurt my friends, they had better be already gone.

I turned the knob and shoved the door open.

CHAPTER 49
ARMED

As soon as the door opened, I rolled inside and a brush flew past my head.

"Cinder," Gus yelled as Jacquetta screamed, what looked like a chair leg in her raised hand before she dropped it back down to her side.

Jacquetta paused mid scream and flung herself forward, followed by Gus who tossed a heavy pot of makeup onto the floor.

"Oh, thank you," I said, my voice a sigh, calling on the same unnamed thing I had before as my body relaxed a fraction.

They slammed into me, wrapping their arms around me with tears streaming down their faces. I dropped my spike to hug them back.

"Where in the hellfire were you?" Jacquetta wailed, hitting me in the arm with her chair leg.

"Stop, ow." I rubbed the spot and took the thing from her before she could hit me again. "I was with Tristan outside the palace. What happened? Are they still here?"

"I don't know," Gus said, and I pushed them away, picking up my spike again and holding the chair leg in the other hand.

"Come on, we need to be quiet." I looked each of them in the eye, trying to imbue them with as much courage as I could.

Gus nodded and picked up the wooden brush. Jacquetta set her face into a mask of fury and grabbed a pair of garment scissors off the bed.

I didn't question their choices of weapons, just motioned for them to get behind me, tucking the front of my dress into my waistband and starting back through the parlor.

"Don't look too closely," I warned in a hush before we left the apartment.

Gus sucked in a breath behind me, but I didn't turn to see how she was handling the carnage in the hall.

Jacquetta darted out from her safer position behind Gus, and grabbed a short sword from the lifeless hand of a guard.

It was a good idea, so I handed the chair leg off to Gus and did the same.

Gus held her two wooden weapons up like she was going to cook with them, but I didn't try and correct her form. As long as she was with me, she was going to be okay. I wouldn't let anyone get close enough for her to need to use either.

A few more paces down the hall and one of them tapped my arm.

Jacquetta pointed at the pale face and white hair of Princess of Fiachra.

Her neck was slit, the blood soaking her from the cut down to the floor where she sat crumpled up against a wall. Her Ladies in Waiting lay dead beside her, and three guards slumped face down in a half circle around them.

I shook my head. There wasn't time to think about the ramifications of her death right now. Or wonder if her Ladies were slaves, led to their deaths by a terrible, foolish woman.

Right now, all I could do was keep moving, find Tristan, and fight anyone who got in my way.

We worked our way down the hall and the stairs, picking our steps carefully around the bodies littered in our path.

I wanted to run, but I needed to think about Gus and Jacquetta in their nightgowns and bare feet.

Finally, we reached the front doors, one of them hanging at an odd angle. Wailing in the courtyard floated through the night paired with barked orders and the sound of hustling, armed people.

All I could do was hope the sounds were from the people on our side. Hope and raise the weapons in my hands into ready position.

We walked out onto the front steps to chaos coated in blood.

But the guards running past with bandages in their arms, carrying injured people, or brandishing weapons belonged to the palace.

I lowered my arms and stood up straight, scanning the scene, looking for one person in particular.

Looking past the wounded, lying bloodied and broken, silent or screaming, I spotted the wailing woman in her servant uniform as she cradled the body of a small child who looked like a stable boy with a sword hilt buried in his chest.

Crouched next to her, with Shield Elio leaning down and patting his shoulder, Tristan had his shirt sleeves pushed up his arms, his cloak gone, blood soaking his chest.

With Shield Elio helping her, Tristan turned and yelled an order at a guard running past who nodded and changed direction. Then he turned and ran toward the doors, toward me.

He spotted me and his steps increased.

I ran to him, the muscles in my shoulders finally releasing some of the tension. If Tristan was checking on the wounded and the dead, then the threat was past. There was no way he would be thinking about them yet if the threat was still in the palace.

We met in the middle of the courtyard. He grabbed me by the arms and pulled me in tight for just a moment before he pulled back again and looked past me to where Gus and Jacquetta were catching up.

"You're alright," we said at the same time.

"Do we know what happened?" I asked, looking around at the devastation I didn't think was possible inside the walls of the Obsidian Palace.

"Not entirely, but we do know that the attackers were all dressed as guards. That's how they got in."

I thought of the bodies I passed in and outside the palace. I wondered how many of them were the real ones, and which ones were part of the attacking force.

"But how do you know if you found all the fake ones?" Gus asked behind me, with her chair leg raised high again as she watched everyone who passed us.

"They couldn't fake the sigil," Tristan said, putting his hand to the place on his chest that the guards wore the Obsidian sigil of the Dragon Kings.

"Good. But at some point, you still need to check every single one with other guards and make sure none got through the cracks," Jacquetta said. Tristan blinked like he was surprised by her comment.

"Yes, you do," I said, looking at the blood on his chest until I was sure it wasn't his, "But what can we do now? How can we help?"

"Unless you know anything about wounds," Tristan ran a hand through his hair, leaving behind a streak of blood on his forehead, "You can go back to your rooms, and wait until we can make a decision about what happens next. I need to check on the other potentials. I have no idea what state the inside of the guest wing is in."

"Not good. Princess Fiachra is dead." There was no point in hiding it from him.

He squeezed his eyes shut, his entire face pinching in.

"Will Corvid want revenge?" I asked. That was the most important part of that news, and the only reason I wasn't asking if this attack was from Corvid.

"I hope not. I'll deal with that, but first I need to check on all the other potentials," he said, putting a hand on my arm like he was going to move past me.

"No." I passed the sword into my hand already holding my spike and put my empty fingers on his. "You go be the King of Onyx and take care of all of this. We can handle ourselves. I'll check on all the potentials."

"But—"

"Go, Tristan. Your duty is out here. Send the Chamberlain, or somebody, if you want, but you're needed here." I nodded and he straightened, his eyes clearing and filling with purpose before he ran off into the night.

"Are we really going to check on everyone?" Gus asked, her voice exhausted.

"Trust me, I don't want to either, but..." I said, turning to face my friends, whose eyes still darted around the courtyard like they were expecting an attack any moment.

"Yes," Jacquetta said. "Let's go and get this over with."

Whatever kept them from panic, they harnessed it as we walked back inside and had to move through the grisly gauntlet of blood and death again.

"Do we even know which rooms are occupied?" Gus asked at the top of the stairs.

"No, we can assume all the ones with sigils on them, but I don't know if there are some without them." I looked down the long hall, the task in front of me more daunting than I realized when I offered.

"So we're knocking on all of them," Gus said, marching to the first door.

But by the time we got to the third door, all our calls going unanswered, the Chamberlain came into the hall.

The Chamberlain's face was screwed up in distaste, and a phalanx of guards followed. Without a word, the guards began to collect the dead, servants following soon after to start cleaning away the gore.

"Have you found any of the other potentials?" the Chamberlain asked, turning away as a body was hauled past.

"No. We knocked on the first three doors, but we don't know where to look to see if everyone is alright," I said.

"You can go back to your rooms if they're not too destroyed. Thank you." With a nod the Chamberlain moved down the hall a few doors past the one at which we stood and announced the all-clear.

It opened on a trembling Lady in Waiting of Marquessa Ziya who nodded and gave the Chamberlain a tremulous smile before she shut the door again.

The Chamberlain sighed a sound of relief and moved to the next door with a sigil on it.

"Come on, Cinder," Gus said. "There's nothing more you can do."

She was right for now. But as a guard carried the body of Princess Fiachra away, her white hair hanging down over his arm, I knew she would be wrong in the long run.

Because whether Corvid attacked in response to her death or not, someone was behind this. And they were going to pay. I would see to that.

CHAPTER 50
EYES SHUT

We climbed into my bed together, the three of us behind locked doors, with our weapons on the nightstand.

But while Gus and Jacquetta tossed and turned in fitful sleep, I stayed awake and ran through what I knew of the attack, trying to find answers.

As the first of dawn's rays peeked in through the window, lighting the room around me, a quiet knock sounded on the door to the apartment.

I slipped from the bed, careful not to jostle them, and ran to the door.

There was only one person who would be knocking at that time, but I had my spike in my hand just in case I was wrong.

Opening it, I found I was right.

Tristan leaned against the wall with one hand, the other on his face.

He was soaked in dried blood, his hair sticking up all over his head. Even the way he leaned looked like he was about to fall asleep standing up.

"Come inside," I said, my voice a hushed whisper.

He dropped the hand from his face, his eyes meeting mine, but he looked through me for a moment before focusing.

"If I come in there, I will fall asleep."

"That's understandable." I stepped back and opened the door wider, gesturing for him to enter.

For a second, I thought he would say no, but he smiled a wan, painful smile and walked inside.

Looking down the hall, the bodies were all cleared, and some servants were still scrubbing walls of the marks left by death. I shut the door.

In the parlor, Tristan stood looking down at the sofa, which I righted earlier along with all the other furniture—except the stool to my vanity which was missing all its legs.

"It's good the attackers didn't get in here," he said, and I raised an eyebrow.

"But they did. Jacquetta and Gus hid in my room. They broke into one of the bedrooms, shredded the bedclothes, and tried to break into my room. I don't know why they stopped." I took his hand and tugged him down to sit on the sofa with me.

"We put all the furniture back where it belonged, too," I said.

The look on his face as he scanned the room, taking in the blood on the wall and the damage done to the doors as if he was looking at a puzzle he didn't have any clue how to unlock.

"None of the other potential's rooms were attacked. I thought maybe Princess Fiachra was the target, but she just got caught out in the open." His voice was low and grave.

"Do…" I wasn't sure I could ask the question. Not when the answer seemed ludicrous.

"Do I think you were the target?" he asked, speaking my thoughts out loud.

"I'm no threat to anyone. That doesn't even make sense." I shook my head. I was a huge threat, but not as Lady Cinder a potential queen, just as my brother's sword arm. And no one knew about that side of my existence.

"Cinder," he said, turning to look at me, biting his lip, "I know of one way that people see you as a threat."

"Only the targets in the training grounds think I'm dangerous at the palace." I shook my head, but the way he looked at me, even through the exhaustion, made me want to run away.

His hand lifted, tucking a wayward hair behind my ear, the heat of his hand as he let it linger on my jaw sending a surge of warmth down my body.

"You need to sleep," I said, my voice hoarse, my breathing shallow.

He dropped his hand, wrapping it around mine, his head leaning back on the cushion of the sofa. His eyes didn't leave mine as they closed and stayed shut. His breathing evened out. He sunk further into the cushions, but his hand kept a hold on mine.

Somehow, while I broke all the rules Madam laid out for me, I became someone who mattered in some way to him. To the King.

And if others thought I was a threat it had to be in the time we spent together, and the way Jacquetta and Gus managed to get so many on my side.

But I wasn't going to be Queen. I didn't want to be. This version of me, the one in the pretty dresses and the perfect manners wasn't who I was. My brother was the only one who knew who I was.

His sword arm.

Tristan, this man in front of me, asleep and vulnerable, had no idea that the spike he saw me holding—that rested on a table nearby—was meant to be shoved into his heart.

My brother wanted me to kill him. Still.

The reasons for me to do it were deep in my bones. And the reasons for me not to weren't nearly as clear. Nor as easy to face. They were just impressions from my time here.

Just the way his hand was warm in mine and his face open and troubled in his sleep.

I reached out and rubbed a thumb along his brow, straightening out the furrow in the middle until he looked at peace.

But even as I held his hand, leaned against him, and felt the warm air of his breath on my skin, I wanted to check that his heart was intact, that I hadn't stopped it from beating.

Placing my hand on his chest, right over his heart, on top of the blood-crusted shirt, I felt his heartbeat.

It was strong and steady, the heat from him so warm I didn't want to let go.

Leaning my head against his chest, heedless of the grime and gore covering him, I let my eyes fall shut. The music of the blood in his veins sang me to sleep even as the scratch of the blood on his clothes reminded me of the mission I ignored.

Heat traced a pattern along my hairline and down my back. It made a track running the same path over and over again until I opened my eyes.

For a moment I forgot where I was and what happened the night before.

Opening my eyes, the first thing I saw was Tristan's bloodied chest.

I sat up, sucking in a breath, panic ratcheting through my body like I was struck by lightning.

"Tristan," I said, pawing at him, checking every bit I could reach, looking for the wound.

"Cinder, it's okay," he said, sitting up and grabbing my hands.

Breathing too fast, I looked into his eyes, searching for the explanation until the memories slammed into me, and I crumpled into him while he held me tight.

"It's okay," he said. "You're okay."

"For a minute I thought you were hurt." For a minute I thought I killed him. I clung to him and tried to force the blood in my body to slow down.

He ran a hand along my back, the heat from it chasing away the last of the shock to my system.

Tristan was silent for so long, just holding me, and staying still except his hands. I pulled back and scooted away from him on the sofa thinking he must be embarrassed for me.

I shook my head, and he grabbed my hand, leaning over to reach me as I looked up to find him smiling.

"You're laughing at me," I said.

"No. I'm not at all. Come here," he said, tugging on my hand.

Biting my lip, I moved a fraction closer, enough for him to sit up.

"After last night, I feel guilty," he said, wiping my cheek that was probably smeared with dried blood from resting on his chest.

"Why? It isn't your fault the attack happened."

"I feel guilty being as happy as I am right now," he said, and I gulped down a wavering breath.

He looked at me, the smile on his face holding a promise I couldn't keep, and his eyes dropped to my mouth.

The door to my bedroom opened behind me and I smiled.

"Come on out," I said, hopping up from the sofa, never more thrilled to be interrupted by my friends as they peeked out from the door.

"Are you sure?" Gus asked, her grin wicked.

"We can go back to bed," Jacquetta said, the somber look on her face failing to hide the glee in her eyes.

"No, no," Tristan said, getting up and rolling his shoulders, "I need to go. There is too much to do, but thank you all for letting me use your parlor. I'll get out of your way."

He bowed to Gus and Jacquetta who curtsied in their night-gowns, and when he turned to me, his eyes were shining.

"If there's anything you need," I said, taking his hand and squeezing it.

One side of Tristan's mouth quirked up and he looked at my mouth again.

I let go, stepping back.

"As soon as I know more, I'll let you know." He stepped close to me, kissing my forehead and lingering with the heat of his lips running through my body.

But then he was gone, shutting the door behind him.

"So, you for sure kissed him." Gus bounded out of the doorway to the bedroom, grabbing my hand and pulling me back down to the sofa as I shook my head.

"And he proposed, right?" Jacquetta asked, jumping to my other side, her mask of fake sadness long gone.

"No. We didn't kiss, no one proposed. He fell asleep because he was tired. He just wanted to check that we were okay." I raised my chin in the air and they made noises like they didn't believe me.

But if I was in their position, I wouldn't have believed me either.

I didn't know how I was going to go home to Ash. He would figure out I was lying, and that I had more than one opportunity to kill Tristan.

I just...didn't.

And I wasn't sure I was capable of it.

CHAPTER 51
FAULT

Our doors were replaced, the blood was cleared from the wall, my vanity stool was restored, and days went by without Tristan.

I didn't know if I was supposed to train without him with the state of the guards all on high alert. They might have been training all night long.

Maybe I could have found out from General Pace, but she didn't come either.

Their absences made sense, but I started to go a little more than weird stuck in our rooms all the time. Especially after Jacquetta and Gus found my bag of destroyed clothes.

Complaining the entire time, they spent the whole of the next two days sewing and cutting and remaking the dresses. They even fixed my old cloak and sent my sodden clothes to be washed.

At least I still had the short swords we stole from the guards.

While my friends slept in my room, I snuck out of the bed and trained with the swords every night in the parlor.

My muscles were starting to bounce back after far too long

not working with a blade, but I wanted out of the beautiful cage I was in.

The night after they fixed my cloak, I trained. After I was done and the muscles in my body were screaming at me, I turned off the lights in the parlor and spotted the old cloak sitting folded on the table as the darkness took over.

It needed to be put back in my trunk. Holding it in my hands made me think of the first part of that clandestine night out with Tristan. The good part.

Eventually I needed to have someone to tell the story of climbing out the window to, because I still thought it was amazing that I survived on clothes alone.

When I picked it up, though, I spotted something on the floor under the edge of the table leg that glinted in the moonlight.

I pulled it out, the metal cold in my hand.

Bringing it over to the window to see it better, I saw the sigil of the flames of Lehar. It was my mother's sigil ring, and my blood went as cold as the metal it was made of.

Running to my bedroom door, looking over at Gus and Jacquetta, watching close as their chests rose and fell, I had to stop myself from running down the hall and finding Tristan to check on him, too.

Folding my fingers over the ring and gripping it tight, I knew what it meant.

The ring wasn't with me when I got to the palace. There were only two of the flame sigil rings in the world.

My brother had the other one on his hand. He had worn it since the day our parents died, and he became Duke.

Our parents didn't always wear theirs, but Ash did.

He said it was to remind himself at all times why he did what he did. For them. For revenge.

Now, he attacked the palace, lost far too many people from

Lehar in the process, and did it all just to drive home to me that I needed to kill the King and fulfill my assignment.

Princess Fiachra died, the little boy in the courtyard lost his life, and so many others were gone forever, just for Ash to remind me.

He always used pain.

This time, instead of fists causing me physical pain, he used the pain of others.

Gus and Jacquetta slept, completely unaware that because they were my Ladies in Waiting, he threatened them, too.

But Ash was wrong.

No matter how hard he tried to remind me, I never forgot.

And no matter how loud the threat to my friends, I wasn't going to let them feel the pain of this.

Even if I had to disappear and never return, they wouldn't be a casualty of Ash's relentless press for me to get our revenge.

I took the ring, the sting of the message making it hard to clutch so tight, and put it in my trunk with my mother's shoes.

My brother saved my life in so many ways after our parents died. I believed in him. But he wasn't here.

No matter what he thought happened in the last war, I knew more now.

And he was wrong.

I climbed into bed with my friends, hoping I would be able to protect them, and hoping that I would be able to get up the courage to leave them.

Because I was starting to think there was no other way for me to avoid doing what I was sent to do.

What Ash didn't know, what he would never understand, was that the pain of worrying about them, and the pain of worrying about Tristan, was good.

He taught me how bad pain could be, and these people taught me how good it could be.

I hurt thinking about them, thinking about absence from them.

But I hurt far worse thinking about their deaths.

Somehow, I needed to go home, face him, and stop this.

Onyx needed us.

And I needed to remind my brother of that.

Killing for him, being his sword arm, wasn't going to be part of my life here at the palace. No matter how much Ash wanted it to be.

I fell asleep, more at peace than I had been in a long time.

The next day, General Pace came to the door.

"We're having a service for Princess Fiachra tomorrow. People are supposed to wear black because it was her color. Supposedly some Corvid dignitaries are coming, too." She stalked, rigid as one of the towers on the palace, back and forth across the room.

"Do you think it's dangerous?" I asked, Gus and Jacquetta's eyes going wide.

She turned and looked at me, her face back to the mask she put on when we first arrived.

"Yes," she admitted, but it cost her something to say.

"No matter what happens, it isn't your fault," I said. She squeezed her eyes shut, but the mask didn't falter.

"Is everyone going to be there?" Jacquetta asked, and by 'everyone' I heard 'the potentials.'

"The ones remaining, yes."

"How many are remaining?" Gus asked, leaning on the table in front of her.

"Lady Cinder, are you staying?" General Pace asked in as neutral a tone as I thought she was able to.

I smiled and shook my head. If she or Corvid thought they could chase me away from protecting my friends now, they weren't paying attention.

"Of course I am."

The general released a breath, the set of her shoulders relaxing a bit.

"We have four potentials who aren't leaving then," she said, and it was like she dropped a bucket of hellfire water into the middle of the room.

"Four?" I asked, my mouth dropping open.

"How many are from Onyx?" Jacquetta asked.

"Cinder, I don't care what Corvid pulls. You can't leave now," Gus said.

"Marquessa Ziya is the only potential remaining from outside Onyx," the General said. Then, as if that was all the additional information we needed, she turned and walked to the window.

I followed her while Gus and Jacquetta fell into a conversation about how to get Tristan and I to spend more time together.

Outside, in the courtyard, carriages were lined up again, a flurry of activity surrounding them.

Tristan stood near the head of the line, talking to Shield Elio and the Chamberlain.

My heart twisted watching him. With Corvid coming, no matter how hard he tried, this service might end in disaster for the kingdom.

"How many Corvids are coming? Do we know? And where will they be staying?" I whispered to the general.

"From what I understand, they aren't staying." Her voice was acid, letting all the anger from the situation pour out in the sound if not the words.

"Which only makes it more dangerous for all of us," I said, and she nodded.

It didn't matter if Ash intended for the attack to end in

Princess Fiachra's death, Corvid wouldn't care about why it happened.

"They can try and take their revenge, but they will fail," I said, my voice low and as sharp as the spike strapped to my leg.

General Pace merely nodded.

CHAPTER 52
PLEASE

"When did this happen?" I asked, touching a finger to the velvet of the gown laid out on the bed.

"It was one of the only black dresses left that wasn't sacrificed to your ridiculous hatred of them," Jacquetta said, yanking on my hair a bit harder than she needed to.

"How you missed this one, I don't know. But I'm glad it was in there. It isn't the best of them, but that's fine." Gus shook her head, her red hair shining against her own black dress.

"Are you both sure you won't stay in here today?" I asked again, looking at them both in their beautiful dresses and perfect hair I helped them with. I tried to imagine how I would protect them and Tristan at the same time. It left my hands balled into fists in my lap.

"Cinder, we are coming with you." Jacquetta raised her brow at me and turned into her mother.

"So stop asking." Gus pointed the makeup brush at me, and I nodded.

"Besides," Jacquetta said, grinning, "We're armed and dangerous now."

"Yeah," Gus said, "Just let those Corvids think they can threaten any of us."

I shook my head as much as I was able, these fierce friends of mine—armed with the short swords we stole sewed into pockets in their dresses—thought they were invincible. And it only made them more vulnerable in my mind.

There was no choice, though. I wouldn't order them to stay back. I wasn't in charge of them.

And there was no way I was going to send them into this situation without some kind of protection that wasn't me.

We finished with my hair, pinned back by red gems so it formed a tight, contained, long cascade down the open back of my dress.

Jacquetta and Gus were right that this dress was simple in its construction, body hugging, long sleeves, covered to the neck in the front and open in the back with a slit up one side. But being covered in black velvet was striking no matter the simplicity.

And at the cuff of both sleeves, black embroidery of the sigil of the Dragon Kings marked me as Onyx as clear as the obsidian sigils the guards wore.

I stood tall in it and in front of the girls, strapped on my spike, putting it on the leg that was exposed by the dress.

Gus swallowed, looking at me with wide eyes.

Jacquetta took a deep breath and touched the pocket holding her sword.

"No point in making them think I'm a good target," I said, straightening up. Especially important for me to seem at least somewhat formidable when Jacquetta and Gus would be behind me.

"Okay, we're ready," Jacquetta said, her voice breathy.

"Yep. Early, too," Gus said, trying for nonchalance and winding up closer to sounding trepidatious.

I nodded and pulled out a deck of playing cards, smiling at them and hoping it would work as a distraction.

They smiled back and we went to the table in the parlor, but someone knocked on the door before I could sit down.

Making my way to it, my hand ready to grab my spike, while my friends shuffled and dealt behind me, I wondered at how safe this same place once felt.

Opening the door revealed Tristan in all black formal attire except for the heels he never wore, his jaw clenched.

He looked at me and the set of his mouth relaxed.

"You don't have to come to this today," he said, pleading in his voice.

"But I do." I opened the door further, and leaned against it. "If you're going to be there, surrounded by Corvids, then I'm going to be there too."

Shaking his head, his hands wringing together in front of him, he looked down at the floor, and stopped when he got to my spike, his held tilting to the side.

"What's that?" he asked, gesturing to my leg.

I smiled, and pulled it out, holding it up for him to see.

"This is my almost constant companion," I said, not bothering to explain any further because he didn't need to know that part.

"Almost constant? So, have you been wearing that the whole time you've been at the palace?" He didn't ask it like he was even remotely suspicious of my motivations, or the fact that I had a specialized weapon he never saw before. But like he was amused.

"Every now and then I left it behind, but most of the time, yeah." I looked at the spike, turning it in my hand, and then put it back in place. "You see, everyone should be happy I just threw one knife."

He laughed, but it was short lived before he stopped himself and his face dropped back to worry.

"Do you need to be down there today?" I asked, hoping he understood that I meant when they arrived.

"Yes. But I really would prefer if you stayed away from the Corvids today." He looked at me. A line between his brows and his eyes pinched at the corners, and it dawned on me that this seemed like more than just the usual threat they posed.

"Tristan," I said, stepping closer and lowering my voice, "Is there something you're not telling me?"

His eyes went blank, and he raised his brows as he shook his head.

"For a king, you're a shitty liar."

His mouth popped open at that, but I went on.

"Are you asking the other potentials to stay away from them?"

With a sigh, he pressed his eyes shut and shook his head.

"No, because they weren't specifically mentioned in Princess Fiachra's letters home."

"Oh." There wasn't much else to say to that. The raven bitch hated me, and I returned the favor. It shouldn't have been a surprise that she was petty enough to mention it, or that the palace was reading our letters. I thought as much when I sent mine to Ash.

Knowing beyond a doubt that the Corvids not only knew who I was, but that they were told about me in a negative light, made me look back to Gus and Jacquetta playing at the table.

"It isn't just you I'm worried about, but all the people connected to you," Tristan said, his voice low and careful.

Turning back to him, I narrowed my eyes.

"Are you actually an accomplished liar, telling me this so I worry about them and stay away?" I asked, my voice a hiss.

"No." He ran a hand through his hair, making it stick up at an odd angle.

I couldn't stop myself. I reached out and straightened his hair, but he caught my hand and held it to his chest. The heat of him radiating out through his clothes and down my arm.

"Cinder, please, I just want you to be safe."

"But the safest the *country* will be is if I'm near you. Even if that puts me near them." I turned my hand in his, folding my fingers over his and holding on tight.

As much as I wanted to protect Gus and Jacquetta, I knew what I said was true. The most important person to protect today wasn't me, and it wasn't my friends. It was the King.

His face crumpled like he failed, and he pulled my hand up to his mouth, kissing the back of it.

For the first time, the heat of his lips was so intense it was almost painful. But I stepped closer, pulling him to me and wrapping my arms around him.

"No matter what happens today, it isn't your fault. You're doing the best you can in a shit situation," I whispered into his ear.

He let go of my hand and wrapped his arms around me, burying his face in my neck.

"Please be okay," he said, like a prayer directed at me.

I let him go, stepping back and running my hand through his hair to fix it.

"Go. Be the King." I smiled and he nodded, looking into my eyes like he wanted to memorize me.

Finally, he turned and walked down the hall. I had to stop myself from running after him.

CHAPTER 53
DEFENESTRATION

In the courtyard, black carriages pulled up in a line. They looked like Onyx carriages, like the one I arrived in, but maybe they had similar ones. Ten carriages with more than the usual number of footmen holding onto the back, and three people packed into the driver's seat.

Corvid dignitaries, whatever that meant, poured out.

"There are so many of them," Gus said, her voice a wisp of sound.

"How many will there be of us?" Jacquetta asked, her voice barely more than an impression in the air.

I didn't know how to answer them.

Guards lined the courtyard, more than I had ever seen collected there at once, and General Pace stood next to Tristan on the steps.

One of the guards left the line and marched to the gate of the palace.

All I could do was hope he was calling up more from the barracks.

No matter how prepared they thought they were, if the

Corvids came with revenge on their minds, and they were actually as magical as everyone said then we had a problem.

"Please stay up here today," I said, looking at my friends crowded around the window with me.

"Cinder," Gus said, but the tremor in her hand belied her petulant tone.

"We can't stay up here if something goes bad again," Jacquetta said, her eyes darting to the door of the apartment.

I nodded.

As much as I wanted them hidden away, the thought of being back in the place I was that night when I saw the bodies on the stairs, not knowing if they were dead or alive, made me touch the spike on my leg.

"So, we're going down there now, right?" Gus straightened up and walked toward the door, her hand on her pocket.

"Let's go," Jacquetta said, following after her.

"I'm sitting near Tristan," I said, and they nodded.

We walked in a line—I was at the front, and they flanked me. Although I would have preferred to have them behind me, they held their heads high and didn't move from their positions.

Everyone had a hierarchy of importance in their mind, and I knew where I was in theirs. But under no circumstances was I going to let one of them go down instead of me.

First, Tristan was getting out of this. Second, they were.

The world needed more of them, and a lot fewer Corvids. If the Corvids attacked, I was prepared to make that a reality.

Making our way down the staircase in the grand foyer was like walking into the barracks itself. Guards lined every wall and stood in the doorways of every room and hallway except to block the doors leading into the grand ballroom.

I touched Gus and Jacquetta's hands, leading them through the wide-open doors of the ballroom. The Corvids had spread out.

While our guards were thick in here too, the Corvids sat in pairs in every row of seats, rendering any move the guards made too slow.

Tristan was at the front, sitting next to General Pace and a Corvid in full black court finery complete with the ridiculous heels and feathers hanging off him.

Looking at my friends one more time, I took a deep breath and moved to the outside rows of chairs, skirting between them and the guards along the wall.

We made our way to the front, to the second row back. I stepped into the row first, positioning myself between them and the nearest Corvid. The ones in the row behind us were on the inside of that row and the ones in front were almost directly in front of me.

Of all the places in the room, next to the doors was probably safest. This was the second-best option to protect my friends. And it was the only option to afford me a chance to watch out for them and Tristan at the same time.

More people filled in the rest of the seats. The normal rustling and hushed mutterings were less than most other gatherings I had been to. But they all noticed the security posture in the room even if they didn't realize just how ominous the Corvid actions were.

The other potentials, much to my relief, sat in back next to the doors.

If the worst happened, the guards there and in the foyer should be able to usher them to safety.

Before taking her seat with the others, Marquessa Ziya—in a purple and black striped dress that looked comical—made her way to the front and curtsied to the Corvid sitting next to Tristan.

"My condolences," she said, her eyes downcast. "The death of your niece is a great loss to everyone."

The Corvid man nodded and smiled at her, although it looked uncomfortable on his face like his muscles weren't sure how to do it.

She tilted her head to Tristan and went back to sit among the others.

"Interesting," Jacquetta whispered.

"What in the hellfires was that?" Gus muttered.

Even if she seemed innocent, for the Marquessa to slight Tristan with her little tip of the head while she curtsied to the enemy in front of the Corvids was enough for me to want to send her home with them. Preferably in a coffin.

Finally, General Pace nodded and leaned over to tell Tristan something.

He stood up and moved to the middle of the dais.

"Thank you all for coming." His voice was strong as he welcomed the contingent from Corvid, looking at each of the pairs in the crowd for long moments.

I held back my smile as people shifted in their seats, realizing where they were sitting.

With Tristan's warning in a simple look, he gave everyone a better chance.

Every word of his touching tribute to Princess Fiachra was a lie. She wasn't warm and inviting, nor was she happy to know more about the people and customs of Onyx.

And it couldn't have been further from the truth that she would be remembered like one of our own since she spent her last breath on Onyx soil.

But he had to say it.

It was a smart political speech, even if it was complete crap. More interesting to me, was the fact that no one watching would have thought he was lying.

Which meant he was terrible at lying to me, or he was pretending to be terrible at lying earlier just like I thought.

Tristan finished and bowed his head to the crowd, speaking Princess Fiachra's whole name and title before he returned to his seat.

Some in the crowd followed his example. The Corvids didn't, so I kept my eyes up.

Her uncle stood next, moving to the same place on the dais Tristan occupied moments before, and raising his hands out from his body, palms up.

The entire energy of the room changed. It grew charged with power that made me expect my hair to stand on end.

Jacquetta sucked in a breath and Gus stiffened.

Breaking my study of the Corvid for a second, I saw the panic in Tristan's eyes and the set of his jaw. I pulled my spike, Jacquetta and Gus pulled their short swords beside me, and held them against their legs, hidden by the folds of their skirts.

"As we all do, my niece has returned to the skies," the Corvid yelled, his face turning into a sneering mask, and turned his palms down.

The Corvids in the row in front of me expanded, the black of their hair and their clothes molding together into a blur of darkness, and erupting into giant crows who lashed out with their talons and their beaks.

Screams erupted in the ballroom, and I drove my spike into the eye of one of the birds in front of me, shoving the body off when I was done.

Guards moved in, but the melee had begun.

The other bird in front of me burst into the air, and I leapt over the chair it had just occupied, through the blood of the wailing man it had partially disemboweled, intent on not looking at Tristan's guts spilling out of a wound.

"Jacquetta, Gus, get down, and raise your swords," I screamed, trying to be heard over the cacophony of agony and fear in the room.

Another bird dove for Tristan who, standing back-to-back with the General already, had a feathered body at his feet.

They didn't see the bird coming, falling fast from the ceiling straight at him, their focus on the ground and the horror there.

I jumped onto the dais, grabbed his shoulder, and launched myself into the air spike first.

With a flurry of feathers and screeching, the crow turned in the air and flew off toward the back of the room where people poured out into the foyer.

"Come on," I yelled at them after I landed on the balls of my feet, my hand bracing me on the front edge of the platform.

Jumping back down to the ground, I snatched a short sword from the lifeless hand of a guard whose head was no longer fully attached to his neck, and a handful of the throwing knives on the inside of his jacket that was torn open along with his abdomen. They were slick with blood.

Checking the room, I saw only three birds still circling inside. One was surrounded by guards.

"Gus, Jacquetta," I yelled.

"Here," they called, popping up from under a disconnected wing they shoved off of themselves, their swords red and dripping.

"Anteroom," I yelled, and they ran that direction without being told again.

I watched them go, making sure they got the door shut behind them before I turned my attention to the chaos spreading outside.

"Cinder," Tristan yelled behind me.

Looking up, I raised the sword, and another bird changed direction in midair. It sent wind at high speed into my face as it backed up like it thought it would just wait for its moment.

Behind the bird, a window looked out on the courtyard, and

dark shapes darted through the sky, diving at people in the courtyard.

"Your raven princess bitch got what she deserved," I screamed, throwing one of my knives, hitting the bird in a wing, sending it reeling back, into, and through the window. Shattering it, the bird fell on the other side.

"How many?" I called to no one and anyone, looking around the room and checking the ceiling.

"Two in here, but more outside," the General called back, throwing a knife into the air and hitting one of the birds in the rafters in the leg.

It cawed in fury, but circled again.

All the guards who subdued the one on the ground, tying it up like they were going to cook it on a spit, fanned out around the General.

The hunt was on.

But Tristan ran past me, his sword raised as he made his way to where the worst of it was.

"Damn it," I yelled, running after him.

He got away from me when I hit a wall of guards battling a bird. They swung their swords ineffectually up at the bird, barely avoiding each other. None of them knew how to fight something in the air above them, and I didn't blame them.

But they were in my way, and I didn't have time to wait for them to figure it out.

I threw another knife, it buried itself into the stomach of the bird who let out an ear-splitting scream.

"Aim for the eyes, and jab," I yelled, squeezing between them now that their blades weren't swinging around wild, and I ran out the front doors.

The courtyard was even worse than I thought.

Corvids who must not have been able to turn were on the ground, fighting in human form, marked by black feathers on the shoulders of their clothes and in some of their hair. They fought with guards who also had to cover themselves from the attacks from above.

Just to the side of the stairs, someone shot an arrow that went right through the eye of a crow dive bombing a group of guards. The bird twisted and fell from the sky, landing in a crumpled heap at the feet of the people it was attacking.

I leaned over the railing of the stairs to find Tristan, bow in hand, unloading arrow after arrow into the Corvids.

But one of the unshifted ones ran at him while he wasn't paying attention to the ground around him, their sword lifted, elbow bent, and blade down to strike him in the heart.

CHAPTER 54
FLIGHT

Bracing one hand on the railing of the stairs, I leapt over it, the skirt of my dress flying up around me like my own black wings.

I landed on the advancing attacker, grabbing his chin, wrapping my leg around his chest and slitting his throat as he tried to scream.

Riding his body down to the ground, his sword clattering on the cobblestones as it landed, I looked up to see Tristan staring, eyes wide.

Above him, another Corvid bird headed straight for him.

"Heads up," I yelled, throwing my last stolen throwing knife, slicing along the bird's neck, but missing anything vital.

It screeched, but Tristan buried three arrows in it then jumped out of the way before it crashed to the ground in blood and feathers.

"You stay here. Keep your eyes up," I yelled, but he grabbed my arm before I could run back into the fighting.

"Where did you learn to do that?" he asked, his voice full of awe and reverence even as black-winged death rained down around us.

"I told you. I train on one thing, obsessively, until I get it right." I smiled, pulling my spike from its holster and raising it like a salute, and ran off.

A bird flew down and drove its beak into the chest of a guard, its great wings flapping and sending bits of dirt flying.

Raising my arm to block the rocks and dust from my eyes, I doubled my speed, ducking beneath a pair of clashing spears, dragging the tip of my spike along the abdomen of the Corvid wielding one of the spears. I jumped and landed on the back of the bird, driving my spike into its shoulder to give me a handle.

It screamed—a sound so human that it set my teeth on edge —and started to lift us into the sky.

On the way by a running guard with a short sword and a spear, I grabbed their spear out of their hands, yanking so hard that the bird I rode veered to the side, slamming into a Corvid on foot.

Tucking the sword under the arm I latched onto my spike with, I held the spear tight against my body.

The Corvid we knocked over was attacked by multiple guards, turning into a human version of the target Tristan unloaded his quiver into.

Squeezing my legs tighter around the bird, the sleek feathers not giving me much purchase as we rose into the air, I tried to take stock of the scene below.

We were winning, but the losses were far too great.

Not enough guards were using bows or even throwing knives, relying on their swords and spears. It allowed the damn birds to get too close for the guards to fight back well enough. Especially because the birds seemed to focus their attacks on the people who were engaged with their forces on the ground.

Another bird circled and aimed for General Pace where she

fought with precision, efficiency of movement, and the rage of a thousand people.

With my stolen spear I leaned to the side and threw, hitting the other bird in the eye, knocking it from the sky.

"Fucking flying rats," I yelled, wishing I had more spears on hand.

"Bitch," the one I rode squawked. "You will die."

Its voice was a strange version of a raven's. Obvious words, but they were hidden deep within the more recognizable sounds of a bird.

"Try me," I said, leaning forward until I was right next to where its ear was hidden in its feathers.

But a second later, I regretted my taunt when the bird tipped, flying sideways.

I dug my feet into the bird's belly, squeezing my legs as tight as I could, hanging onto the spike in its shoulder, and grabbing the sword with my other hand before it could drop.

"Fall," it said.

Maybe it didn't say that, but it was close enough and it was what I heard.

"No," I screamed through clenched teeth, the muscles in my arm and legs knotting up.

"Get off me." It definitely said that, flipping so I was completely upside down for a moment.

"Stop it."

Wrong thing to say, the bird made a choking sound resembling laughter, and then did it again, rolling through the air, heading toward the ground at the same time.

"Cinder." Over the wind in my ears and the sounds of the clashing on the ground, I heard Tristan call my name.

I heaved up on the spike until I was eye-to-eye with the crow.

Everything else about the Corvids may have changed into birds, but the eye that I looked into was human.

I punched it in the face with my sword hand, the weight of the sword making the strike stronger.

We veered to the side, not wholly in control of the flight anymore. Not me, or the bird I was on. A gust from somewhere shoved us back the other way, almost toppling me as I adjusted my grip.

Finally, the bird regained control and flew back to edge of the courtyard.

My heart hammered in my chest, but I didn't want it to back off. The last thing I wanted was for it to just sit up here flapping its wings out of the way. I wanted to get back in the fight. This was only supposed to be a temporary ride for reconnaissance, not a retreat from the field.

Damn it. How was I going to send it back down?

"You a coward, duck? Afraid of King Tristan's arrows?" I pulled on the spike, causing it as much pain as possible.

"I'm not a duck, fire bitch."

But it didn't work. The damn bird just dipped in the sky and didn't dive bomb him like I wanted it to.

"You know it was my brother's troops who killed your little duck princess, right?"

The bird screamed a sound so full of pain it should have made me feel bad, but I had no feelings for these slavers and attackers.

"He did it while I was spending time alone with King Tristan. Maybe she would still be alive, but he wants to spend so much time with me."

My voice in the bird's ear was acid disguised as secret sugar, and it fell for it.

It screamed, flew in a circle, and dove for Tristan who was busy shooting its friends and family out of the sky.

Waiting until the precise time was the hardest thing I had ever done. Sitting on its back while it got closer to killing Tristan stole my breath and made me grind my teeth. Moments away from slamming into Tristan, I let go of the bird with my legs and stood on its back, holding onto the spike.

A second later and it was time.

I screamed, slamming the short sword into the bird's eye, the point bursting out of the other side of its head in an explosion of blood, brain matter, and gore.

"Tristan, move." My voice was raw and full of terror.

He didn't second guess. He didn't even bother to look where I was or what I was warning, he dove to the side. His bow and arrows went tumbling along the cobblestones.

But when the bird I rode hit the spot Tristan was just in, he wasn't there, and I was able to leap from the bird's back, rolling to a crouch.

"Cinder," Tristan yelled, not scared, not checking on me. He was furious.

"No time. Get more archers. They're killing us from the sky."

CHAPTER 55

BLIND WITH BLOOD

I jumped up and ran to the wall in the training grounds, taking every single throwing knife I could carry. I shoved them through the velvet of my gown, using it as the holster for the blades, heedless of the fact that I cut myself a couple times in the process.

I ran to the other wall, grabbing up another sword, this one a hand-and-a-half sword, before I darted back out into the fray.

Snatching the first guard I saw by the collar, I swung his face around.

"Get a bow, aim high," I screamed at him and pointed with my sword to the birds overhead.

We ran in different directions, I screamed the same instructions at every guard I passed, only hoping some of them heeded me.

A bird went to attack a guard from behind whose sword was occupied with a Corvid human on the ground.

I pulled a knife out of my dress and threw, hitting the bird in the eye, earning a scream from it. It fell back and flapped in spasms until I brought my sword down on its neck, the black head rolling away at an odd tilt because the short hilt of the knife stuck out of it.

The guard turned as if he was checking it was gone, and opened himself up in the process to the Corvid human he had been fighting.

"Damn it," I yelled, jumping forward and cutting down the Corvid man, driving my sword all the way through his shoulder and into his chest.

Blood soaked my velvet dress, dripping off my hands, making me tighten my grip.

I brought the man down to his knees with my sword steering him like a rudder, his eyes wide and empty. On the ground, I planted my foot on his other shoulder, yanking the blade from his body.

The guard I saved turned suddenly and stabbed another Corvid in the stomach.

Good, he could handle himself after all.

With my sword ready, I tried to locate General Pace again.

If anyone could call the order to arm some with bows and start shooting arrows, she could.

A guard moved and I spotted her.

She was still in a group of guards, falling as many enemies as they could while protecting each other.

But she was halfway across the courtyard from me.

I started toward her, but five Corvids surrounded me, their stupid feathers bent and broken, marking them as food for my blade.

Taking three throwing knives out of my dress, I held two folded into my palm and the third at the ready between my thumb and fore finger. I put my throwing arm up in a blocking brace position and laid the flat of the sword along my arm.

I crouched low and turned slowly, kicking out my dress with my leg as I did, taking them in.

One of them had a spear, but the rest wielded short swords.

Circling above us, a bird cackled that ugly bird laugh and I smiled.

They thought I was a good target now, that they had me surrounded and would win this little skirmish.

But my smile made one of the ones with a sword hesitate a step.

It was my opening.

Dropping the sword down to my side, I spun, using the weight of the sword as my pivot point, and threw my ready knife into the neck of the one with the spear.

He dropped his weapon, choking on his own blood, and clawed at his throat.

Grinning, I moved another knife into my fingers, and ducked a swing from another Corvid's sword, driving up with my sword to bury it in his chest.

As I let him drop, I pulled his short sword from him.

The next Corvid yelled as he ran up behind me, a truly stupid decision.

But I bent my knees and arched my back, dropping below the sweep of his wild swing, and stabbed him with his friend's sword.

I followed through, grabbing onto him and shoving my feet off the ground, flipping over the man entirely to wind up back on my feet, distanced from my attackers, pulling my stolen sword out of their friend's chest as he died on the cobblestones below me.

Raising my head, I took stock of where we were in the battle.

Some of the Corvids were trying to fight their way out of the gate, but General Pace and her team were dropping them all.

A few birds still flew overhead, but there were more feathered bodies on the ground.

"Good work. You showed us your magic," I yelled to the

skies, the birds all focusing on me. "Now, if you attack again, we'll know to come armed with bows soaked in hellfire water. I'll bring the hellfire."

The Corvid humans in front of me shrank back and looked above them, telling me something else they probably didn't want anyone to know.

Of all the Corvids who came, most were on the ground, but none of them were in charge. The birds were.

"Cinder," one of the birds screamed, diving for me. The Corvids on the ground advanced at the same time.

An arrow sliced through the air and sank to the fletching in the bird's eye, the obsidian arrowhead slamming out the other side. The force of the shot sent the bird reeling. Its body bashed into one of the obsidian walls of the palace, falling to the court-yard below.

Throwing another knife, I hit one of my attackers in his eye, but he didn't die at first. He dropped his sword and brought his hands to his face, blood spraying from between his fingers.

Someone on the other side of him drove a sword into his back, the point thrusting out of his chest.

But with the other two on me, I couldn't watch as that man fell.

My sword clashed with one man's, the ring of steel singing like none of their birds did.

The other man thought he could get at me while I was engaged and swung his sword, but I let go of mine and crouched down, sweeping out a leg to send him toppling over. Unable to stop the momentum of his swing, he cut his own soldier almost in half.

Guts and blood rained down on my head, blocking my vision.

I rolled and swiped at my eyes with a sleeve already sodden with blood, only making it harder to see.

All I had left for weapons was a single throwing knife and now I was blind.

Making a grab for my skirt, I tried to clear my eyes, but it was only in time to see another bird diving at me and feel the press of another Corvid human pounding across the courtyard at my back.

I flattened on the rough ground and rolled, throwing my knife into the person running up behind me.

But the wind of the approaching bird was on me, and there was nothing left to fight it with.

CHAPTER 56
SEVEN YEARS

I scrabbled along the ground and found the spear of the first man I killed, raising it just in time to slam it into the bird's open beak.

The force of the hit lifted me from the cobblestones and threw me tumbling through the air to land in a heap, bashing my elbow and my knees in the process.

A jolt went up my arm as it took the worst of it and my face was so close to the cobblestones that I tasted dirt.

But sitting up, I realized that all the birds were out of the sky, all the Corvid humans were done fighting, and Tristan stood with his bow and arrow hanging limp in his hands, staring at me.

My breath was ragged. Every tiny bit of energy was gone from my body, but I bowed my head.

"King Tristan," I said, my voice harsh and half hoarse.

"Cinder," he said. Just my name, and I couldn't make out the meaning behind it, what he thought of me now.

I wasn't a Lady. I wasn't a sword arm. I was a weapon.

A weapon covered in the blood of the enemies of Onyx, but dangerous nonetheless. And now he knew it.

The pounding of feet brought my eyes back up, but not my body.

Pain shot through every part of me and screamed up my arm from my elbow.

Somewhere, I heard my name again, but my eyes were closed. No amount of willpower could open them.

I woke up again. Night had fallen, and the room was dark.

Heat traced along my hairline, and the surface I laid on was soft.

The next time I woke up, there was light enough to tell me I was in my room in the palace and in my bed.

Instead of sitting up, or alerting anyone to my state, I took stock.

My body ached, but my arm was the worst. There were bandages all over me. At least I was pretty sure I was clean. There was no sticky residue of the blood that coated me, and there was no dirt and grime digging into my palms.

"The physician says her elbow should be broken, but it is not. She just bruised the bone." The voice wasn't someone I recognized, but they were near the door and my hearing was distorted by a ringing headache.

"Are there any other major injuries?" Tristan asked, his voice hoarse and wan.

"No. All the cuts are minor, and the blood seemed to all be from other people."

"See?" Jacquetta said, her tone irritated, "I told everyone that after we got her cleaned."

"Lady Cinder is just exhausted from exertion," Gus said, her voice as proper as Madam's ever was, and just as superior.

I couldn't help it. I smiled and rolled my head to look at the group gathered at the door.

"You're awake," Jacquetta cried, running to the edge of the bed, dropping all the echoes of her mother.

"We were worried about you," Gus said, kneeling down next to Jacquetta, folding her hands and resting her smiling face on them to look me in the eye.

"Sorry I worried you." I looked past them to Tristan whose blinks grew longer as I watched.

The person he was talking to, who I didn't know, looked like a nurse. But he was turned and speaking quietly to General Pace.

"How are you?" I asked him, my voice an ugly croak.

"You need this," Jacquetta said, grabbing a glass of water from the nightstand.

Gus moved behind me and helped me sit up, propping pillows behind me.

My head spun and the ringing got louder, but I drank down the entire glass in three gulps, and the sound started to fade.

Resting back against the pillows, I allowed myself a few deep breaths with my eyes closed before I focused on Tristan again.

"Now you know," I said, and he straightened, biting his lip.

Jacquetta and Gus looked at each other and left the room, taking General Pace with them and shutting the door.

"They're still not subtle," he said, tilting his head toward the door.

"Likely never will be. And I love them just as they are." I smiled and he came toward me, perching himself on the edge of the bed.

"Are you sure you're okay?" he asked, searching my face.

"Yes, mostly. I'm really sore, but I think that's to be expected." I had never fought so many people at once. Even sparring with Ash's soldiers in their protective gear and my foils with their blunted edges, I never fought for so long with so many foes all coming at me.

"Well, you did ride a Corvid," he said, smiling back.

Finally, with his smile and little joke, I could take a real breath.

"Right." I nodded looking down at the bedclothes covering me, acutely aware that I was not wearing anything beneath them.

I furrowed my brow and cocked my head, pulling my arms out of the blankets and pressing them closer to my chest before I looked up at him again.

"Were you here when they gave me a bath and bandaged me?"

"Oh," he laughed, "No. I wasn't. Which is good because it gave me time to do all the other things I needed to do."

"I don't know what that means, but I'm sure there was a lot that needed your attention. How long have I been out?" I shook my head and tried to pay attention to what I was missing, this heaviness coming from him. It might have been just the aftermath of the battle, but it seemed like there was more.

"You've only been asleep for two days, but I..." He rubbed the back of his neck and looked out the window before he looked back at me. "After I did the first things I had to elsewhere, I sort of set up a command center in your parlor so I could be here all the time. I've been here ever since."

"Ever since?" My voice was barely there, but he nodded, running a hand along mine, sending heat running up my arm and easing some of the ache in my elbow.

"Were..." I tried to remember everything, and I had a moment, just a tiny bit of time I thought was real, but I wasn't sure. "Were you here in the night? Did you touch my hair?"

He smiled, and put his hand on mine.

"Yes. I needed to be sure you were real."

"Real?" I didn't seem to be able to do anything other than ask him questions back.

"See, I watched this woman I knew to be someone who liked training, and had an uncanny ability to do things like swim rivers—although it made no sense—suddenly turn into an army in a dress."

I smiled. Even though I wasn't sure he wanted me to be an army in a dress, I liked that comparison.

"Then, as if she was magic that came out to save me and the country, she passed out and stayed out. Like the magic was spent. So, I needed to make sure that you were still you and that you would wake up again."

"I'm sorry that I surprised you. But, if it makes you feel any better, I surprised myself." Only the parts where I flew on the back of a magical bird person, and then I passed out for two days. But he didn't need to know that.

His smile was soft and brilliant, like he was in awe and still couldn't believe I was real.

"Eventually, you'll have to explain to me the weapon you carry and the training regimen you do." He shook his head.

"The training I do…" I couldn't explain the spike, but I could tell him about the training, at least in part. And maybe if I did, he would fully understand that it wasn't good for the country to have a weapon as Queen. "My parents died seven years ago in a war that came to my home."

His eyes grew grave, and he nodded while I took a deep breath and sat up a little further, holding tight to my blankets.

"I never wanted to be unable to defend my home again. So, my training is seven years, twelve hours a day, every single day, one discipline at a time." The only part I left out were the times I was on assignment, killing someone. But I tried to make it enough. Enough for him to understand.

"Cinder," he said, his face full of pain and grief, "My parents died the same day. I wish I had known that it haunted you that much. I…" He looked up at me, his mouth working to find the words. "I don't know what I would have done to make it better. But I would have tried something."

Leaning over, he kissed my forehead, the warmth of him chasing the last of my headache away and making all the aches in my body ease.

"Tristan, it isn't your fault. None of it is." And I believed that. Finally, I believed it all the way. Even if it meant that Ash would kill me or disown me, I knew he was wrong about Tristan.

He stared at me, a small, pained smile on his face as he held my hand.

But his blinks were growing longer and the dark circles under his eyes were so pronounced it looked like he was bruised.

"Go, get some sleep. I'll be here when you wake up," I said.

Smiling, he kissed the back of my hand and nodded, getting up from the bed.

"I'll be back soon," he said, and walked out the door leaving behind the feeling that something was still different. And it wasn't my less aching body.

CHAPTER 57
DEAD DREAMS

"**A**re you sure you want to?" Gus asked, still reaching for me to help me up.

"Yes. I have to get dressed, and be up and around again." If I didn't get up, I was likely to start throwing things at everyone who came to see me. No one wanted that.

"Why can't you just give us one day where we don't have to worry about you?" Jacquetta asked, wrapping a bath sheet around my naked and bandaged body.

"Why are you worrying about me?" I stopped in the middle of the room, looking at each of them.

Gus screwed her mouth to the side and Jacquetta crossed her arms to stare back at me.

"Seriously, what are those looks for?" Holding the bath sheet tighter, I shook my head and stalked into the bathroom.

They followed me into the bathroom and shut the door, turning on the water in the tub.

"Get in there," Jacquetta said, pointing.

"And stop talking. It's time to listen and answer some questions," Gus said, planting herself on the bench next to the tub.

"Well, shit." I dropped my bath sheet and climbed into the tub, bandages and all.

"Yeah, shit. What in the hellfires was that? And don't tell me it was just because you like training." Gus yanked the bandage off my elbow, stinging my skin.

"King Tristan may believe you, but you knew it was coming before anyone else did. And the way you climbed him and General Pace to go after that bird? No way. You've killed before." Jacquetta brought the creams, herbs, and flower petals her mother used to heal my little wounds and scars over to the bath while she yelled at me.

"I..." There was no way to answer their questions. Even while they yelled them at me, and were clearly angry that I kept something from them, they still loved me enough to take care of me. But would they still love me if they knew the truth? Even part of it?

Both of them stared at me, waiting for me to tell them something.

My lips trembled as I opened my mouth, and my vision went blurry with tears.

"I can't tell you," I said, my voice thick and cracking on can't.

"Cinder," Gus said, leaning over and taking my hand, all the anger gone from her face.

"Yes. You can," Jacquetta said, uncrossing her arms and leaning against the tub, her eyes watery too.

Trying to catch my breath, it came in fits and starts, my chest felt like it was cracked in half as I stared at the bath filling up around me, making the bandages fall away.

"Ash, my brother, I am his sword arm," I said, my voice so quiet I wasn't sure they heard me over the sound of the water.

"What does that mean?" Gus asked, her voice low too.

"It means that...it means," tears dripped down my cheeks, splashing into the water I was sure was washing away the only friendships I had ever had, "When he tells me to kill someone, I do it."

"No," Jacquetta said, her face crumpling as she cried.

"Cinder, he can't do that to you," Gus said. The anger was back, but now it was *for* me, not at me.

"Why aren't you walking out?" I asked, my voice a croak and their faces swimming in my salty eyes.

"Because you big dipshit, we love you," Gus said, splashing water at me.

"And we know you're a good person," Jacquetta said, tucking my hair behind my ear.

"I'm not, though. I'm a killer. I'm good at it. And I like it. That makes me a terrible person." My tears didn't stop, they only flowed more. I tried, I really tried to get them to listen. To get them to understand.

"We're glad you're good at it," Jacquetta said, her voice fierce.

"If you weren't then we would be dead, and so would King Tristan," Gus said.

And I broke, my tears turning into sobs that wracked my body and made me feel like my chest was turning inside out as I choked down any air I could get.

"Shhh," Gus said, petting the hair back on my head.

"Please, Cinder, it's okay," Jacquetta said, rubbing a hand up and down my back.

But it wasn't. And it would never be. Not really.

Everyone, including them and Tristan wouldn't have been so close to death if it wasn't for me.

Ash killed Fiachra, and that set off everything else.

How was I ever going to be able to forgive myself for my role in that? Because I was his faulty sword arm, my brother put them all at risk.

"Cinder, just because someone attacked because of you, and

the raven bitch died in the attack, doesn't mean that's your fault," Gus said.

I looked up, frozen.

"You know?" I asked, my voice a squeak.

"We know the attack targeted you, so you blame yourself. It isn't hard to figure out. But it isn't your fault. It's the fault of whatever asshole mounted the attack," Jacquetta said.

Squeezing my eyes shut, I focused on that idea, trying to make it hurt less and *feel* like it was true that it wasn't my fault.

No matter how hard I tried, guilt tore a hole in my heart.

But I was able to stop crying, and I opened my eyes.

Gus and Jacquetta smiled at me, as if it was all okay now and we could just keep going like it never happened.

Even though I knew it wasn't true, I tried to pretend to believe.

They coaxed the other bandages off of me, washed my hair, and let me soak in the hot water, allowing the mixture in it to tingle along all my scrapes, bruises, and cuts, helping them heal.

I leaned back when they were done with my hair, staring at the ceiling while they talked about joining me for training so they could learn how to better protect themselves.

But I wasn't paying attention.

My brother was at home, expecting word of Tristan's untimely death.

What was Ash's next move? What would he do when he found out I fought at the king's side, that I saved his life more than once?

Nothing about the situation was comforting, no matter how much comfort floated in the water with me, and floated in the air from my friends.

Tristan had to send me home or cut me from the potential list.

It was the only way I was going to be able to keep protecting him: get far away from him.

And there was little in the world I wanted less than for Tristan to send me off.

No, I wanted him to hold me closer.

But killers didn't get happy endings or dreams coming true.

Too many people were out there whose dreams I cut short, and there were still too many after that whose dreams died with their loved ones.

CHAPTER 58
LANGUAGE

"**D**o we even have any black dresses left?" Jacquetta asked, digging in my trunk.

"Why don't I just wear my training clothes?" Perched on the vanity stool in my bath sheet with Gus working on my hair seemed like a bad time to explain that I just wanted to put on my pants and go home to face my punishment.

"Because you're still Lady Cinder, a potential queen," Gus said, shaking her head like I was daft.

Maybe I was, because I didn't think I was Lady Cinder anymore. Not when the entire palace, including the other potentials knew what I was capable of while my friends seemed to think that was fine.

"Unless you two let me out of this room, no one is probably going to see me today, anyway."

"First of all," Jacquetta said, pulling a gown from the trunk and smiling at it, "Yes, they will because we are going to make sure they know you're fine."

"And second, even if we kept you in here, King Tristan will be back," Gus said while Jacquetta nodded at her.

"Especially since we are going to join you in training from now on." Jacquetta brought the dress over to the bed, laying it out.

"No, you're not." In what world did they think I was going to put them in even more danger?

"Yes," Gus said, turning my face to look at her, "We are because we want to be able to defend ourselves better."

"But you did fine. You killed a bird." And hacked off a wing to hide under, which was brilliant.

"We got lucky," Jacquetta said, standing next to Gus, "We stabbed it in the back. If it was coming at us, we would probably be dead."

"I wouldn't let that happen." How did they not see what I would do to keep them safe?

"Cinder, you can't be with us all the time." Gus smiled a gentle smile like she understood, but she didn't. I shook my head.

"King Tristan needs you at his back. We have to come second to that." Jacquetta had the same smile as Gus, and I thought about sending them to the anteroom so I could go after Tristan.

I turned back to the mirror, looking at my reflection. Just me, one person, and too many allegiances. I nodded. No matter how much I thought training them would give them just enough skill to land them in trouble, I couldn't leave them defenseless anymore.

They grinned and got to work, talking about how we were going to get Marquessa Ziya away from the palace after her stunt at the service. But I was thinking about the Corvids, and what they would do now.

War seemed to be inevitable. And even I wasn't ready for a war with the birds.

"Don't you think it's a problem to wear that color?" Gus asked, a hairpin in her mouth, muffling her diction.

"What color?" I asked, but Jacquetta raised an eyebrow as she brought a brush with makeup on it toward my face.

I closed my eyes again, and went back to holding still for her.

"At first I thought you should wear black because you kicked so much ass in your last black dress. But I think we should stay away from it because it's a Corvid color. So, I decided you should wear the King's color."

My eyes popped open, and Jacquetta's mouth set in a line as she raised her eyebrows at me.

Taking a deep breath, I closed my eyes again.

"But I don't want to make it harder for Tristan to send me away. He needs to have a queen, not a weapon," I said.

Silence reigned. My friends didn't move, and I couldn't even hear them breathe.

Opening my eyes, one at a time, I realized they were both standing with their mouths hanging open and shock in their eyes.

"What?" I asked, my voice a whisper.

"You're an idiot," Jacquetta said, shaking her head.

"A Dragon King is a weapon himself. They should have a queen who is as deadly as they are," Gus said.

They shook their heads and went back to getting me ready, but now my mind was stuck on Dragon Kings lore. It was junk. Everyone knew it wasn't real.

But people said the same thing about the Corvid magic. And I knew better now.

Could Tristan really have been a descendant of dragons? And what did that say about the lack of any powers for generations?

Finally, I was done, and Jacquetta and Gus got me into a dress of the deep red Tristan loved, this one with flat silver gems in a line down the back like dragon scales. It had lace sleeves in a flame pattern that ended in points on my hands. The lace wrapped the low neckline. The rest of the dress a soft, form-fitting satin with a slit up one leg that moved as I did.

It was beautiful in the way a Damascus blade was.

"And Tristan says you two don't know how to be subtle," I said, staring at myself in the mirror, none of my cuts and bruises showing.

"Pfft." Gus shook her head.

"Subtlety is overrated." Jacquetta flung her hair over her shoulder, and I couldn't help laughing.

"Maybe I should leave my spike here. It will probably show through this dress." I turned my leg so it peeked out, showing the scrape and bruise on my knee even though they were less noticeable than they were before the bath.

"No. Put your spike on that leg." Gus picked it up off the nightstand and handed it to me.

"Everyone needs to be reminded what you did." Jacquetta smiled and I strapped on my spike.

Looking at the dress now, the blood red of it, and the sharp edges of the lace paired with the spike made me look even more like a weapon.

"Fashion can be a language," Jacquetta said, her voice low and imbued with a weight that sounded like secrets.

"And we have a lot to say," Gus said, sounding as fierce as she ever had.

They turned and headed for the door, leaving me to follow.

But in my mind, I was stuck on what they were saying through my clothes. It was a language I wasn't fluent in, and I was afraid they were putting words in my mouth when I didn't understand the context.

Guards were posted at regular intervals in the hall, their presence driving home how thin the edge was that we walked on toward war.

One by one, as they saw me, realized who I was, their eyes

brightened, smiles bloomed on their faces, and they saluted. Placing a palm in the middle of their chest with their fingers spread wide in a salute, they added the touch they never did in concert with the other except to the king: They bowed.

I sucked in a breath while Jacquetta and Gus stood taller beside me and smiled.

All down the hall, every guard we passed did the same as if I was Tristan. As if they coordinated it.

By the time we got down the stairs, my knees felt like they might buckle, sweat collected in the small of my back, my smile was long gone, and I struggled to pull in a full breath.

These people, these guards who signed up to devote their lives to protecting the country, our King, and our people, were honoring me.

An assassin.

CHAPTER 59
NOT GOOD ENOUGH

Jacquetta and Gus headed toward the open doors and noise of the grand ballroom, while I veered left to the front doors of the palace.

I needed air.

On the front steps, I realized I was wrong. This was the last thing I needed.

Guards were everywhere. Equipment was in large stacks like they were taking stock. The General marched up and down the line of piles with aides running in her wake.

I tried to turn around. To go back inside. To get away from everyone and everything. I was so wrong. Staying in bed seemed like a perfect plan and I should have followed it.

But Jacquetta and Gus each grabbed one of my elbows, forcing me to stay rooted to the spot at the top of the stairs, flanked by the giant open doors of the palace.

People in the courtyard caught on to my presence, it spread like spilled hellfire water from one to another.

The people who weren't part of the guard bowed while the

guard, every single one of them, placed their hand on their heart and bent at the waist.

Even General Pace.

When the General straightened up, she was smiling. But I wasn't.

Nothing about this was right. Nothing about this could be allowed to stand. I had to stop it. To stop *them*.

I opened my mouth, but a throat cleared behind me.

Jacquetta and Gus let me go so I could turn to find Tristan standing in the doorway, his hand on his heart.

Behind me the sounds of the courtyard were still too hushed for me to turn and face any of them. This was too much, and I couldn't find the words to make them stop. Least of all with Tristan in front of me.

He stepped toward me, taking my hand and placing it in the crook of his elbow.

"Some of them want to name you a Shield," he said, leaning down and whispering in my ear.

"I'm not one of them. I'm ineligible." Like it mattered. The world was upside down. An assassin was being celebrated like a hero.

"Don't worry. I won't let anyone force you to retire to some spring somewhere." He grinned like this was all a big joke, something funny for me to talk about later like the time Gus laughed so hard water came out of her nose.

"Tristan, this has to stop. I don't deserve this," I said. And it was an understatement.

"Cinder, let them have this. You give them hope. A Lady from Lehar outfought the Corvid and the guard itself. They are thrilled. And the story is spreading. We have more women signing up for service than we have since my mother died." He looked at me like I was some kind of rare jewel when I felt like gold plated shit.

"Please come with me," he said, leading me into the grand ballroom.

No dining table was set up in it now. No band was in the corner. And no one was dancing.

The grand ballroom was turned into an infirmary.

Where only a little while ago blood soaked the floor, and Corvids turned into birds while we honored one of their own, people laid in beds placed in neat rows and healers walked among them.

"I can't," I said, tugging my hand out of his elbow to run in the other direction.

"You can. They need this," he said, snatching my hand back, folding it on his arm and latching onto it like he knew I would make another break for the door.

We walked out into the space. The healthier ones smiled. One young woman—who couldn't have been old enough to have done much fighting—waved with her good hand. Her other was in a sling.

"People of Onyx, Lady Cinder came to show you she healed. And I know you will, too," Tristan said, putting far too much weight on me.

I shrank under it, but I tried to smile.

Whatever I was to them, I did want them to get better. I didn't want to lose any more to the Corvid's. Or have any more lives on my conscience.

These people weren't Lord Fall. They were innocents caught in my terrible wake.

Finally, the itching in my legs to turn around and leave grew to be too much.

"Really, I can't anymore," I whispered, and Tristan nodded.

He waved to the people and turned me around, not letting go of my hand.

We walked back to my room, and I breathed a fraction better when the guards didn't repeat their performance in the hallway.

Once we got inside my apartment I folded, falling to my knees and putting my face in my hands.

"None of that was good." I spoke into my hands, but I was close to screaming. I knew they heard me.

"After all of that, how can you think that?" Tristan bent down and ran a hand down my cheek.

"She thinks she doesn't deserve it," Gus said.

"That she isn't good enough," Jacquetta added, the click of the door following her statement.

"Cinder," Tristan said, his voice soft, he pulled me forward, so I ended up in his lap with his arms around me. The warmth of him soaking into my body and easing some of the shaking in my nerves.

I kept my eyes shut, but dropped my hands.

He touched my cheek again and sighed.

"Maybe you need a break. This has been a lot," he said.

Opening my eyes, I looked into his, lost in the kaleidoscope of colors, and the way he looked back at me.

Like a magic only he had, in a look he made it seem as if he knew I wasn't what they thought I was, but that it was okay.

"We'll just stay in here for a while," I said, my words hushed, "You have too much responsibility on your shoulders already for you to have to walk me back here all the time."

His smile was sad, tinged in the hours he spent dealing with the aftermath of the attack.

"Okay, but is it alright if I come up here sometimes?"

"Tristan," I said, cupping his cheek, the scruff of too many days spent taking care if everyone else rough against my palm, "You can come to me anytime."

Eyes wide, he swallowed and nodded.

Closing his eyes tight like he held back tears, he kissed my forehead, stood me up before he got up himself, and left without looking at me again.

"Did you mean that?" Jacquetta asked.

"Mean what? That I don't want to go back out there for a while? Yeah." I made my way to the sofa and flopped down onto it.

"I'm pretty sure the King heard you say that you want to hide from everyone except him," Gus said, plopping down next to me.

Furrowing my brow, I ran through my words and sat up straight.

"Damn it, I meant I would help him. That I supported him. Shit." Leaning my head back on the cushion, I stared at the ceiling.

No matter what I did, I screwed it up and dug myself deeper. This had to stop. I needed to get out of the palace.

And yet, I didn't walk out. I couldn't bring myself to abandon Tristan with the Corvid threat upon us. And the last thing I really wanted to do was face my brother. I couldn't go home, not really. But I couldn't be here either.

CHAPTER 60
MIDNIGHT

Tristan came to me at night.

After he was done being King all day, he came to my door, his face fallen, his gaze long, and his shoulders slumped.

I let him in and led him to the sofa, expecting him to want to talk.

But, instead, Tristan wrapped his arms around me, kissed my forehead, sighed and fell asleep.

Every night for a week, he did the same thing. While I hid in my rooms with Gus and Jacquetta, he did the work.

One night, while he slept, I moved so I could look at him.

"You're a better person than I am," I whispered, running my hand along his jaw, "You deserve better than me."

And I asked my mother and father for a way to let him go when he found the right queen.

In the morning, like always, he was gone with only a note left behind.

My Dearest Cinder,

Thank you. Hopefully I will be done with this flurry of activity soon.

Sincerely, Tristan

The notes were always variations of the same. And every one of them went into my trunk with my mother's shoes. Even though I knew I couldn't keep them. Not once I was home. Not where Ash might find them.

Finally, one night a note came instead of Tristan.

Jacquetta read the note and told us what it said as it wasn't a letter only to me.

"We need to be at a statement tomorrow in the courtyard." She lowered the paper, her brow furrowed.

"Does it say what the statement will be about? Or why it's in the courtyard?" Gus asked, while I got up and went to the window.

Outside, the courtyard looked much like it did before the Corvid attack. The weapons were gone, and the extra patrols of the guards someone might not notice if they weren't paying attention.

"It's in the courtyard because the grand ballroom is still in use and he wants to talk to more than just the potentials," I said, not turning around, or even caring what his statement was going to be.

"Maybe he's finally going to propose to Cinder," Jacquetta said, and I shook my head.

Unless his statement was a proposal—which I had no idea how to deal with and didn't think he would just spring on someone—what more he could say that would be a surprise?

He wasn't going to send me home.

Which might have been best since Ash probably wanted to kill me.

The only thing I could think of was that we were going to war. Which wasn't a surprise at all. As much as I was prepared to do that, the idea of another war, of so many more orphans Tristan would need to open more Shield Homes, and trying to protect him through that just made me tired. Tired and sad.

In the morning, waking up on the sofa, after waiting for Tristan to show and not seeing him, I stretched and tried not to worry what his absence the night before meant.

Gus and Jacquetta whispered about me as they got me ready for the statement.

"You see what I mean?"

"Do you think she even knows she acts like this?"

"What are we going to do if…"

They still weren't subtle, these friends of mine.

But they were ready, and had me ready. This time the dress wasn't red.

"Are we sure we aren't just making it a little obvious now?" I loved the silver tank dress covered in gems with green flames creeping up the bottom of the skirt in colored gems and a dragon in still more black gems down the back that was positioned like it set the bottom on fire. And at least they left my hair down in waves without any adornment. But this was too much.

"No. This is perfect." Jacquetta sighed, cocking her head to the side as she stared at me.

"It's going to dazzle in the sunlight," Gus said.

And it was going to leave me freezing cold in the courtyard. Sunlight or not, it was thick winter now, the air tasted like snow, and I wasn't a human-shaped heater like Tristan.

But we didn't have time to argue.

We left the apartment, Gus in a green gown that suited her just like I thought it would, and Jacquetta in a brighter green that somehow made her seem even more like a calla lily—long and statuesque—than she normally did.

Guards still lined the hallways, but all they did was nod as we passed. I breathed a bit easier. A nod I could handle.

Leaving the grand foyer into the courtyard, confirmed my suspicions that this was more than just a little statement to a small group.

We made our way down the steps to where General Pace stood in front of a large contingent of guard, many of them officers.

All of the other potentials stood among the courtiers, but I preferred to be with the guard, people more like me than the other Ladies of the Court.

The guard members directly around us all stood even taller and straighter as I came to the General's side.

"Lady Cinder," General Pace said, placing her hand on her heart with a smile on her face.

"General, please," I whispered, trying not to upset her or let the stinging nerves running through me make me fidget.

"Any idea what this is?" Jacquetta asked.

"Send off for some of the guard," the General said, raising her chin and dropping her smile, every inch the officer.

Moments later, Tristan walked out onto the stairs.

He managed to still look tired, but less exhausted and haggard than he had every other time I saw him this week.

A nod from Tristan, and the regular hum of conversation around us fell silent.

He found me in the crowd, a smile playing on the edges of his lips and turned back to the rest of the gathering.

"Everyone, in the wake of the events last week, I have ordered the guard to send re-enforcements out to strategic locations in Onyx. They leave today. Let's wish them all the best on their mission as they protect us all," he said, and the people gathered cheered.

The guard behind me sent up their yells more enthusiastically than anyone else, and I hoped those would be the last yells they would give for their time away.

I wanted them to end up bored. If they were bored then Onyx was in a good position, but I understood their need to psych themselves up.

"Now," Tristan took a deep breath, any hint of joviality for the guard's moral dropping from his face, "I must implore my councilors, for the safety of all involved, to end the hunt for a potential queen, and send all the participants home."

All? Did he mean me? After wanting him to send me home all this time? Now that I didn't want to go, was he sending me away?

AFTERWORD

Thank you for reading!
If you enjoyed this book, please leave a review at your favorite bookseller.
Don't forget to go to jdarleneeverly.com and sign up for the newsletter to be the first to know about all the updates on this series. The second book, Heart of Shattered Glass is available for preorder now and comes out in January 2022.

As a special exclusive for those who sign up for the newsletter, the author is giving away and exclusive prequel in this series, as well as an exclusive free book in another story world and more.

ACKNOWLEDGMENTS

A whole hearted thank you to Bean, the Rottens, and all of my friends and family. A big bag of thanks to Jupiter Alley and Krystal for their help in making this happen, Heather Cardona for all she does, Miblart for the gorgeous cover, as well as the team at Wishing Well.

ABOUT THE AUTHOR

J. Darlene Everly is an author of sci-fi and fantasy stories. Her serial, Crossroad Inn, is available on Vella, her debut trilogy, The Grimm Star Saga: First Light is available everywhere, and two new series will begin in 2o22. Keep an eye out for Major Arcana, and The Grimm Star Saga and keep reading for all of Cinder's story.

  facebook.com/jdarleneeverly
  instagram.com/everlystories
  patreon.com/Everly

CHAPTER 1: MESSAGE

It was too hot.

Too hot to train with this heavy sword. I kept dipping the end toward the ground instead of lifting it and holding it in the proper position.

"Again, Cinder. It needs to be right," my father said, staying in his position and giving me that perpetually patient look.

I hated that look when we were training because it meant I was failing.

"Dad," I said, swiping sweat off my forehead, my arms and shoulders screaming from the work we had already done, "Can't I throw knives today? It's so hot and I'm good at that."

He smiled and charged at me, giving me seconds to raise my sword and block him.

The wood of our training swords slammed together with a force that reverberated up my arms.

But he stepped back and took my training sword from me, the weights down the center of it shining in the midday sun.

"Good. That last block was good, and you did it on instinct without needing to think about it. When you're actually faced with an attacker, you can't be thinking through your moves. You have to get to the point where your moves are in reaction to theirs and on instinct. If you know the proper counters in response to what they do, the ways in through their guard, and how to protect yourself, then all you have to worry about is finding your opening."

He left out that I needed to worry about finding an opening, hope the person had one, wasn't as good as Dad at closing them down, that I was better conditioned than my opponent, and I wouldn't just run out of energy before I could make a move.

Dad put a hand on my shoulder and smiled at me, holding both the heavy swords with one hand, no sweat beading on his brow.

I wasn't sure I would ever be as good as he was, nor so strong I could do this all day. Especially not in the middle of summer. But I wanted to be.

"How long did it take you?" I asked, walking with him to the weapons shed and grabbing a glass of water. Beads of condensation sluiced down the glass as soon as I touched them.

Putting the outside of the glass to my forehead sent a wash of relief through me, a cool kiss after the torching heat raging through my veins from exertion.

"You're not going to like the answer." He laughed and took a drink himself, perching on a bench that ran along the outside wall of the shed. The climbing roses that covered so many of the walls of the manor and the outbuildings framed him like he was posing for a portrait.

"Come on, it can't be that bad." I guzzled down the rest of my glass, leaving me breathing heavily.

"Well, I think that someone could train their entire lives and still meet someone who could best them," he said.

And he was right. I didn't like it. I hated it.

"Don't look at me like that, Cinder. Everyone has pulls on their time. You have your studies, and I know you don't care, but they're to get you ready to be a Lady of the Court one day. It simply makes sense that there isn't enough time for you to train enough to be unbeatable. That isn't how the world works. Unless someone makes it their whole life. And that isn't healthy."

He stood up and planted that big hand on my shoulder, steering me toward the door of the manor all the way across the grounds while I scowled and tried to figure out a way that I could devote more time to training.

Learning how to be a Lady of the Court was stupid. It wasn't like I was planning on being at court for more than the required month when I was old enough in a couple years. Mom just made a bigger deal out of learning all the details about the different royals than I thought was necessary.

I wasn't planning on marrying some Lord somewhere and being the usual royal wife. I wanted to have a life like my mother's. One where I could have my own interests, and lead my own troops to defend the kingdom. I wanted to have a husband who loved me and looked at me like I was magic.

And if that wasn't something I found, then I would just stay a Lady of Lehar and lead our forces here when they needed it.

Eventually Mom and Dad wouldn't be able to. Everyone knew my brother Ash—who would be Duke one day—would make a terrible leader in battle.

He never trained. After he learned enough in hand-to-hand to make specific painful blows, he never came back to the training yard.

Other than the time he caught the kittens of the barn cat...Father banned him from ever using a bow again. And I had nightmares for a year.

But Ash swore he would never do that again, and so far, he held to his word.

I still wasn't ready to pick up a bow and arrows again either. My skills were less than mediocre in the discipline, even though Mom excelled at it.

When I trained with her, we used throwing knives. Which I was good at.

Maybe I wasn't a master like Mom, but it wasn't bragging to say I was good. It was just fact.

Inside, the manor was so much cooler. The sweat along my body turned into a chill and I shivered, wrapping my arms around myself.

"Go down to the pools. Get washed up." He patted my shoulder and walked away, probably to find Mom.

Before I did as he suggested, I needed to get something to eat.

Wandering through the main hall to the family dining room—the smaller of our two dining rooms and the only one we ever used unless some dignitary or royal showed up—I replayed our sparring session in my head, looking for the mistakes I made.

According to Mom, I was a baby the last time we really needed to use the formal dining hall. The King and Queen were here to do something with my parents about the hellfire water we mined here in Lehar and provided to the rest of the country.

Grabbing something from the fruit bowl on the table in the dining room, I slumped down onto a chair.

One of the pears from the orchards near our manor wasn't going to last me long after the workout I got sparring. The sweet juice of the flesh was too good to pass up, and I didn't want to take the time to go get something more substantial.

While I sat, thinking about how I could get better at sparring while still doing all the things Mother expected me to, the sounds of feet started pounding through the halls outside the dining room.

People were running somewhere. I assumed a horse got out or something as mundane as it always was.

Moments later, Ash slammed into the dining room, storm clouds in his eyes and his mouth in a sneer. His dark hair was long over his eyes, hiding the severe set of his brow I knew was under there when his eyes looked that way.

I sunk down in my seat, Ash wasn't great to be around when he looked this way. If I made myself small enough, maybe he wouldn't notice me. After all, I was the stupid kid sister—four years younger, and I irritated him too much.

At least, that's what he usually told me.

Which sucked, because Ash was my first friend and I wanted to go back to the days when he took me swimming in the deep pools beneath the manor and we played sea monster as he tried to catch me.

He hadn't done that since I was eight. He said it wasn't fun anymore because he never caught me.

But, as long as I could remember he couldn't catch me, so that was just an excuse to leave his kid sister behind and spend more time with his cruel friends like Brix.

Now, though, Ash grabbed an apple and pulled out his knife, peeling it in one long curl as he turned it in his hands.

Part of me wanted to ask him what was going on. But when he looked like that, it was better to let Ash speak to me first.

I took another bite of my pear, making a study of the fingernail I broke in training and wondering if Mother would be irritated anew that I never could grow them out.

"Cinder," Ash said. Keeping my head down, I raised my eyes to him and tried to look as nonchalant as possible, "When was the last time messengers came from the Obsidian Palace?"

"Obsidian Palace? Did the King and Queen send a message?" I asked.

His knife slipped, cutting the apple peel, and his eyes narrowed at me.

"Sorry, Ash. Stupid question. The last time a message came that wasn't a response to something from Mom and Dad sent was when they were invited as part of Solaria's month at court."

Solaria was our cousin, and her time last year as a Lady of the Court included Mom and Dad and Ash going to a ball in honor of her and the other young women there at the same time. Of course, I didn't get to go. I was too young.

No matter how much I wanted to go and see something like the palace, I always ended up stuck with the Governess and left out of the fun stuff.

"Well, we don't have any other cousins, so any guesses what a message would be about this time?" He raised a brow at me, his mouth pinched.

I shook my head, a sinking feeling making the pear heavy in my stomach.

"And why wouldn't it be delivered by a messenger?" he asked, and I set the rest of my pear down, shaking my head again.

"No? How about why would it be sent by a guard?"

I sucked in a breath and Ash nodded, settling back into his seat and staring at the wall in front of him.

Messages sent by a guard could only mean one thing: Onyx was under attack.

Pushing myself up from the chair, I caught the pause in Ash's movements.

"Are you going to come with me and find out exactly what's going on, or not?" I asked.

He cocked his head to the side, slicing off a piece of apple that he held with the knife and his thumb until he got it into his mouth.

"Why would they answer questions from you when they made me leave the room?" His voice sounded mild and calm. If I didn't know him better I would have assumed it was just a question with nothing else behind it.

But as innocuous as the words sounded, the careful containment of Ash's whole body set off every alarm in me.

"I don't know, but if we are both at the door the second the guard leaves, they might tell us what's going on, then." I held still as he continued in the implacable blank stare while eating his apple. I waited for him to decide what I should do next.

"Okay. Let's go," he said, putting down his partially eaten apple and knife as he pushed his chair back from the table.

Leaving the dining room and heading for the receiving hall, I took deep breaths, allowing myself the comfort of knowing I passed one of Ash's little tests.

We got to the receiving hall just as a guard walked out, his black uniform coated in the road dust. He dipped his head to us, Ash returned the gesture, and I bobbed in the appropriately small curtsy.

I always curtsied when it was expected, even when I was wearing pants and thought it looked ridiculous.

But just beyond the doors to the receiving room, I realized that whatever we thought the message was, it was worse.

The Captain of our forces was taking notes and nodding as Father spoke while Mother was in a huddle with three of the counselors for the duchy. They were just as careful in taking stock of her words as the Captain was of Father's.

"Ash?" I asked, my voice small and tight.

He reached out a hand and took mine, squeezing it as he pulled me forward with him.

Maybe we would be able to hear what they were saying. I appreciated my mercurial brother's support, but part of me wanted to run in the other direction and pretend this wasn't my idea. Was I really ready to hear the details of an attack somewhere in Onyx?

'Too late,' I thought as we hovered at the edge of the gaggle.

"What do we need to bring those people in?" Mother asked.

"I've already sent a runner to spread the word."

"Do we have enough stores for that? For the influx of the people?" Mother chewed on the inside of her cheek and tapped two fingers against her side. I leaned closer to Ash.

Mother didn't tap unless she was plotting and running through complex things in her mind. She didn't chew on the inside of her cheek unless she was almost desperate with worry. If she had not been talking with the others, and needing to stay there to get through it all, she would have been pacing.

Ash leaned back against me, propping me up, and patted my hand with his free one.

"How close are they?"

The question made my hearing go out of focus, and it was suddenly as if I was in a swarm of bugs. I swallowed.

"We aren't sure. They were a few measures away from the border of our lands, but they might be headed this way right now." Mother's voice was low and as sharp as her throwing knives.

"Are we sure it's Amethyst?"

I sucked in a breath. It stabbed into me, and the small pear I ate roiled in my stomach.

"Yes. We are at war."

CPSIA information can be obtained
at www.ICGtesting.com
Printed in the USA
BVHW030853191021
619299BV00015B/546/J